Acclaim for the authors of
REGENCY CHRISTMAS PROPOSALS

GAYLE WILSON
Anne's Perfect Husband
"This high-action plot careens along the edge between traditional Regency and gritty, intense historical. This innovative mix carries themes on the healing powers of love and survival."
—*RT Book Reviews*

The Heart's Wager
"Gayle Wilson has achieved an uncommon, and uncommonly successful, hybrid of Regency, action-adventure and romance that makes for nonstop entertainment."
—*RT Book Reviews*

AMANDA McCABE
High Seas Stowaway
"Amanda McCabe has gifted us twice over—nothing is better than hearing about friends from other stories. *High Seas Stowaway* is a fast-paced, exciting novel. Amanda McCabe has done it again— a wonderful tale!"
—*Cataromance*

A Sinful Alliance
"Richly detailed and brimming with historical events and personages, McCabe's tale weaves together history and passion perfectly."
—*RT Book Reviews*

CAROLE MORTIMER
Lady Arabella's Scandalous Marriage
"Mortimer excels at producing strong, independent heroines, and Arabella fits the bill when she comes up against London's most notorious rake."
—*RT Book Reviews*

Snowbound with the Billionaire
"[This] novella…is an excellent example of this international bestselling author's storytelling prowess!"
—*Cataromance*

GAYLE WILSON

is a two-time RITA® Award winner. In addition to this, Gayle's books have garnered more than fifty other awards and nominations, including the Daphne du Maurier Award for the Best Single Title Romantic Suspense of 2008, awarded to *Victim,* her most recent novel from MIRA Books.

Gayle has written forty-one novels and four novellas for Harlequin Enterprises, including works for Harlequin Historical, Harlequin Intrigue, Special Releases, HQN Books and MIRA. Please visit her website at www.BooksByGayleWilson.com.

AMANDA McCABE

wrote her first romance at the age of sixteen—a vast epic, starring all her friends as the characters, written secretly during algebra class. She's never since used algebra, but her books have been nominated for many awards, including a RITA® Award, an *RT Book Reviews* Reviewers' Choice Award, a Booksellers Best, a National Readers' Choice Award, and a Holt Medallion. She lives in Oklahoma with a menagerie of animals and loves dance classes, collecting cheesy travel souvenirs, and watching the Food Network—even though she doesn't cook. Visit her at www.ammandamccabe.com and www.riskyregencies.blogspot.com

CAROLE MORTIMER

USA TODAY international bestselling author Carole Mortimer was born in England, the youngest of three children. She began writing in 1978, and has now written more than one hundred and fifty books for Harlequin Enterprises. Carole has six sons: Matthew, Joshua, Timothy, Michael, David and Peter. She says, "I'm happily married to Peter senior; we're best friends, as well as lovers, which is probably the best recipe for a successful relationship. We live in a lovely part of England."

Regency
Christmas Proposals

GAYLE WILSON · AMANDA MCCABE
CAROLE MORTIMER

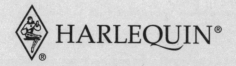

HARLEQUIN®

TORONTO • NEW YORK • LONDON
AMSTERDAM • PARIS • SYDNEY • HAMBURG
STOCKHOLM • ATHENS • TOKYO • MILAN • MADRID
PRAGUE • WARSAW • BUDAPEST • AUCKLAND

ISBN-13: 978-0-373-29615-6

REGENCY CHRISTMAS PROPOSALS
Copyright © 2010 by Harlequin Books S.A.

The publisher acknowledges the copyright
holders of the individual works as follows:

THE SOLDIER'S CHRISTMAS MIRACLE
Copyright © 2010 by Mona Gay Thomas

SNOWBOUND AND SEDUCED
Copyright © 2010 by Ammanda McCabe

CHRISTMAS AT MULBERRY HALL
Copyright © 2010 by Carole Mortimer

Recycling programs
for this product may
not exist in your area.

CONTENTS

THE SOLDIER'S CHRISTMAS MIRACLE

Gayle Wilson

Dear Reader,

Although I've written several novellas through the years, this is the first Christmas anthology I've been privileged to be part of. Like so many of you, however, I, too, love to read the seasonal stories these contain because this time of year is so very special. It always evokes memories of my childhood and particularly of my father, who made sure that no matter how trying the times or how little we had materially, we still were able to enjoy the rich traditions of this holiday. Christmas was, and always will be for me, a season of love and miracles.

The Soldier's Christmas Miracle celebrates both. Brutalized by battle, Guy Wakefield has known the depths of suffering and despair. But because of the whispered words of a stranger, he has never lost faith in his ability to overcome whatever obstacles life throws in his path. The courage of Isabella Stowe has also been severely tested, not only by war but by the deprivations and loneliness of its aftermath, creating a singularly strong and determined woman. The trials these two endured have stripped from them everything except their pride—something both cling to desperately, despite the threat it offers to their one true chance at happiness.

I hope you will enjoy Guy and Isabella's journey of discovery. I also hope that your own Christmas will be filled with love, peace and joy—miracles enough, I think, for all of us!

Sincerely,

Gayle

First, last, and always, to my own soldier hero

Prologue

'It's water.'

A gentle hand raised his head as the rim of a metal cup was placed against his parched lips. He drank greedily, only now aware of the depth of his thirst—a sensation that had been buried under the pain of the burns and his other wounds.

When the cup was taken away, he asked the question he'd wondered about for hours. 'Is it morning?'

'It's still night,' the same voice answered.

Feminine. English. And cultured, he assessed automatically.

'More?'

'Please.' The need to keep her beside him—to keep the darkness at bay—was greater even than his thirst.

They had bandaged his eyes shortly after the battle, but by then the darkness had already closed around him. And it was that and that alone he feared.

When the cup was removed from his lips a second time, he knew that she would leave him, too. Just like the friends who'd brought him here to await the ships that would take the wounded back to England.

And when she was gone the terrifying blackness would become omnipresent again.

'Could you stay a while?' he heard himself beg, although he recognised the request for the cowardice it represented. 'Unless there are others who need water…?'

'No, you're the last,' the woman said, not unkindly.

'I could hear it,' he said, to keep her talking. 'The sound the cup makes against the side of the bucket. But then no one came.'

'You were so still, I think everyone believed you were sleeping.'

Given the extent of his injuries, they would probably have considered that a blessing. It would have been, of course, but he hadn't been able to sleep. The thought of what might lie ahead had destroyed any hope of that.

He had promised himself that no one would ever hear him complain. He was, after all, a soldier, and others had suffered far more than he.

But now, whether it was the thought of home or the anonymity of their situation, he found that he needed to tell her. To acknowledge, if only to this unknown voice in his darkness, the true depth of his cowardice.

His lips began to tilt upward at the ridiculousness of what he was about to say. That movement was halted by the painful pull on the burned skin of his cheek, but the words of his confession spilled out almost of their own accord.

'Like a child, I find I'm afraid of the dark.'

He waited, expecting some bracing homily or even a rebuke for his weakness. She was silent instead, for so long that he was once more aware of the sounds of human suffering that surrounded them.

'You would willingly accept water from my hand, but not its guidance?'

'Not if…' He hesitated, and then said what he knew to be the truth. 'Not if I were *always* to be guided.'

Never to ride again. Or to dance. Never to walk unfettered through a meadow. Never to see the faces of his children.

His throat thickened with that thought, although he could not remember thinking about his future progeny before in his entire life. There had always been other things more pressing. Friends. His regiment. The intoxicating pull of the dangers they faced daily, often with a confidence that bordered on insanity.

Now a vision of the remaining years of his life stretched before him—a montage of dependence and invalidism. Death, even here, far from everything he had ever known or loved, would be preferable to that.

'Because that would make you less of a man?'

Was that what he feared? Emasculation by infirmity?

'Would it?' he asked.

She was a woman. Surely she could provide the answer to that question better than he.

'I think that would depend upon the man you were before.'

He examined the words, using the mental exercise it offered to keep the relentless pain at bay. He knew his reputation, of course. Fearless. It was a word that had been used often enough to describe some reckless endeavour he'd undertaken without a second's thought.

And that was the crux. He had never thought beyond that moment between life and death. Had never considered the possibility of a life unlike the one he'd known. Did he have courage enough to live under the restraints he'd been imagining since they'd wrapped the cloth around his eyes?

'It's easy enough to live young and free and strong.' The voice beside him echoed his thoughts. 'But without any one of those... I think *that* life would require a man of remarkable courage.' The last had been so softly spoken he'd had to strain to hear the final word.

And then, in the stillness that had finally fallen among the wounded, came the sound of distant bells, their joyous clarity vastly different from the noises of the suffering.

A celebration? Some hard-won victory in a battle he had not been part of?

'What is it? What's happening?'

'Christmas.' The woman's voice was filled with wonder. 'It's

Christmas morning. I had forgotten.' The last words contained a breath of amusement.

'Christmas,' he echoed softly.

Memories evoked by the word invaded his brain, pushing out the darkness that had seemed to swallow up all the goodness he had known in his life. A thousand images, foreign to those of the last few years, bright and gay and dearly familiar, were there instead.

'The season of miracles,' she said. 'Perhaps…'

Again the words faded, but there was no longer any need of them. She had already uttered the only ones that mattered.

Through the long days and longer nights that followed, he clung to them rather than to the unspoken suggestion that miracles still sometimes occurred. *I think that life would require a man of remarkable courage.*

And in the years that followed, that dauntless courage and it alone was all he asked for in his prayers.

Chapter One

'**A** post, my lord. I believe it may be the reply you've been awaiting.'

Rodgers' words created a tightness in Guy Wakefield's chest he couldn't quite explain. While it was true he'd been waiting for a response to an enquiry he'd made, he had no reason to believe that this, any more than the dozens of other avenues he'd pursued during the last five years, would provide the information he sought.

'Would you read it to me, Rodgers?' He was pleased that his voice reflected none of his inner turmoil.

'Of course, my lord.' There was a slight delay before his butler added, 'The candles, my lord. If I may?'

'Of course,' Guy agreed, waiting again until Rodgers had lit enough to read the letter by.

The butler cleared his throat before he began, the unfamiliar words laboriously sounded out, while the easier ones were rushed. Rodgers was proud of his ability to read, unusual for someone in service, and it had proved invaluable to his master since his return from the Peninsula.

Major General Roland Abernathy's first paragraph said all that was polite regarding the Viscount Easton's military record, and expressed a hope for his lordship's continued good health. It wasn't until the second paragraph that the reason for their correspondence was addressed. And, despite Rodgers' stumbling performance, the answer Guy had sought was rather quickly delivered.

If one could consider five years 'quickly.'

'The only English gentlewoman I am aware of in St Jean de Luz during the period about which you enquire was Captain William Stowe's wife, Isabella. I cannot, of course, be certain this is the lady you seek, but I can tell you that on several occasions Mrs Stowe, whose grandmother was Portuguese, proved invaluable to the allied efforts. I am also unable to provide you with Mrs Stowe's location. As she is now a widow, and entitled to her husband's pension, it is quite possible Captain Stowe's regiment may be able to give you her direction.'

Although Rodgers continued to read the Major General's closing remarks, Guy found that his mind had stuck on those salient to his quest. He now had a name for the woman whom he credited with saving his life that December night. Isabella Stowe, whose grandmother had been Portuguese. And who was now a widow.

The images that formed in his brain as a result of that information were contrary to those he had previously entertained. Whatever else she might be, the woman whose words had rescued him from what could only be described as the depths of despair was unlikely to be typically English. Other than in one important respect.

Like hundreds of others widowed by the war against Napoleon, she might very well be living in straitened circumstances. That, at least, was a situation he could do something about.

And even if she were not, he could at last express his gratitude for what she had done for him. That, of course, was the impulse that had driven his enquiries. Now that he had a name, the object of his search seemed finally within his grasp.

* * *

Isabella lowered her head, closing her eyes with her thumb and forefinger. It didn't help her headache. Or the reality the stack of bills before her represented.

There *was* no help for those, it seemed. Not in her late husband's pension and certainly not in her own failed efforts to supplement that meagre income. And if she could no longer put food on the table—

'A good cup a tea will soon put you to rights, my dear.' Her housekeeper pushed aside the shopkeepers' duns with the familiarity of long service to set the teapot down on the desk before her. 'Storm's a-brewing. That's all that's wrong with your head,' she went on cheerfully as she poured. 'My grandfather was the same way. He could always tell you about the weather.'

There *was* a storm brewing, all right, Isabella acknowledged as she lifted the steaming cup. One that didn't involve wind or rain.

'What did Mr Winters say to you when he delivered this?' She raised her eyes to assess the honesty of her servant's reply.

'I gave him a piece of my mind, I did,' Hannah said stoutly. 'The likes of *him* making demands on Mrs Stowe, I said. You should be ashamed, I told him. And he should be.'

'For wanting to be paid? You can hardly blame him for that. He has a family to feed.'

'And have you ever *not* paid him? As long as we've given him our trade? He'll get his money. I told him so, too.'

Except this time there was a very real possibility that he wouldn't, Isabella acknowledged. Neither he nor the others who had given her credit through the winter. A winter during which the roof had had to be replaced and the apothecary had been called for both Hannah and her husband, who saw to the workings of her household beyond the kitchen and the parlour.

After five years there was nothing left of William's estate—no income at all other than the pittance due her from his regiment because of his service. And that was nowhere near enough to maintain this house, small though it was, or provide a livelihood for her staff.

'There now,' Hannah said. 'That's better, isn't it?'

'Thank you.' Isabella managed to find a smile for the house-keeper, who had been like family these last few years.

How Hannah and Ned would get on if she were forced to sell the house, Isabella couldn't imagine. They were well up in years and, as evidenced by this past winter's illnesses, no longer strong enough for the demands of service.

Perhaps she would raise enough from the sale to buy them a cottage where they could live out their days? Unconsciously she shook her head, knowing that even if she were by some miracle able to provide a roof over their heads, she could not support them as well as herself.

She must have made some sound in response to the realisation. Hannah turned from the fire she'd been building up to look at her.

'Shall I rub your temples? Or perhaps a kerchief dipped in vinegar? My mother swore by that. Troubled by headaches, she was, until the day she died.'

'It isn't my head,' Isabella confessed. 'In truth…' She hesitated, hating to share the very painful realisations she herself had been forced to face this morning. 'I don't know how we shall get on,' she finished weakly.

It wasn't for herself that she feared. Not only was she well-born, she had also been well-educated. And she had travelled extensively during a period when that pastime had been denied to most Englishwomen. Even in these troubling economic times she had no doubt she could find a position as a companion or even as a governess, although her experience with children was very limited. Hannah and Ned, on the other hand…

'We'll be fine, love. Don't you trouble your head about us. As long as we've a roof over our heads and something for our tea, why, what more could we want? Ned was saying just the other day that plot to the side that gets the morning sun would be perfect for planting some more vegetables. There's no telling what else he could grow if he set his mind to it.'

The knock at the front door took them both by surprise. Hannah put down the poker she'd been wielding to wipe her hands on her apron. 'Now, who could that be in this rain?'

She was right, Isabella realised. The storm now pounded against the new roof. She said a silent prayer that the costly repair would hold against it as Hannah disappeared towards the front of the house.

Her eyes fell to the stack of bills again. *Please, God, it's not one of these demanding payment.*

She could hear Hannah's voice, but not that of the caller. A neighbour, perhaps? Or a traveller seeking directions? Apparently not the dunning she had feared.

'A gentleman, Mrs Stowe,' Hannah said as she re-entered the room. 'He insists on speaking to you.'

'Did he give you his name?'

'Wakefield, he said. Doesn't seem to be from around these parts. Too fine, if you take my meaning.'

Isabella wasn't sure she did, but she rose, brushing at the wrinkles in her skirt. It was her second-best dress, but it had already been carefully darned. If the gentleman at the door was as fine as Hannah indicated, then she should have had the house-keeper direct him to the parlour. She didn't do that because she couldn't imagine a real gentleman would come calling on her.

More than likely he'd been sent by someone whose accounts she'd been trying to figure out how to pay. If that were the case...

'I'll go to him,' she announced.

The housekeeper's mouth opened and then closed, but by that time Isabella had already pushed by her to walk towards the front door. Hannah was right, she decided as she got her first glimpse of their visitor. He *was* too fine to fit into any of the categories she had mentally assigned him.

Although she'd hesitated before entering the hallway where the housekeeper had left him, the man somehow became aware of her presence. He turned to face her, destroying the lingering possibility that he might be some tradesman's messenger.

From the intricately tied cravat to the gleaming Hessians he was every inch the gentleman. The beaver he held in his hands had probably cost more than she'd spent maintaining her household during the past year.

'Mrs Stowe?'

'Yes?'

The quick upward tilt of his lips caused a very peculiar sensation in the pit of Isabella's stomach. Not only was her visitor impeccably turned out, he was rather shockingly handsome.

His coal-black hair was touched with grey at the temples, which seemed to belie the youthfulness of his features. The most striking of which, she realised, was a pair of blue eyes rimmed with lashes that would have been the envy of any London beauty.

'How may I help you, Mr…Wakefield, is it?' Although her hand had nervously found the throat of her gown, she managed to resist the ridiculous impulse to touch her hair, which she knew was in complete disarray.

There was a brief hesitation before her caller responded. 'That's right.' As he agreed, he stepped towards her.

It was only then that she saw the scars, which had been concealed by the dim light of the hallway until now.

'I know you,' she whispered.

She did. This was the boy she'd given water to while he'd awaited transport at the harbour of St Jean de Luz.

A boy no more, she acknowledged. *If* he had been then.

One long-fingered hand lifted to touch the marred area on his right cheek. 'I wasn't certain you'd remember.'

'Of course I remember.' She was beginning to get her bearings, finally able to put this into perspective.

Mr Wakefield was here because she had attempted to succour him in an hour of need. Just as she had done with so many others during the years she'd spent in Iberia.

He was not the first of those to seek her out. Especially after William's death had become known to the soldiers who had fought with him.

'I see you have recovered from your injuries,' she said with a smile. It was always gratifying to see someone who'd survived, given the rather ghastly odds against it.

'Despite my fears.'

The answering tilt of his lips disturbed the emotional equilibrium she had just congratulated herself on achieving. And she couldn't quite decide why.

'If I remember correctly, those fears were well justified.'

'Perhaps, but…' He hesitated again, the smile in his eyes fading. 'If it were not for you—'

'I offered you water and some words of comfort,' she interrupted briskly, well accustomed to dealing with unwanted gratitude. 'I wish I could claim that I believed them, but I had in all probability offered the same meaningless phrases to the man lying beside you.'

'Possibly.'

He smiled at her again, something she found she was enjoying a little too much. Too long out of the company of attractive men. Out of the company of *any* men, she amended.

It's amazing I'm not bowled over by the butcher. And if I pretended to be would he give us something for the table?

She tried to arrange her features into some appropriately sincere mode, determined to let Mr Wakefield express his gratitude as he'd clearly come here to do. When he had done so, there would be time to decide what to do about the butcher.

'I am not, however, so certain of that as you seem to be,' he continued. 'Our conversation was quite specific, I assure you. And your remarks too apt to be given by rote.'

'Or perhaps I had grown very good at telling sorely wounded men what they needed to hear.' A skill she had rather not have had occasion to develop.

'I was taught never to argue with a lady. And I promise you that debating our memories isn't why I've come.'

'Whatever you've come for—' she began, only to be interrupted.

'I had hoped to express my gratitude in some…tangible way.'

'I'm afraid I don't understand.'

Actually, she was very much afraid that she did. And, despite the stack of duns on the table in the kitchen, she felt her temper rise.

'I was told your husband succumbed to a fever in the last days of the war.'

'A pinprick.' Her bitterness over the stupidity of it came through in her tone. 'All the times he'd been injured… This was nothing. Less than nothing. Maybe if it had been he would have let me see to it in the beginning. Instead…' She paused again to control her emotions. 'Instead the wound began to suppurate, and there was nothing I could do to stop it. My husband was gone in three days, his body burning up before my eyes.'

Only the prolonged silence after her words made her realise that she had told this stranger more about William's death than she had ever confessed to anyone else.

'I'm truly sorry,' he said softly. 'From all accounts he was a fine man. And a fine officer.'

'Yes, he was.' Unconsciously she lifted her chin, a reaction to her embarrassing display. Was she not a soldier's wife?

'It can't have been easy for you since his death.'

Her chin inched upward another notch. 'Thank you for your very kind concern, Mr Wakefield, but I assure you it is quite unnecessary. My husband provided for me very well. You need have no fear on that account.'

Another silence, during which she held his eyes, daring him to offer an additional bit of unwanted solicitude. Thank God the man had sense enough to realise he had overstepped his bounds.

She held out her hand, suddenly eager to be done with this. 'Thank you for coming to see me. I'm so very glad that what you feared that night did not come to pass.'

Again there was a heartbeat's hesitation, and then he touched her outstretched hand, bringing it to his lips. They brushed her skin, lingering not a second longer than politeness dictated.

'Thank *you* for my life, Mrs Stowe. I confess I should have been very loath to lose it.'

'You give me too much credit, Mr Wakefield. Please know,

however, that although I deny any role in your survival I am very glad it came about.'

He smiled at her again, a hint of genuine amusement in the depths of those remarkable blue eyes. 'Then…until we meet again.'

It seemed almost a question, but before she had time to think of an appropriate answer he had let himself out through the front door, stepping forward into the deluge. The door of the black closed carriage pulled up before her cottage was immediately opened to receive him, and her gentleman caller was swallowed up into its elegance so quickly she doubted his clothing would even be damp when he arrived at his destination.

And that is that, she thought decisively. She realised her hand was still hovering in mid-air, in approximately the same place where her guest had released it.

She retrieved it before stepping forward to close the door against the wind. Instead of doing so, however, she stood a moment watching Mr Wakefield's carriage drive smartly away, despite the condition of the lane.

As she turned to go back to the kitchen her eyes were drawn to the mirror over the hall table. It was exactly as she had feared.

Too late, she used her fingers to tame a few of the most recalcitrant strands of hair before she gave the exercise up as futile. The black gown drained all colour from her cheeks, and her lips matched the chapped condition of her hands.

At that thought her eyes fell from her unappealing reflection to stare at the fingers her visitor had so recently held. It seemed as if she could still feel the warmth of his wrapped around her own. Suddenly she drew her outstretched fingers into a fist, as if to hide their embarrassing condition.

What could it possibly matter? she demanded of herself brusquely. All this had been was an unexpectedly diverting interlude in an otherwise dreary day.

As William had so often reminded her during the deprivations campaigning had imposed, one should be grateful for small favours. The lovely Mr Wakefield had introduced a bit of romance into her rather bleak existence.

One that would, she reckoned, have to last her a depressingly long time.

Guy rested his head against the deeply padded seat of his carriage and closed his eyes. The long day of travel yesterday, added to the excitement of finally completing his quest, had conspired to produce another of the megrims that had periodically felled him since he'd regained his sight. And, since he refused any further doses of the laudanum that was all his physicians could offer for them, there was no help for what lay ahead.

Eyes still closed, he concentrated on remembering each detail of his meeting with Mrs Stowe. Those memories wouldn't stop the pain, of course, but they would—if briefly—take his mind off its impending attack.

He had known from General Abernathy's description that Isabella Stowe would not be the typical English beauty. What he hadn't been prepared for was the very atypical nature of her attraction.

Dark hair and eyes. The latter far too direct for polite society. A classically oval face, whose perfection might by some be considered marred by the high cheekbones and strong chin. His lips curved in remembrance of the proud tilt of her head on that swan-like neck.

Not beautiful, he conceded. Handsome would be a more appropriate description. Or perhaps, given the slightly foreign cast of her features, striking.

He could almost feel the fine bones of the hand she had given him. The skin that covered them had been cold and reddened from work. Hardly the hand of a lady, but the surge of pure sexual attraction that had jolted through his body when he'd touched it had been unlike anything he'd ever experienced.

She had accused him of misplaced gratitude, an emotion he readily admitted to. One that did not, however, come close to explaining the effect she had had on him.

If she were right, then the effort he had made to track her

down and his professed thanks should satisfy any obligation he might feel. He very much doubted that would be the case, but there would be time enough to determine that when they met again.

Because there was now, of course, no doubt in his mind that they would.

Chapter Two

Two days later, his mind occupied with the problem of finding a believable excuse for calling again on Mrs Stowe, Guy almost bumped into a slight figure hovering near the door to the public room of the inn where he had taken up residence. He looked down to make his apologies—and straight into the face that had haunted his dreams.

'Mrs Stowe?'

Her eyes widened with recognition. 'Mr Wakefield. Forgive me, but I believed from our conversation that you were not from the area.'

'London. And Hertfordshire. As I have business in the district, I'm stopping here a few days.

'I see. Two birds with one stone?' she suggested, with a touch of asperity.

'Have I offended you?'

'Of course not. I simply was not aware of your additional… engagements. I hope your accommodation is a pleasant one. The Wren's Nest is reputed to be one of the finest inns in the area.'

'Thank you, yes, but…' Puzzled by her presence at the public house so early in the day, Guy glanced around the bustling inn in an attempt to find some explanation for it. The sight of a servant carrying baggage out the main door made him realise what that must be.

'You're waiting for the stage?'

'I have some shopping to do for which I'm afraid our local establishments won't suffice.'

'Newark?' he guessed. 'Then allow me to offer what I'm sure will prove to be a more comfortable means of transportation to your destination.'

Her gaze moved to the wide doorway, crowded with those waiting to board the public conveyance. When it came back to his face, she said, 'Thank you, Mr Wakefield, but I'm quite accustomed to travelling by stage. And quite content with my experiences.'

Guy raised his own eyes, letting his gaze linger meaningfully on the throng by the front doors. A nursemaid struggled to control a couple of rambunctious boys determined to play tag, despite the close confines of the hallway. Beside her a farmer, who wore a great deal of his fields on his boots and trousers, was smoking a malodorous pipe. A large red-haired woman, whose muddy footwear marked her as very possibly his wife, held by their necks a duo of freshly killed chickens. The birds swung back and forth as she conversed with the wizened cleric at her side—a conversation of great interest to the three louts standing behind them. Through the open door he could see the coachmen loading a pile of bags and boxes, presumably belonging to the motley assemblage waiting to board, onto the already laden coach.

Guy looked back down, his brows raised in question. 'Is it always so crowded?'

Her eyes focused briefly on the coach before returning to his face. 'I believe there is a market today.'

'Ah,' he said with a smile. 'Then all the more reason to avoid the crush. I should be delighted to convey you to whatever shops you wish to visit.'

'I would not dream of troubling you.'

'It is no trouble, I assure you. I am going to Newark on business. As are you. Why should you not travel there in comfort?'

Her eyes reflected her disbelief. 'You *intended* to drive to Newark?'

'Indeed.'

'This very morning?'

'Mrs Stowe, are you doubting my veracity?'

'Mr Wakefield, do you think me so gullible as to believe such a happy coincidence?'

'Then you admit such a coincidence *would* be happy?'

'A figure of speech. As you well know.'

'Not in my case. *I* should be delighted to see you safely to your destination.' He touched her elbow, gesturing as he did so towards the crowded doorway of the inn.

Her eyes followed the direction of his hand. 'I cannot—'

'But you *can*. It is merely a matter of walking with me past those attempting to board the stage and out to my carriage, which I can assure you is warmer, better sprung, and far less crowded than the one on which they will ride. Come, Mrs Stowe. I took you for a practical woman. I shan't bite you, you know.'

'You are not foolish enough, I hope, to think I am *afraid* of you.' Her gaze, now challenging, came back to his face.

'What else am I to think?' Perhaps the thought that he *might* believe it would convince her.

'That I don't like to feel under obligation to anyone. I seriously doubt you have business in Newark, Mr Wakefield.'

'Doubt it if you wish, but I give you my word as a gentleman that is the case.'

She held his eyes a long moment.

Before she broke the contact between them, he knew he had won. It was all Guy could do not to gloat as he led her down the crowded hall and into the fresh air.

When he held out his hand to help her into his carriage she met his eyes again. 'It wasn't this, I assure you. However elegant it may be.'

'I beg your pardon?'

'It was the birds. Irrational, I know, but I never could abide them.'

'Chickens?' A woman who had endured the worst of war was afraid of a few dead fowls?

'It was my task as a child to bring in the eggs. The wretched hens would never give them up without a fight. I still have scars on my hands.' As she said the last, she placed her gloved fingers into his, her eyes alight with amusement.

'I believe you are teasing me, Mrs Stowe.'

'Indeed not, Mr Wakefield. A lady's delicate sensibilities are so easily overset.'

She turned to step up into the coach, leaving him standing alone in the crowded yard, stifling the urge to laugh. He succeeded in that endeavour by stepping to the front of the carriage in order to change his previous instructions.

'To Newark.'

The coachman's eyes widened slightly, but he was too well trained to respond with anything but what he should say. 'Of course, my lord.'

'And we have precious cargo, John. A smooth journey, if you please.'

The coachman's grin showed he was up to the task. 'Smooth as silk, my lord.'

'I'm counting on you.'

The trip was exactly what John Coachman had promised, with the matched bays bowling along the road as if the recent rain had never occurred. Guy's only complaint was that the time he spent with his unexpected guest was far too brief.

For two people with shared experiences of war, despite the fact those had taken place more than five years before, conversation came easily. Having reluctantly agreed to his offer, Mrs Stowe seemed immediately to relax into the luxury offered by his carriage.

They spent the first few minutes exploring acquaintances they had in common, only to discover that far too many of those had perished on the Continent. Afraid that realisation would remind her of her own loss, Guy undertook to lighten the mood by recalling the outrageous antics of the group of men he was honoured to have called comrades-in-arms as well as friends.

She readily matched his best stories about life as a member of Wellington's diverse and sometimes eccentric staff with others concerning men under her husband's command. Her understanding of reckless young soldiers was both generous and forgiving. In short, Guy found himself laughing more than he had in years.

'And his lordship never discovered who had left her chemise in his headquarters?' she asked at the end of his narrative about one of the most memorable episodes of the type of teasing so prevalent among the staff.

'As he included my name in the dispatches from the next battle, I'm certain he had no inkling of who was involved. If he had, I promise you we should not be having this conversation today.'

'Then I am grateful to your fellows for keeping your secret.'

The laughter that had sparkled in her eyes during most of the trip was suddenly replaced by a sincerity that took his breath. Guy searched for a response that, in spite of what he had just seen in them, wouldn't indicate he'd read too much into her simple statement.

'Believe me, I was grateful, too,' he said, smiling at her. 'Then *and* now.'

She lowered her eyes to adjust the fit of her gloves. They both looked up as the carriage began to slow.

'It seems we've arrived,' she said, glancing out of the window.

The strength of Guy's disappointment in that surprised him. He couldn't remember a more enjoyable hour since those long-ago days spent among his comrades.

'Is there a particular shop you wish to visit first?' he asked.

'Instruct your driver to stop at the town's centre, if you please. I fear my list of errands is not only quite extensive, but varied.'

'Then perhaps I might offer my services in carrying your packages?'

'I could not think of delaying you from seeing to your business, Mr Wakefield. I shall do very well on my own, I promise you.'

Hoist by his own petard, Guy gave up the battle in order to continue the war. 'Then if you'll suggest a time at which your shopping might be completed—?'

'Oh, no. I shan't trouble you with *that*. The stage will do very well for my return.' She looked up to smile at him. 'I suspect the hens will have been sold long before the afternoon's run.'

'Forgive me, Mrs Stowe, but I had thought you, too, had enjoyed our journey. As I am spending several days in the area, I will, of course, be returning to the Wren's Nest this afternoon. I had looked forward to continuing our conversation on the way.'

She held out her hand, which he took automatically. 'You have been everything that is kind, Mr Wakefield. I can't remember when I've more enjoyed reminiscing about my campaigning days. As you can imagine, there has been little opportunity for that since William's death. Now, however…' Her eyes returned to the window as the carriage bumped to a halt. 'Yes, this will do nicely. Thank you for allowing me to join you. Perhaps we shall meet again before you return home?'

'I look forward to that,' Guy managed, before the door opened and the steps were lowered. He jumped out to offer his hand.

When she was safely on the ground, she lifted the skirt of the black bombazine to shake out its wrinkles. 'Until then,' she said, looking up with another smile.

Before he could think of an appropriate attempt to delay the inevitable, she was walking away from him up the crowded street. He motioned to his tiger, perched on the back of the carriage. The lad hopped down with alacrity.

Guy caught him by the shoulder, pulling him close. 'Follow the lady. I want to know where she goes and what she does, but she must not be aware that you're watching her. There's a guinea in it if you manage both.'

The boy's eyes widened at the promise, and he quickly nodded. 'Right you are, my lord. I'll be her shadow. But she won't know I'm around, I swear to you.'

'See that she doesn't.'

As he watched his tiger rush off to follow his prey, Guy felt like a spy. He was probably making too much of Mrs Stowe's reluctance to have him accompany her on her shopping. Perhaps she was simply tired of his company.

The memory of the ready laughter in her eyes and of her responses to his stories belied that explanation. Something else was going on with Captain Stowe's widow and, whether his pursuit was entirely honourable or not, Guy was determined to discover what it was.

'And you're sure the situation is that dire?'

Guy's fingers played idly with the gold locket he had purchased from the jeweller in Newark as he awaited an answer from his man of business. Although the wedding ring Mrs Stowe had sold, along with a necklace and a brooch, also lay on the table before him, he was reluctant to touch it.

He was now aware—because he had taken pains to find out—how small William Stowe's regimental pension was. Still, despite that, and Isabella's decision to sell her jewellery, he was surprised at the bleakness of the report he'd just been given.

Mrs Stowe was heavily in debt. Not, according to Benton, through any profligacy on her part, but rather through a series of wrenching choices that had forced her to put the welfare of her dependents ahead of her own economic well-being.

'It could hardly be worse, my lord. Given the extremely depressed value of all property now, even the sale of the house may not cover what she owes. She has her husband's pension, of course, but as far as being able to provide a living for the couple she currently supports…' Benton's shrug was eloquent.

'Can you obtain a list of her obligations? Without, of course, letting her know the information is being collected.'

'Easily, since I suspect it will contain the names of most of the tradesmen in the district.'

'If that is the case, then discharge her debts to them,' Guy ordered softly.

'But if I depend upon *their* accounting, without corresponding corroboration from her, there will be no way to prevent the unscrupulous among them from padding their bills.'

'Pay whatever they ask.'

'Forgive me, my lord, but that's hardly the wisest way to do business.'

'But it *is* the quickest.'

'And speed is important?' Benton's tone was sceptical.

'In this instance. I want the matter handled before Mrs Stowe has any inkling of what you're about.'

His man of business knew Guy too well to press the point. Besides, debts that must seem crippling to a widow living on a soldier's pension were a trifle to the sums his estate routinely incurred. He had never blinked at those.

Benton was almost to the door of his office when the Viscount stopped him. 'And it must be done anonymously, Benton. That's most important.'

'Of course, my lord. She *will* find out, you know,' Benton warned.

Guy raised his eyes to focus on the piercing ones behind the spectacles. 'But not, I believe, before your task can be accomplished. Especially not if you begin at once.'

Chapter Three

Lost in the same troubling thoughts that had occupied her mind for the last two days, Isabella was unaware that a carriage had slowed to a snail's pace beside her until its occupant spoke.

'May I offer you a ride, Mrs Stowe?'

She looked up to find Mr Wakefield looking at her out of the window of his coach. She was suddenly aware that the hem of her gown was thick with mud and its style years out of date. Something a man of his refinement would certainly be aware of.

'Thank you, no. I find a walk often clears the head. Especially after being shut inside for a few days.'

'You are undoubtedly right,' he returned pleasantly before tapping on the roof of the carriage with his stick.

Instead of driving on, as she had anticipated, the coach stopped, allowing its passenger to descend. He smiled at her as he took his place beside her.

'Today's sun is a pleasant change,' he offered.

'Indeed.' They walked a few paces before she turned her eyes towards him. 'Your animals are beautiful. And superbly conditioned.'

'Thank you. I confess to a weakness for good horseflesh, as well as an uncommon admiration for it.'

'No doubt your experiences on the Peninsula account for that. If your life has ever depended on the courage of your mount, I suspect you never feel the same about horses.'

'Exactly. Do you ride, Mrs Stowe?'

'Not for a long time.' One of many things she could no longer afford.

And in a country where children starve to death, what can that possibly matter?

'Would you join me tomorrow? I'm sure there's a suitable lady's mare to be found nearby.'

She laughed, thinking of the magnificent beasts that had carried her safely through the wildest regions of Iberia. It was a point of pride that there had not been a so-called 'lady's mare' among them.

'Although I'm delighted to have amused you,' her companion said, 'I do wonder what I've said to provoke your laughter.'

'Forgive me. Yours is a natural assumption, I suppose, but I'm not accustomed to riding mounts designated as fit *only* for ladies.'

'A horsewoman, then?' His lips curved slightly, but there was no ridicule in his tone.

'I believe so.' Hers contained a touch of pride.

'All the better. Shall we say…seven?'

The words of denial were on the tip of her tongue. Considering all the difficult decisions that had been forced upon her during the past few days, she found it impossible to utter them. One last ride on a horse worthy of the name. What could it hurt?

'If you wish. There is, however, a spot I'm particularly fond of from which to watch the sunrise.'

'And how early should one be to accomplish that?'

'If you are at my door at five, I believe you will be in for a treat. I realise those aren't London hours…'

'I beg you to remember that I was one of Hooky's aides, Mrs Stowe. I assure you I've seen many a sunrise.'

'Five,' she repeated, throwing what was intended to be a

warning glance at him. At some point in the process, it became a smile instead.

He returned it before he tipped the beaver she'd admired on the day of his call, bidding her farewell before he climbed back into his coach.

And when he had driven away, leaving her quite alone again on the muddy lane, she was hard pressed to explain the sense of loss that descended on her spirits.

'Worth leaving your bed so early?' Isabella asked her companion.

Mr Wakefield's eyes remained locked on the vista before them, but a muscle tightened in the strong line of his jaw. 'Can you doubt it?'

She turned back to face the rising sun, which had first painted the scene below a faint rose that was now shading to old gold. With the overlying mist, this morning's subtle colours heightened the sense of wonder she always experienced here. 'There *are* those who would see no magic in this.'

'Not if they had ever been unable to see,' he responded softly.

She'd almost forgotten the circumstances of their initial meeting. Because he no longer seemed either young or vulnerable?

'I'm sorry. I didn't think.'

'Why should you?' He turned to smile at her. 'It was a very long time ago.'

Bothered by some shadow in those remarkable eyes, she turned back to contemplate the remainder of the miracle she had brought him here to view. Her mount, as prime a piece of horseflesh as she'd ever ridden, tossed its head at the enforced inactivity.

Although she quickly re-established control, she could sympathise with the gelding's impatience. After all, they had not yet fully tested one another. Not to either's satisfaction.

'I believe he wants a run.' Although there was no hint of challenge in his voice, Mr Wakefield was not quite able to control the line of his lips.

'I believe you are right, sir.'

She began to turn the animal, intending to send him down the gentle slope they had climbed and then out onto the wide meadow below. A gloved hand over hers prevented the movement. She raised her crop, the gesture more reflex than temper—although that, too, had begun to rise.

'Forgive me, Mrs Stowe,' Wakefield said. 'I feel I must warn you—'

'Remove your hand, Mr Wakefield.'

Their eyes locked for a fraction of a second, but only that. Then the fingers that had impeded her were released. Anger heating her blood, Isabella dug in her heels, sending the roan racing down the hill.

Excitement flowed through her veins like an elixir. Caged too long by worry and circumstance, she had missed the exhilaration this offered. To become one with the animal and yet to know that its power was fully in her control.

As was almost nothing else.

She banished the unwanted thought, leaning forward over the neck of the gelding. She was aware on some level of the rider who followed, but she ignored his presence, too, relishing the unaccustomed feeling of freedom.

She didn't slow her mount until she felt the first tremble of fatigue in its powerful legs. As soon as she did, she began gradually to pull up, until they had once more achieved a sedate amble.

She was running her gloved hand over the gleaming neck of the horse and whispering endearments when her companion drew alongside. She turned to smile at him, her pleasure as heady as new wine.

'Thank you, Mr Wakefield.'

'You're very welcome, Mrs Stowe. And it's Guy.'

'I beg your pardon?'

'My name is Guy.'

With the exertion of their ride, fresh colour stained his cheeks. It made the scars on the right more visible, but she found they in no way detracted from his attractiveness.

'I believe we are not on such familiar terms.' She lowered her eyes, again running a soothing hand over her mount's neck. Its breathing had returned to normal, as had her own.

'Forgive me. I had hoped we were. You know, the gentleman who owns the gelding would be delighted to have you ride again.'

She glanced up at his offer, weighing it in her mind. How much it would mean to have this avenue of escape from the worry that seemed to depress her spirits more every day.

But, although tempting, she didn't want to be beholden to either Mr Wakefield or the owner of this magnificent animal. She had had her treat. One she would never have believed available to her only a few days ago.

Before the elegant Mr Wakefield had appeared at her door. And in her life.

'I don't believe I shall have time for that, but do express my gratitude to him for today.' She didn't dare raise her eyes for fear her companion would read the truth in them. 'I am so very grateful to you both.'

'Should I believe, Mrs Stowe, that the gelding may have satisfied your stipulation of "no lady's mare"?'

Although Mr Wakefield's voice was rich with humour, it wasn't at her expense, Isabella decided. She lifted her eyes to smile at him, and surprised a look in his that didn't fit with the lightness of his remark.

A downward sweep of his lashes quickly hid what she had seen. Only with her hesitation in answering did he raise them again, but all she saw there now was polite enquiry.

'He is everything I could have wished for and more. Thank you again for knowing exactly what I meant.'

'Another "happy coincidence," perhaps?' he said with a smile.

He immediately turned the subject then, commenting on the profusion of wildflowers the recent rains had produced and asking her to name them for him, so that they were able to chat quite easily about nothing at all on the way home.

When he had seen her safely inside her house, Isabella leaned against the door, for the first time allowing herself to recreate in her mind's eye what she had glimpsed in his.

She was no green girl, but a woman who had been happily married for eight years to a man she'd adored. A man who had fully awakened her to carnal pleasure.

She drew a long breath, feeling her body unwillingly respond to the memory of the desire she had clearly read in Guy Wakefield's eyes.

Ridiculous, she thought determinedly. He was years younger than she. And, as Hannah had so aptly put it, far too fine. Too much the London gentleman.

Besides, if he desired her—and she was too experienced at *being* desired to have mistaken that emotion—it was not in the way William had. No, Mr Wakefield had no doubt made the same mistake a few of her husband's compatriots had made when they'd discovered the Captain's wife had come campaigning with him.

If Guy Wakefield believed that she could be had in exchange for a morning ride and some words of gratitude, he would soon realise his mistake. Of course, she acknowledged with a slight smile as she pushed away from the door, she *would* have to give him credit for the rather singular nature of his courtship.

Chapter Four

'He's here again,' Hannah said, *sotto voce*.

'Who?' Her intellect completely occupied by the difficulty, despite the sale of her jewellery, in making so little money satisfy so many debts, Isabella truly had no clue what the housekeeper meant.

'The London gentleman.'

'Mr Wakefield?'

It had been two days since their dawn ride, and, given her abrupt denial of his offer to repeat the experience, she'd not been surprised when she had not heard from him again. She had even wondered—despite having vowed to put all thoughts of the man from her mind—if the business that had brought him to the area had at last been completed.

Apparently not, she thought with a flutter of something that felt annoyingly like anticipation in her chest.

She stood, stripping off the apron she'd donned that morning to help Hannah with the cleaning. As she laid it on the back of her chair, she realised her fingers were ink-stained and more reddened than usual from their immersion in the soapy water she and the housekeeper had used to scrub the floors. Once again Mr Wakefield had caught her at her worst.

'The same.' Hannah reached out to straighten her collar. 'And *this* time he's brought flowers,' the housekeeper added, a smile tugging at her wrinkled lips.

'Flowers?' Although she had no doubt as to what she'd seen in Guy Wakefield's eyes that morning, Isabella had believed she'd been discouraging enough that she would not have to deal with this sort of romantic nonsense. 'Oh, for heaven's sake…'

She stormed towards the hall, only to have Hannah call after her, 'He's in the parlour.'

At least after their morning's labours the room was clean, she thought as she marched resolutely to where her unwanted suitor awaited. If she had not been forceful enough before—

She stopped on the threshold, the peculiar sensation she'd experienced during his first visit roiling in her stomach again. Guy Wakefield stood with his back to her, looking out on the front garden.

The breadth of his shoulders was clearly delineated by the impeccable cut of his jacket. Just as the muscles of his long legs were revealed by skin-tight pantaloons that disappeared into the tops of his Hessians. His hair gleamed blue-black in the light from the window.

Every inch the London gentleman, she thought again.

Then she remembered, despite his age, the broad sweep of grey at his temples—something that indicated as surely as did the fading scars on his cheek—that there was more to him than the shallow man-about-town his dress indicated.

And no longer the frightened boy she had comforted all those years ago.

He must have sensed her presence. He turned to smile at her, holding out a bouquet of field flowers tied together with a blade of grass.

'I couldn't resist,' he said, blue eyes twinkling. 'You particularly admired these during our ride, and they seemed to be blooming even more prolifically this afternoon. It seemed a shame you couldn't enjoy them, too.'

Her mouth had been opened to give him the set-down she had

come to deliver, but something about that endearingly bedraggled collection of wildflowers made her close it again.

'What are you doing?' she asked instead.

He didn't pretend not to understand. 'I am attempting to win the favour of a lady I admire.'

'Why?' She schooled her features to express displeasure, although surprisingly that was not the only emotion she felt.

'Because I find I very much desire her favour.' The soft words were almost apologetic.

'I believe that what you *desire*, sir, is the lady,' she said bluntly.

His silence lasted so long she became aware of the pounding of her heart. Why *did* he have this effect on her?

'Forgive me, Mrs Stowe, but I cannot deny the truth of that. Nor would I wish to,' he added.

'Whatever fault of character you may have read in my having accompanied my husband to Iberia, it is, I assure you—'

His face changed abruptly. He took a step forward, the outstretched bouquet allowed to fall to his side. 'You could not be more mistaken, ma'am, in thinking I have found *any* fault in your character. Indeed…' He hesitated before finishing earnestly, 'the fact that you accompanied your husband to war only increases my admiration.'

'It was not an admiration of character I saw in your eyes the day of our ride, Mr Wakefield.'

The stern line of his lips ticked upward slightly, but he quickly controlled what appeared to be an impulse to smile. 'I confess. It is not *only* your character I am enamoured of.'

'Are you bowled over by my beauty or my charm?' As if to emphasise her point, she spread the meagre skirt of her gown, a dark grey bombazine, and dropped a low curtsy.

'Is that so difficult for you to believe?'

'Impossible,' she said succinctly. 'I can tell you the true source of your infatuation, Mr Wakefield. Even a blind man could see it.'

Although her choice of words had been deliberate, she regretted them immediately. His face closed, hardening so that for the

first time she could imagine him carrying out the highly dangerous missions he would have undertaken as one of Wellington's
aides.

'You have come to believe that I played some role in your
survival and subsequent recovery,' she went on ruthlessly. 'You
are, understandably, grateful for both, but I assure you I had no
more to do with either than did the bells we heard. Whatever I
said or did that encouraged you was a fortunate accident at best.
And nothing I hadn't said or done for dozens of other wounded
men. Many of whom *didn't* survive, despite my miraculous presence at their side. And now, if you'll excuse me, I have household
matters to attend to. Hannah will see you to the door.'

She was halfway to the hall before his words stopped her.

'I have no right to ask it, I know, but I'd be very grateful if
you would hear me out.'

She turned. 'I think you've been *quite* grateful enough, Mr
Wakefield.'

'I can hardly deny my gratitude, since I readily admitted it to
you the first time I came.'

She inclined her head, feeling vindicated by this confession.

Until he added, 'That wasn't, however, why I returned.'

She hesitated, waiting for him to go on. When he didn't, she
was forced to voice the question that begged to be asked. 'Then
why *did* you return?'

He lifted the bedraggled bouquet, the gesture unthinking,
before he shook his head. 'Because I have never in my life felt
about a woman as I feel about you.'

Exasperated, she looked down at her fingers, tightly inter-
twined at her waist. She lifted her joined hands, holding them
together at heart's level. 'You are infatuated with something that
does not exist.'

'*You* exist.'

'Not as you believe me to be.'

'And what do I believe you to be?'

She ignored the amusement in his voice to plough on. 'Some
sort of romantic figure you've created in your head. Some-

one responsible for your survival. Someone to whom you owe something. *None* of that is true.'

'No, it is not.'

Caught in mid-tirade, it took a moment for her to register his agreement. 'I beg your pardon?'

'None of those things are, true. Or at least if they are they are not the reasons for how I feel.'

She swallowed against the unexpected surge of emotion his denial created. 'Then to what do you attribute your...?' She hesitated, beginning to fear that she was making a fool of herself by having read too much into a bunch of wildflowers and a pretty sentiment.

Because I have never in my life felt about a woman as I feel about you. What other interpretation could she possibly put on that? Had she been out of society so long that she had forgotten what being courted felt like?

'My attraction to you?' he finished for her.

She allowed her hands to separate, holding them out before her, palms up. 'You can't possibly be attracted to me.'

'Why not?' This time he made no attempt to conceal his amusement.

'Because...' She shook her head, for some reason unwilling to list for him all the faults she had quite forthrightly been cataloguing to herself since she had met him. 'We do not suit, Mr Wakefield.'

'Believe me, you suit me very well, Mrs Stowe.'

'I am older than you.'

'And undoubtedly wiser. My family would not find that amiss, I promise you.' The curve of his lips increased slightly.

'Are you mocking me, sir?'

'Only myself, Mrs Stowe. Is age the only impediment you see to my courtship? If so—'

'Our positions, of course. I am not...in society. Actually, I have never been in society. I married young. You know what my life was like before William's death.'

Something shifted in his eyes. His body, which had been

relaxed despite the strong tension in hers, straightened. 'Forgive me. I had hoped that five years would be long enough...'

His words trailed, and her mind struggled to finish his thought. When she finally realised what he believed, she wondered if that would be enough to put an end to this. But for some reason— perhaps her inherent aversion to lies—she could not bring herself to use the weapon he had placed in her hands.

'There is no one who would wish for my future happiness more than my late husband, Mr Wakefield. I loved him deeply. Too much so to falsely claim that what we shared would keep me from falling in love with another man. That is the last thing William would have wanted.'

'*Another* man? But not with me? Should you like a letter of recommendation from my commanding officer, Mrs Stowe? I promise you I served my country to the best of my ability.'

'I'm sure you did. That isn't what I meant. I meant to a man I loved.'

'The ultimate impediment,' he said. 'An undeniable one, I admit, which is why I'm trying so hard to win your favour. If you tell me what you find objectionable about my suit or my person, I promise I shall try to remedy it.'

'I don't find you objectionable, Mr Wakefield.' *Quite the contrary*, she thought, before she banished that admission from her mind. 'It's just that we do not suit. There is too wide a gap between us.' She braced for his denial, and was surprised when it did not come.

'Am I allowed to try and bridge that gap?' he asked instead. When she hesitated, he added, 'Please understand that today's attempt is far from my best effort. I did not wish to frighten you off by rushing you. Perhaps I could bring you a bouquet from a conservatory the next time?'

She raised her eyes to find that he was again holding out the roadside flowers, which were now even more bedraggled than when they had begun this conversation.

'You cannot court me, Mr Wakefield.'

'I can indeed, Mrs Stowe. You may refuse me, but you cannot

in all good conscience forbid me to try. Not having given me your husband's permission.'

'Did I do that?'

'I believe that you did. Let me look after you as he would surely have wished someone to.' There was no doubting the sincerity in his voice.

Hearing it, she felt her eyes sting with tears she resolutely denied. She could not succumb to that lure. If she gave herself to this man, in spite of all the very good reasons she saw against doing so, then it must be because she loved him as much as she had loved William.

'No,' she said resolutely, and then softened the denial by adding, 'But I will let you give me those.' She gestured towards his offering by tilting her chin at them.

Her voice had been unsteady. His answering smile was not, as he stepped forward to present them to her. 'Only until I can find the conservatory flowers I promised you.'

'Thank you,' she said as she raised the fading blossoms to her face. 'These are lovely. In all honesty, I much prefer them to any others.'

'I suspect that we have a great deal in common. Then…until I am fortunate enough to see you again…' He inclined his head, his eyes holding hers.

'Your business in the district is not yet complete?'

His smile widened. 'No, but I am greatly encouraged that it might yet have a satisfactory resolution. Don't bother your housekeeper. I can see myself out.'

When she heard the front door close behind him, she raised the flowers once more, breathing in so deeply that she sneezed.

A fitting conclusion to a *most* peculiar courtship, she decided. But she was smiling as she returned to the kitchen.

Chapter Five

'I know this is not all that is owed on my account, Mr Carter, but I promise you that the rest will be paid as soon as possible.' Isabella placed the small sack that contained a few carefully counted out coins on the desk between them. 'I have had some unexpected expenses that necessitated the delay in settling with you. However, I do not expect any additional drain on my finances. If I may ask for your continued patience…'

She looked up to find the merchant's eyes on her face, rather than on the money she had just presented to him. In them was a look she had seen before—particularly from those who, as she had accused Guy Wakefield of doing, judged her character based upon her having travelled with Wellington's army. This man might not ever have heard the phrase 'camp follower,' but his eyes indicated that what he was thinking was something very much like that insult.

'Is there some problem, Mr Carter?'

'Not at all, Mrs Stowe. It's just that…' Carter's thick lips pursed as he seemed to weigh his next words. Then, with the back of his hand, he pushed the bag towards her. 'You owe me nothing.'

'But there must be some mistake. I received a bill from you only last week.'

'As you say, a mistake. Businesses make such errors all the time.'

'A mistake?'

'Another customer's purchases credited to your account, perhaps? I shall speak to my bookkeeper to ensure nothing like this happens again.

'Come, Mr Carter, your accounting was *quite* specific. The items listed *were* my purchases. I believe I have brought the bill with me…' She opened her reticule to procure the document.

'Please don't bother, Mrs Stowe. That's all been taken care of.'

'Taken care of?' Her fingers froze around the paper she had sought as she looked up at him. 'I'm not sure I understand.'

'Your account has been paid in full, Mrs Stowe.'

'*Paid?* Paid by whom?'

Nothing about this made sense, she thought in confusion. And then, in some dark corner of her mind, an idea fluttered to life. An idea she had no desire to give credence to.

The merchant shrugged. 'By a gentleman who wished to remain anonymous.'

It was there again. The look she had seen in his eyes before. And it infuriated her.

'*No one* has the right to settle my accounts but me.'

'Come, come, Mrs Stowe. An act of kindness, surely? As you said, you have had some unexpected expenses. Perhaps a friend wished to make things easier for a lady he admires. The scripture tells us—'

'Do *not*, I beg of you, quote scripture to me. Who paid my accounting?' As she made the demand, she laid the bill she had received only a few days ago from this very man between them.

'I was not told his name. As I said, he wished his actions to be anonymous.'

'What did he look like?' Even as she posed the question she already knew the answer.

'A relative, perhaps? What can it matter?'

'It matters a great deal to me, Mr Carter. A description of my benefactor, if you please.'

'I gave him my word, Mrs Stowe. He was quite insistent about that.'

'Well-dressed? With an air that marked him as not local? A citizen of…London, perhaps? Someone with fading burn marks on his face?'

'As I have indicated, the gentleman did not wish to make his kindness known.' The unctuous smile did not quite reach his eyes.

'And you believe that you know why?' she asked. 'Never mind answering that, Mr Carter. It is very clear what you think.' She stood, reaching across his desk to pick up the small sack of coins that symbolised all she had given up through the years in order to keep her independence and protect her pride. 'He is neither a relative nor a friend.' Her voice softened as she added, 'Nor anything *else* you have been imagining him to be.'

He's simply a meddling fool who is far too accustomed to having his own way.

'I will bid you good day, Mr Carter.' She rose, but stood a moment on the other side of the wide desk, looking down on the merchant. 'From now on please remember that my accounts are my concern and mine alone and refrain from making them known to anyone else—no matter how well connected you perceive that person to be. Perception isn't truth. And, whatever you think about the gentleman's reasons, they are, I assure you, as far from the truth as what you have just now been thinking about me.'

She turned towards the door, ignoring his sputtering denials. It didn't matter what he said or thought. The man, as despicable as she found him to be, wasn't the villain of this piece. But she knew exactly where to find the person who was.

'A lady to see you, my lord. A Mrs Stowe. And quite insistent, I might add.'

Although, thanks to the efficiency of his servants, Guy had settled in nicely at the Wren's Nest, he was not opposed to the speed with which his next meeting with Isabella Stowe seemed about to occur. In truth, he had not expected her to discover what he'd done so quickly, but, given the size of the village in which she lived, he probably should have.

'Of course. And Andrews…?'

'Yes, my lord?'

'More light, I think.'

'Of course, my lord.'

As his valet lit candles, Guy felt his anticipation grow. He'd waited so long to find Isabella. He had begun to wonder during the past few days if his frustration with that search had played a role in the effect she had had on him. Even if it had—

'Now, my lord?'

'No title, if you please. The lady believes me to be *Mr* Wakefield.'

'I see, my lord.' Andrews' tone made it clear he did not. 'As you wish, my lord.'

As he turned to usher Isabella in, Guy smiled at his valet's expression. Clearly the fact that he was hiding his position did not sit well with Andrews. He suspected it wasn't the duplicity that annoyed him so much as it was the loss of the cachet Guy's title would normally provide.

'Mrs Stowe, my—sir.'

'Thank you, Andrews. That will be all.'

Isabella waited until the valet had disappeared into the adjoining bedroom. Then she walked across the room, fingering a folded paper out of her reticule as she did so. 'What is the meaning of this?'

Guy glanced down at the document thrust under his nose. 'Forgive me, Mrs Stowe, but I assure you I have no idea what that is.'

'You know very well what it is. It is a household account. One which has been paid. One which *I* did not pay.'

'Ah.'

'Do you still deny that you paid it?'

'Although I am very loath to correct a lady, I don't believe I have denied anything.'

'You said you had no idea what it is.'

The becoming colour he'd noted in her cheeks seemed to be increasing. Of course she was standing very close to him in order to present her evidence. So close, in fact, that he could detect the faintest trace of the scent she wore. Something heady. And as unusual as she was.

'I don't. The damage to my eyes precludes me from being able to read, I'm afraid.'

Her mouth had opened to deliver what was intended to be her next accusation. When the sense of what he'd just said penetrated her anger she closed it again, swallowing hard against an emotion he had never before deliberately tried to evoke in another person. Indeed, he had spent the last five years trying *not* to evoke the sentiment he saw reflected in her eyes.

'Forgive me. I didn't know.' She removed the paper she'd been holding in front of his face, stepping back to increase the distance between them. 'That doesn't, however, change what you have done.'

Her chin had come up again, he noted admiringly. And thankfully the fire was back in her eyes, replacing that flash of pity.

'I merely wanted to express my gratitude for what *you* did for *me*.'

'I gave you water—' she began.

'And hope,' he interrupted. 'A priceless commodity, I promise you, when one has none.'

Her mouth closed again as she considered her next words. 'I did no more for you than for dozens of other men.'

'And I have no doubt any one of them would wish to do as I have done. To thank you. I simply had both the opportunity *and* the means.'

She lowered her eyes to the bill she held in her gloved hand. 'I never wanted your gratitude. I certainly don't want your money.'

He wisely refrained from arguing that it had, in the end, cost him very little to secure her financial security. He reached into his pocket instead, pulling out the locket, brooch and ring he had carried there since he'd retrieved them from the Newark jeweller to whom she'd sold them.

'You would rather give up these than allow me to express my thanks?' He opened his palm, the gold glinting in the candlelight.

Her eyes studied the items a moment before they lifted to his face. 'How did you—?' The question faltered as she worked out exactly how he must have come by her possessions. 'You followed me that day.'

It was clearly an accusation, and one he didn't bother to deny. 'By then I had begun to suspect that your circumstances were...' He stopped, unable to find words that might not give more offence than his actions had already provoked. 'The fact that you were willing to part with these simply confirmed my fears.'

'Those were mine, Mr Wakefield. To dispose of as I saw fit.'

'Despite their sentimental value?'

Her smile was bitter. 'I discovered in Iberia that sentiment is a very unpalatable dish when people you care about are hungry. The choice to sell them was entirely mine. And none of your concern.'

'I only wanted to help. To make things easier for you. As you say yourself, that is what one does when the people one cares about are suffering.'

'I cannot prevent you from feeling whatever you profess to feel for me, but I have not given you the right to interfere in my affairs. A week ago I was a stranger to you—someone you had met briefly a very long time ago. During these last few days I have told you at every turn that I am not interested in furthering our relationship. Instead of abiding by my wishes you have humiliated me before people with whom I am forced to do business.'

'*Humiliated* you? How can what I have done have—?'

'What do *you* think those men believe is the reason you have laid out a goodly sum to pay my debts? Trust me, *they* have no doubt about your motives.'

'That's absurd—' he began, only to be quickly interrupted.

'Can you actually be so insulated by your wealth that you have no idea what a fertile field for gossip a village like this can be? I have little of value, Mr Wakefield, beyond my good name—which you, with your meddling, have now destroyed.'

'I cannot believe your neighbours are so low-minded. But if you do, there is an easy remedy for your concerns.'

'Oh? Pray tell me what that is?'

'Marry me.'

'Mr Wakefield!'

The tone with which she said his name was not one he would have wished to evoke with his proposal, but Guy ploughed on, beginning to realise only now what a botch he had made of this. He had gone about achieving what he wanted—what he had genuinely believed would be to Isabella's advantage—with the same heedless single-mindedness he had too often displayed in his youth.

'I know that I've offended you, and for that I am deeply sorry, but I assure you that was never my intent. I simply want to take care of you. That was my only motivation, believe me.'

'I did not give you the right to "take care of" me. Nor do I need to be taken care of.'

'Then give me the right to love you instead.'

That gave her pause. Her mouth opened and then closed. And for a moment he dared to hope. A hope that was quickly dashed by her response.

'I see that you will not be reasoned with. Please send me a list of the other tradesmen you have given money to in my name, and the amounts you have paid them. I shall see to it that whatever outlay you have made on my behalf is repaid as soon as possible.'

She pushed the bill she had tried to show him back into her bag as she stalked towards the door. She turned before she reached it. 'I do not wish to see you again, Mr Wakefield. If you truly feel any gratitude for what passed between us in France, please do not call upon me before you leave.'

'Isabella.'

Her head came up at his use of her name. 'I have not given you permission to address me so familiarly, and I will not. Please do not do that again. Good day, Mr Wakefield.' She reached out to open the door, finding Andrews standing guard in the hallway.

'Excuse me, please,' she said to him, her voice breaking.

The valet looked towards Guy, his brows lifted in question. 'My lord?'

With those words Isabella turned, her eyes full of disbelief which quickly changed to anger. 'Has there been *anything* in our dealings in which you have *not* been deceitful?'

She turned back to push past the servant, who by now had realised the extent of his mistake.

'There is no deceit in how I feel about you,' Guy said, raising his voice to carry to her as she disappeared into the darkness of the hall.

'I—am so sorry, my lord,' Andrews stuttered. 'Shall I go after her?'

Knowing there was no point, Guy shook his head, looking down on the pieces of jewellery he still held in his hand. He closed his fist around them and brought them hard against his body.

He had done exactly what he always did. He had ridden rough-shod over any and every obstacle that had been placed in his path, convinced that what he wanted could be obtained if only he pursued it as vigorously as he could. That boundless determination had stood him in good stead so many times in his life, but it had obviously been the wrong tactic in winning Isabella Stowe.

She had every right to be angry. He *had* deceived her in regards to his identity. And it had not even once crossed his mind to consider what effect his satisfying her debts might have on her reputation.

He had been arrogant, bull-headed, and incredibly stupid. In the process he had hurt the woman he loved.

And now, despite all his regrets, he had no idea how to undo the unthinking damage he had done.

Chapter Six

Isabella could not have explained what had brought her back to this spot so soon. It was a place that should be filled with nothing but painful memories now, but as the rising sun touched the land below with gilt, she remembered only a man who had been able to feel here what she had always felt.

There are those who would see no magic in this.

Not if they had ever been unable to see.

Was she the one who'd been blind? Would it be such a curse if someone wanted to love and protect her?

If those things came at the cost of my independence.

And will your independence see to Hannah and Ned in their old age? Or fill the lonely days and lonelier nights of the rest of your life?

The last was a question for which she'd not yet given an affirmative answer. Not one she herself could be convinced by.

Her further contemplation of the sunrise was shattered by the sound of a horse being ridden hard up the slope behind her. She turned, watching as its rider directed the animal to the place where she stood.

As horse and rider drew nearer, whatever fleeting doubts she had had as to the identity of the man mounted on the black steed disappeared. She had asked that Guy not call on her before he left. She supposed that in seeking her here he had obeyed the letter of her request, if not its spirit. The fact that he would come to this place, a favourite that she had shared with him in the spirit of friendship, angered her anew.

The stallion's breath clouded the air as he was drawn up beside her. Guy removed his hat and inclined his head in greeting.

The sun was high enough now that it gleamed on his bare head and cruelly exposed the scars on his cheek. The wind ruffled his hair, making him look almost as young as he had on that Christmas Day in France.

'My apologies for disturbing your solitude,' he said.

'You may easily rectify your intrusion.' Deliberately, she turned back to the vista she had come here to enjoy.

Even as she did so, she was very conscious of him. The creak of leather that indicated he was dismounting. The now-familiar fragrance of sandalwood and starch and clean linen as he moved to stand beside her.

She didn't look at him, determined to hold onto her indignation and her sense of being wronged. She knew that if she didn't…

Unconsciously she shook her head, denying what might happen if she didn't remember that this man had both lied to her and opened her up to ridicule from her neighbours.

'I have done what I can to make amends for my stupidity,' he said, almost as if he had read her thoughts.

She kept her eyes resolutely forward, wondering what he thought he could possibly do that would change the situation he had set into motion.

'I have explained to those who might need explanation for my actions that I am indebted to your late husband for events that took place on the Continent and wished to show my gratitude to his widow. I assure you the story was well received. No one seemed to feel that my settling your accounts in any way reflected badly on you or your character.'

'Did you ask for your money back?'

'If I had, I believe it should have made a mockery of my carefully conceived story.'

'Surely not, my lord? I'm sure you, *such* an experienced liar, could have managed it. After all, your lies are so believable. To those who are gullible, at least.'

'I apologise for deceiving you as to my title. Your housekeeper asked for my name. I told her Wakefield. When you repeated it, I saw no reason to correct you, thinking…' He hesitated. 'I'm not sure *what* I was thinking. I suppose at the time I thought it wouldn't matter what you called me. I had intended only to express my gratitude and be on my way.'

'Why didn't you?'

'Go on my way? I think you know the answer to that.'

She laughed, the sound bitter to her own ears. 'Whatever the answer—and I'm sure you could couch that, too, in very reasonable terms—I can't think that it is of any importance now. We have said all that is to be said between us. I wish you a pleasant journey home, my lord.'

'Actually, you wish me to the devil. And I don't know what to do about that.'

'Accept it.' She looked at him then, which was almost her undoing.

His eyes, very blue in the morning light, were filled with something that made her catch her breath. Not desire—at least not the raw, physical kind she had glimpsed there before—but something very different. Something she had sometimes seen in William's when she handed him a steaming cup of tea or pulled off his boots at the end of a long day.

'It seems I have no choice but to accept it. I had hoped…' He shook his head, his gaze now on the scene before them. 'It doesn't matter what I had hoped, I suppose.'

A muscle tightened in his jaw. Then, before she could turn away, he looked down into her eyes.

Despite everything he had done, despite her anger and her humiliation, she could not turn away.

And when she didn't something changed in his face. He grasped her hand, which she did not pull from his grasp.

'I know I've done everything wrong. Ridden roughshod over

your objections and your requests. Courted you when you told me quite plainly you did not wish to entertain my suit. And yet…'

He paused, giving her the opportunity to tell him all that again. She stood mute instead, mesmerised by what she saw in his face.

'And yet for some reason I continue to hope,' he finished, still holding her eyes.

He was too young, she told herself. Too fine. Too rich. Too everything that she was not.

'It will not do,' she managed.

'Why not?'

Apparently emboldened by the fact that she had not removed her hand, he tightened his fingers around hers. She could feel the warmth of them despite the gloves they both wore. And there was no doubting the strength of their hold.

'How old are you, my lord?'

'Twenty-eight,' he said readily.

But then this was familiar territory to him. An argument that had been made and rejected.

'And I am thirty-one.'

In truth she had thought the difference would be more, but then she had believed him a boy that night in France. By that point in the war they had all seemed too young for what fate held in store.

'How old would your husband be now, Mrs Stowe?'

'My husband? What can that possibly matter?'

'If he had lived, what would be your husband's age today?'

It shocked her that she had to think about the answer. 'Thirty-five. Thirty-five next month.'

'That is almost the same difference as in our ages.'

She laughed at the implausibility of his argument. 'Convention decrees a husband should be older than his wife.'

'In order to guide her in the way she should go. Do you feel the need of having someone to guide you, Mrs Stowe?'

Only his eyes were smiling. And she had forgotten how attractive that could be.

'Do *you*?' she asked tartly, and realised too late the trap she had fallen into.

'Apparently so. I realise that directing my path may seem a thankless task, but it is one for which, if you would see fit to undertake it, I should be eternally grateful.'

'We are back to that, it seems.'

'Gratitude? Do you honestly believe that is the primary emotion I feel for you?'

She didn't, she realised. Despite his deceit, she did not doubt the sincerity of his avowal. And had not doubted it from the first.

Because I have never in my life felt about a woman as I feel about you.

'Age is not the only impediment, my lord. What would your family think of my background?'

'I know not. Nor do I care.'

'Ah, but you would. And you would care what your friends think as well. I should stand out like a bramble among the delicate English roses of your circle.'

'Or like a wildflower.' This time his lips curved with his smile. 'But then you are already aware of my fondness for those. Believe me, my dearest Mrs Stowe, as my wife you may be as unusual as you wish. London will worship at your feet. The *ton* enjoys nothing more than the eccentric. Especially if there is a romance involved.'

'And what would your family feel if the woman you choose to take as your wife is unable to give you children?'

Because she had been watching for it, she read quite clearly the surprise in his eyes. When he offered no ready answer to what she had just asked, her chin rose challengingly.

'You have a title, my lord. Surely that signifies the need for an heir to pass it on to?'

'I have younger brothers, Mrs Stowe. If I have no sons, one of them will inherit.'

'And you would not mind if you have no sons? And no daughters?'

'Surely that is in the hands of God?'

'I was married for eight years and never conceived.'

'That does not mean that you cannot.'

'What if it does? If I did not conceive as a girl, what makes you believe I will do so at my age?'

'The ripe old age of thirty-one?' Another smile, one which did not quite reach his eyes.

'What if I am barren?' she pressed, believing that she had at last found the key to forcing him to acknowledge that what he proposed was impossible.

'Then you are barren.' Each word was separately and distinctly enunciated. 'I am not asking you for children, Mrs Stowe. I am asking if you will do me the honour of becoming my wife.'

Time stopped. A million objections ran through her head as his eyes held hers. All her very good reasons to refuse him. Her age, her lack of position, her inmost conviction that she was indeed unable to bear children, her fury with him for deceiving her. The first three he had rejected as unimportant. The latter, which had once burned bright and fierce, now seemed merely ridiculous. Almost contrived.

And still…

'I cannot,' she said, freeing her hand from his with a jerk.

He made an attempt to retake it, but once more she put hers together, intertwining her fingers and pressing her palms against her stomach.

'I have given you my answer. And now, if you please, I should like to be alone.'

'Bella…' He stepped forward to put his hands on her shoulders.

Shocked at the familiarity, she looked up to protest—and straight into his eyes. She swallowed, the rebuke she'd been about to give unspoken.

As she watched, again mesmerised, he bent his head to place his mouth over hers. His right hand fell to the base of her spine, pressing her body against his.

At the first touch of his lips, hers parted. With her response, he deepened the kiss, expertly ravaging her senses so that for a moment she was unable to move or to think. If she didn't—

Realising how dangerous was the trap he was baiting, she raised her hands to put her palms flat against his chest, pushing him away with all her strength. 'Don't. Please, stop.'

He obeyed at once, his breathing as ragged as hers. 'You can't after that deny—'

'No more, my lord, I beg of you. We do not suit. We cannot. That is my last word on the matter.'

She turned, stumbling a little in her haste to be gone. His fingers caught her elbow, holding her until she regained her balance. As soon as she had, she pulled away from him, walking as quickly as she dared over the rough ground.

She expected him to come after her. To ride beside her. To attempt to convince her again that his arguments were rational while hers were not. He did none of those things.

When she reached the broad meadow below, with its profusion of wildflowers, she looked back to the top of the rise. And found it as empty as her heart.

Chapter Seven

Six months later

The snow that blanketed the countryside covered its winter dreariness, but for some reason, despite the undeniable beauty of the scene outside her window, even that failed to work its usual magic on Isabella's spirits.

Hannah had left early this morning to buy the Christmas goose and other items for the feast she was planning to serve in two days. The cottage had already been made festive with the scent of fresh greenery Ned had brought inside.

And, in spite of everything the two of them were doing in preparation for Christmas, Isabella could find not a trace of joy in her heart. She pulled her shawl more closely about her shoulders as she turned away from the parlour window.

Ned and Hannah had undoubtedly been delayed by the condition of the roads. When they returned, the housekeeper would be full of complaints about that, as well as the latest gossip she had picked up in town. All of which would serve as a distraction, and none of which would demand more than the minimal response. Thankfully Hannah would be quite content with the occasional expression of surprise or dismay, as her stories warranted.

Isabella walked across to the fire and bent to add wood from the stack Ned had replenished before he'd brought the pony cart around for his wife. She stood watching as the log caught, its crackle cheerful in the snow-shrouded emptiness of the small house.

For a moment the feelings of despair she had fought for the last six months overwhelmed her resolve. She put her head in her hands as tears welled from behind tightly closed lids. Then, furious with herself, she scrubbed at her cheeks lest sharp-eyed Hannah discern that she'd been crying.

What possible reason did she have to feel sorry for herself? She had a roof over her head, food for her table, two beloved companions who would do anything for her. She should be on her knees thanking God for His many blessings instead of—

The slam of the door chased those thoughts from her head. She pinched her cheeks to give them colour, and then used her handkerchief to wipe any traces of dampness from her nose.

When she walked into the kitchen the housekeeper was unburdening herself of boxes tied with string and sacks that bulged with odd shapes. Snow clung to Hannah's bonnet and dusted the shoulders of her cloak, but she was humming to herself.

'The roads must be a nightmare,' Isabella ventured as she stepped forward to assist in the unpacking.

'Ned had to help Mr Slater free the wheels of his gig,' Hannah looked up to say. 'I'll have a time of it getting the muck out of his coat. Sticky as tar, it is.'

'It's lucky he was there to lend a hand. Especially as cold as it is today.'

'And looks to grow more so. Mark my words, the roads will be frozen solid before this day is done.'

'At least you won't have to venture out again before church on Christmas Day.'

'Thank the Lord,' Hannah agreed, busily placing apples, chestnuts, onions, parsnips and potatoes onto the table. Apparently there was to be no indication in the next two days of the frugality they practised the rest of the year.

'And for His merciful bounty,' Isabella finished. 'Most of

which you seem to have brought home with you. All this for the three of us?'

'And why should we not have a feast? It's Christmas, after all.'

'Yes, it is,' Isabella agreed with a smile.

The plump goose was duly admired. Then Isabella donned an apron to help with the preparation of the Christmas pies, which were to be the first order of business.

As they worked, the familiar camaraderie between the two of them, as well as the housekeeper's pleasure in the meal she planned, dissipated Isabella's earlier melancholia. She was helping peel apples when the sense of the housekeeper's chatter destroyed any illusions she might have had about being content with her life.

'By the by, I heard some gossip in town about your London gentleman. Mind you, Becky Gilbert's tongue has been known to wag at both ends, but she says Mrs Lambert—who she works for, you know—is acquainted with his lordship's cook.'

'Mr Wakefield?' Isabella's heart had stopped with the words 'your London gentleman'. By the time the housekeeper finished her following sentence, it was pounding so hard it seemed in danger of leaping from her chest.

'Lord Easton, he is, dear. Becky was working at the inn when he was there. That's how she came to know his title. Pleasant to her, he was. Not like some of them as stays there. And his man was too—although that one was sometimes quarrelsome about what was or wasn't good enough for his lordship.'

Was he engaged? Married? Dead?

'What did she say about him?'

The words sounded strangled to her ears, but Hannah seemed not to notice. Her knife continued to transform the peel of the apple she held into a long crimson snake.

'Mrs Lambert's acquaintance apparently works in his country house, not in town. Such a shame, she said. But then the good book says—'

Dead, then. Oh, dear God, no.

'What about Lord Easton?'

Hannah's eyes, wide and shocked, came up at Isabella's tone. 'Well, I was about to tell you what about him. If you'll only give me a chance.'

Isabella clamped her lips together, knowing from experience that it would be better to let her housekeeper tell her news in her own way. Questions—although she ached to ask them—would only delay the process.

'There, now.' Hannah inspected the apple she'd peeled and then deftly sliced it into the bowl in front of her. Only then did she look up at her mistress. 'Blind.'

The nod she added to that pronouncement held a trace of satisfaction, but Isabella ignored it, concentrating instead on the single word she had uttered.

'Blind? Are you sure that's what she said?'

He had told her that due to the damage to his eyes he was unable to read, but she had spent too many hours with him to believe that his injuries still affected his sight in any other way.

Had been blind, her searching mind supplied. Someone must have told the cook that, and the information had become garbled when it was relayed to Becky Gilbert's employer. Or to Becky herself.

'Oh, I'd not be mistaking something like that, now, would I?' Hannah went on.

'But whatever damage there had been to his eyes was quite healed. You saw that yourself.' She was clutching at straws, she knew, but straws were all she had.

Blind. The word echoed and re-echoed in her head even as she argued.

'An infection, Becky said. Something to do with what happened to him when he was in the army. Mrs Lambert didn't know the details, her friend not being privy to those. All I'm telling you, love, is what she told me. Make of it what you will. Despite what he done…' Hannah hesitated, looking up at her with sympathy in her eyes. 'I wouldn't wish blindness on anyone. Especially someone so young.'

'What he did? What do you mean?'

'It was plain as the nose on your face that your heart was broken when he left. Mine ached just to see how much you suffered. So maybe it's a rough kind of justice after all. But still… So young.' Hannah shook her head mournfully.

'You could not be more wrong.' Isabella's tone once again caused the housekeeper's eyes to widen. 'He asked me to marry him. I'm the one—' She stopped, her lips clamping shut before she opened them to continue. 'I'm the one who said we should not suit.'

'Not suit? Why ever not? He seemed a fine young man to me.'

'*Too* fine,' Isabella whispered. 'And too young.'

'Whatever do you mean?' Hannah's confusion seemed genuine.

'You said it yourself. That he was too fine. Too much the London gentleman.'

'Oh, love, never say that something *I* said made you go and turn him down? A man like that? Someone who would care for you all your life?'

'We did not suit,' Isabella said again, trying to give the words some validity.

They rang hollow instead. Her heart had known that then, even as her intellect had foolishly tried to make her conform to the opinions of the world.

'Maybe it's for the best.' Hannah had moved around the table to put her arms around her, drawing her close. 'Considering what's happened to him, I mean.'

For a long moment Isabella allowed herself to be comforted by the warmth of the motherly bosom and the familiar scent of lavender water, overlaid now with the smell of cloves. Finally she leaned back, looking into Hannah's face. 'There is no mistake? You're sure?'

'It's what she said. Perhaps if you talked to Mrs Lambert…'

The words trailed as Isabella pulled away from the housekeeper's hold. With trembling fingers she struggled to untie her apron, laying it on top of the waiting apples when she had done so.

'Can I get you something, dear?' Hannah asked. 'A cup of tea? Or a compress for your head, mayhaps?'

'Ned,' Isabella said, trying to think what else she should need.

'Ned?'

'And the pony cart. Do you think the mail coach will run this afternoon?'

'I've never known it not to. But you'll not be needing the mail coach for Mrs Lambert's. Ned can take you straight there, right enough.'

'I'm not going to Mrs Lambert's.'

'Then…why would you need the mail coach?'

'Because I am going to him.'

Chapter Eight

She had sent Hannah to enquire of Becky Gilbert the location of his lordship's residence while she herself threw clothing into William's old portmanteau. She hadn't even allowed Ned to unharness the pony when they'd returned with that information. She had made him turn right around and drive her to the Wren's Nest, where she'd been lucky enough to secure a seat on the fast-moving coach that carried not only the mail but any passengers willing to pay a premium for its speed.

Although she'd been infinitely grateful to have secured an inside seat, even there, somewhat protected from the elements, the cold had seeped through her clothing and chilled her to the bone. And that had been before the brunt of the storm had struck, hiding the highway under mounds of snow.

Now, after more than twenty hours on the road, half of them spent in a coach caught in snow drifts or in walking up icy hills in order to spare the horses, she was at last standing in the courtyard of the inn at Welwyn. And once more assailed by doubt.

No matter what she said to him, Guy would know why she had come. And she knew exactly how he would react.

She had refused him for reasons that were far less important than those he would mount against her. *If* he bothered to

make those arguments. After all, he might not even agree to
see her—

Only as the words formed in her head did her resolve strength-
en. It didn't matter what he thought about why she was here.
Given the opportunity, she knew she could prove to him that
this had nothing to do with pity and everything to do with her
realisation of what a fool she had been.

She turned and marched inside. The ticket agent was engaged
with the last of the passengers for the outgoing coach, so she
waited until he was free before she made her enquiry.

'I wish to hire a conveyance to take me to Woodhall Park.' Her
manner, learned in far more difficult dealings with recalcitrant
innkeepers on the Continent, was so deliberately confident as to
be commanding.

'They're not expecting you, then?' The agent's eyes considered
her, no doubt judging her acceptability to the occupants of the
Hall.

'If they were, they should, of course, have sent a carriage to
meet me.'

One of the man's brows lifted. 'Acquainted with the family,
are you, miss?'

'With Lord Easton. *If* that is any of your concern.'

'His lordship is very well thought of by folks around here.'

'I should imagine that he would be. Now, is there a chaise
available for hire, or must I enquire elsewhere?'

'Why don't I send someone up to the house to tell them you're
here? Then they can send something for you more comfortable
than a yellow bounder.'

There was little to be gained by continuing to argue, Isabella
decided. She could always appeal to the innkeeper, but she suspected the outcome of that conversation would be no different.

She even wondered briefly if it might not be better to let Guy
make that decision, rather than arrive unbidden on his doorstep.
But if she did, and he then refused her, she would lose the opportunity to convince him of her true motives in coming.

'The chaise, I believe,' she said decisively. 'But thank you for
your very kind advice.'

She could not be sure what won the day—her tone of command or the fact that under her cloak she was wearing the first new dress she had purchased in more than five years, a mulberry worsted that she was pleased to think complemented her colouring. For whatever reason, the agent motioned for one of the post boys, giving him instructions to have a chaise brought round.

'Thank you,' she said again as the boy disappeared into the courtyard.

'As I said, we think highly of his lordship around these parts. One of the Iron Duke's aides, he was. Mentioned in dispatches, you know.'

'I did know, actually.' Isabella's lips tilted with the memory of the story Guy had told her concerning Wellington and the Spanish lady's chemise. 'At Salamanca, I believe.'

The man's brows lifted again before he said, his manner far friendlier than it had been before, 'I'll see to it there's plenty of rugs in the chaise, miss. It's brutal cold out. You wait here in the warm, and I'll let you know when they're ready.'

The guests in attendance for the Christmas Eve dinner at Woodhall Park were all family. Even so, when seated they numbered thirty-four.

The second course was being just brought round when one of the footmen entered the dining room. He whispered something into the ear of the butler, who was supervising service.

Guy assumed from Rodgers' expression in response that there was some issue with the staff. He was surprised, therefore, when the butler approached his place at the head of the table.

Rodgers bent, his words discreet enough not to be overheard. 'You have a visitor, my lord.'

Guy briefly considered which of his acquaintances might be unthinking enough to show up uninvited on Christmas Eve. Unable to conceive of any one of them doing so, he looked up to question, 'Someone to see *me*? Are you sure?'

'Quite sure, my lord. A lady, my lord.' Although his features were now perfectly composed, Rodgers still managed to suggest his strong disapproval of the entire matter. 'One who seems a bit…travel-worn, if I may be so bold.'

'Did she give her name?'

'A Mrs Stowe, my lord. I have instructed the driver of the chaise she arrived in…'

The butler's last faltering sentence was addressed to Guy's back as he made his way towards the dining room door. He was aware of his mother's raised brows as he passed her end of the table, but he ignored the message they were intended to convey.

He was halfway down the hall before intellect prevailed upon his emotions, urging him to slow down and think. Isabella had accused him of being too young. Too rich. Of having a title. Of being deceitful. And, at least by implication, of being more interested in acquiring an heir than the woman he loved.

Now it seemed her objections had miraculously been swept away, so that she had come here. And he was terribly afraid that he knew precisely what had accomplished that. His only surprise should be that it had taken so long for the gossip to reach her.

She would undoubtedly have been placed in the small ante-room where questionable guests were left to cool their heels as the staff secured instructions as to their proper reception. What was she thinking as she waited? That someone would eventually bring her to him? Or that some servant would lead him by the hand to this confrontation?

Because by now Guy understood that was exactly what this meeting would be. A confrontation.

He drew a breath, steeling himself for the sight of her. As he walked across the expanse of the marble floor, his heels echoed in the silence of the vast entrance hall, at least providing her some warning.

Isabella was standing in the middle of the room, one gloved hand resting atop its only piece of furniture—a round table that held a small Grecian marble. A priceless *objet d'art*, which she was pretending to admire.

The footman who had admitted her had not even taken

her cloak. Given the chill of the room, that was probably a blessing.

'Mrs Stowe? You have had a very long, cold journey.'

The strain of it was evident when she turned. The delicate skin under her eyes appeared bruised, the area beneath the high cheekbones shadowed.

He fought the urge to gather her into his arms. To do as he had wanted to do almost from the day he had found her again. *To protect her. To have the right to protect her.*

'And on Christmas Eve,' he added, when she continued to say nothing.

Her eyes searched his face. Since he knew quite well what she was looking for, he smiled at her. 'Let me take you somewhere warm.'

He held out his hand, but for several heartbeats she didn't move, her stillness so complete it was almost frightening. Only then did he realise that the hem of her gown was trembling with the fine vibration of her body.

Was she shivering from the cold? Or from the realisation of the mistake she had made?

'I thought—' Her tongue touched lips chapped from their exposure to the relentless winter wind.

His chest tightened with the need to touch her. To soften her mouth against his.

'I was told—' she began again.

'Let me take you somewhere warmer. We can talk there.'

Her lips closed, the reason for her journey still undisclosed. Her eyes clung to his, asking the question her mouth had not.

That he didn't answer it was a deception far greater than that which he had practised before. One he prayed she would never discover.

'Forgive me,' she whispered, the words little more than a breath.

For an instant he had thought she meant something very different. Only when she started towards the door behind him did he understand for what she was apologising.

'You can't mean to leave,' he protested, although if she did it would be the safest thing for him.

'I shouldn't have come. Please forgive my intrusion.'

'You're always welcome, Mrs Stowe. We are, I hope, still friends. And as your friend I must insist that you stay. At least for tonight, if no longer.'

She shook her head. 'I cannot. You must know that.'

'Shall I ask my mother to come to you? Or take you to her? We've just now sat down to dinner. You must be hungry as well as cold. It's only the family.' He moved to take her elbow, but she drew back to avoid him.

'You cannot believe that I wish to trouble your mother. I assure you I did not come for that.'

'Then may I take you where there's a fire? I can't think why they would have left you here.' He glanced around the cold, empty room to make his point.

'They left me here because despite my dress, which I had thought very smart, they judged me as someone who should wait in an anteroom. What do you suppose gave me away?'

She was beginning to regain her equilibrium—much more like the Isabella he'd fallen in love with.

'The indomitable Mrs Stowe,' he said with a smile.

'Hardly.' Along with the note of self-deprecation, there was now a hint of amusement in her voice.

She didn't resist this time as he took her arm, which gave him to understand exactly how exhausted she must be. He guided her up the stairs to his mother's sitting room—the only place he could be sure they would not be interrupted by the dispersal of his guests after they had finished their meal.

Although generously proportioned, Lady Easton's very private domain was small enough not to be overwhelming, and one of his favourite rooms in the entire house. His mother's taste was reflected everywhere—both in the furnishings and the fabrics. Even in the art that graced the walls and the elegantly placed bric-a-brac.

Ignoring all of that, Isabella walked to the fireplace, holding her hands out to its welcoming blaze. After a moment she pulled off her gloves, laying them on the mantel. As she untied her bonnet, she turned to face him.

There was a small silence, which he broke by walking across to the bell on the table beside his mother's chair. He rang it sharply, waiting until one of the girls entered and dropped a curtsy.

'Would you bring us a pot of strong tea, please, Ellen?'

'Yes, my lord.'

'And a light repast for Mrs Stowe. Cook will know the kind of thing I want. She's had a long, tiring journey.'

Isabella's 'Nothing for me, thank you' was spoken almost simultaneously with the girl's 'Of course, my lord.'

Guy ignored her protest, knowing that his orders would be carried out no matter what his guest had said. He placed the bell back on the table and looked up to find Isabella's eyes again on his face.

The woman he'd fallen in love with was no fool. He would play her for one at his peril.

'How have you been?' As he asked the question he indicated the wing chair on the other side of the small tea table before the fire.

Isabella tilted her head to him before she walked over and sat down. He bent to pick up the footstool that stood in front of his mother's chair and placed it at her feet.

'Thank you,' she said, and then, after a long moment spent contemplating her surroundings, 'This is a pleasant room.'

Apparently the conversation between them was to be confined to polite inanities. An art at which he was undoubtedly more skilled than she.

'My mother's sitting room. I loved coming here as a child. It's exactly like her. Bright and gay and full of life. In stark contrast, I fear, to the rest of this pile.'

'Yes, well, quite frankly, Woodhall Park does not quite convey "the rest".'

'You dislike it?' His voice was flat as he made that observation. But, after all, what could it matter whether she approved of his home or not?

'On the contrary. It's most impressive. I simply wasn't prepared for its grandeur. When the chaise rounded the last curve in the drive, the house appeared before us like a castle out of a fairytale.'

'Hardly that,' he said with a laugh.

'*Exactly* that.' The amusement he'd glimpsed in her eyes had disappeared.

'You can't hold me responsible for the place of my birth.'

'Or the condition of your birth, apparently.'

'Still disapproving, I see. So…why *did* you come, Bella? Forgive me—I should say Mrs Stowe.'

She shook her head. 'A whim. A foolish one, it seems.'

'Why foolish?'

'Because I see that I was not mistaken in the objections I made before. If anything—'

She was interrupted by the girl with the tea. The tray she brought was so heavily laden it was almost too much for her to carry.

Isabella quickly swept up the bonnet she'd laid on the table between them, smiling up at the maid as she deposited her burden. 'Thank you. This looks wonderful.'

The girl curtsied before she cut her eyes to him. 'Will that be all, my lord?'

'Thank you, Ellen. For the time being.'

'Yes, my lord. Oh, and your mother's asking for you.'

'Would you tell her I have a guest? Perhaps after dinner she would come up to meet her.'

'I'll tell her, my lord.'

She wouldn't, of course. She would simply pass his message up the chain of command, and Rodgers would eventually whisper it into his mother's ear.

They were silent during the few seconds it took for the maid to leave. As Guy turned back from watching her departure, he found Isabella's considering eyes on him once more.

'Will you pour?' he suggested, easing down into his mother's chair.

She picked up the pot to obey. 'Hannah would think this

very wasteful for only two people.' She nodded at the delicacies arranged on the caddy.

'How is Hannah?'

'Almost assuredly thinking I should be consigned to Bedlam.' She handed him the cup she'd just filled.

'Because she isn't accustomed to your acting on…whims?'

She glanced up from pouring her own tea, her eyes slightly widened.

'Careful,' he warned as the hot liquid overflowed.

'Apparently I shall drink my tea from the saucer, like Ned,' she said with a laugh.

Putting down his cup, Guy lifted hers and laid one of the linen napkins over the spill. When that had been soaked up, he put the stained cloth on the edge of the silver tray and handed the tea to her.

'That's ruined, you know.' She looked at him over the top of the cup as she took her first sip.

'The napkin? I'm sure they'll be able to clean it.'

'Your servants?'

'Yes.' An attempt to make him feel guilty for who and what he was?

'If not, I know of a very good treatment for linen. Your mother may write to me about it.' The flash of amusement in her eyes was quickly hidden by a downward sweep of her lashes.

'I'll tell her.'

There was a small, almost companionable silence as they sipped.

'The tea is excellent.'

'Thank you. I'll tell my mother that as well.'

Another sip. Another upward glance.

'In truth…' she began, and then allowed the words to trail away.

'In truth?'

'It doesn't matter.' She shook her head slightly. 'I never thought we should be having tea.'

'Why not? Are we not friends, Mrs Stowe?'

'I think not, Lord Easton.'

'I had thought we were. I'm very sorry if it's not so.'

She smiled. 'As am I.'

She put her cup and saucer down on the tray and picked up her bonnet. 'Thank you for the tea. It has caused me to feel much revived. Would you be kind enough to ask someone to tell my driver to bring round the chaise?'

He had stood when she did, so that now they were facing one another over the untouched feast he'd sent for. 'You can't possibly intend to turn around and start back now.'

'The sooner the better,' she said. 'I know that now.'

'You will make yourself ill if you persist in this.'

'Then you can rush to *my* side to succour *me*.' This last remark was spoken as she walked towards the mantel to retrieve her gloves. She turned, pulling them on almost angrily. '"Folly must be paid for, and the coin required is always your most precious." My mother used to say that. I wasn't sure what she meant until now.'

'Bella—'

'I was told that you were blind. And without bothering to verify the truth of what I'd been told I rushed across the county to…' She hesitated, shaking her head. 'I'm not sure what I intended. All I know is that I felt I had to come to you.' She laughed. 'And when I arrive I find you quite hale and enjoying dinner with your family.'

'Bella—'

'And all this…' Her hand made an encompassing gesture that seemed to include the room, the tea tray and him. '*Nothing* has changed.'

'No,' he said softly. 'Would you prefer that it had?'

The question stopped her. Her lips parted slightly as she thought about what he had asked.

'No,' she whispered finally. 'No, of course not.'

'But if I *were* blind… It *would* have made a difference in how you feel about me?'

'No.'

'But you had not come before.'

'I thought… I don't know what I thought. Maybe…'

He waited, watching her fingers tear at the ribbon of her hat.

And then her gaze lifted again. 'I thought you might need me.'

'I *do* need you. I always have.'

She shook her head, turning to look at the door rather than meet his eyes. 'That wasn't what I meant.'

'Ah, yes. I had forgotten. You deal in hope. And encouragement. And what was the phrase you used? Telling sorely wounded men what they need to hear.'

Stung, she turned to him then. 'I did not ask for your thanks. I never have. I did no more for you—'

'Than you had done for a hundred others. I know. So you told me.'

'Why are you saying all this?'

'Can you not deal with a man who doesn't need your comfort, Mrs Stowe? Must we be prostrate in order to be attractive to you? Or merely blind?'

The silence this time was awful with the knowledge that he had gone too far. Then into its bitter coldness walked his mother, her pale blue gown and soft blonde curls an unforgivable contrast to the tall, dark woman in the ill-fitting woollen dress.

'Forgive me,' Lady Easton said, 'but I heard your voices in the hall. And if *I* can hear them, my dear, believe me, the servants will.'

The last was addressed to him, but she turned immediately to smile at Isabella.

'Mother, may I introduce Mrs Stowe. Isabella, my mother, Lady Easton.'

'Oh, my dear! Has he said something unpardonable?' his mother asked. 'But of course he has. Men are all the same, you know. His father drove me to tears too many times to count.'

She was right, Guy realised. Isabella was crying. And it was nothing like the pretty tears his mother shed, to be delicately wiped away with the scrap of lace she carried once they had made her point.

Isabella's nose was red, and moisture tracked down her cheeks.

She scrubbed at the tears with both hands, but the leather gloves she had donned rendered her attempts worse than useless.

'Bella.'

'Don't,' she demanded. 'Just…' She drew a trembling breath to appeal to his mother. 'I came in a hired chaise. A hideous yellow thing. Could you please have someone bring it to the door?'

His mother's gaze moved to his face, and then back to hers. 'But you've only just arrived. Surely—'

'I have to go. This was all a terrible mistake. I thought… It doesn't matter what I thought. Please.' The imploring word was full of desperation.

'I'll see to it,' Guy said.

He had learned all he needed to know. There was little to be gained by drawing out this farce any longer.

'Guy!' His mother's protest followed him down the stairs, but he ignored it.

He dispatched servants: one to fetch the chaise, another to bring rugs, and a third for a warming pan. By the time his mother escorted Isabella downstairs everything had been made ready for her departure.

The tears had been controlled, all evidence of them removed. Considering the scene upstairs, she appeared remarkably contained.

She held her hand out to him. After a moment's hesitation he took it, his hold on her fingers deliberately light.

'I'm sorry for my intrusion on your dinner. Thank you for your kindness, Lord Easton.'

He inclined his head, but made no other response, leaving his mother to take matters into her own hands.

'Any acquaintance of Guy's is always welcome, my dear. I don't know why you should rush off, but—' She held up one soft white hand to stave off the anticipated protest, 'I understand that you feel you must. Please do come again. Stowe, did you say? I know I have heard your name before, but I cannot place in what context. Guy?' The wide blue eyes appealed.

'France,' he said. 'Mrs Stowe was the woman who assured me that my life was not over because I had lost my sight.'

'Stowe. Of course. How *could* I have forgotten? Guy has talked of you so often. Why, he searched for you for years. And here you are.' His mother took both of Isabella's hands in hers. 'But you *must* stay. We haven't had time to properly thank you. Guy, make her stay.'

'I'm afraid Mrs Stowe can be remarkably determined once her mind is made up. She doesn't want to be here.'

His mother turned to look at Isabella again, her brow furrowed. 'Surely you can stay the night? It's almost dark. And it's snowing again.'

'You are very kind, but I can't.' Isabella pulled her hands free and stepped out onto the portico.

A footman opened the door of the chaise and helped her up its steps. Another placed the warming pan at her feet and positioned a rug over her lap. In a matter of seconds the lumbering vehicle was pulling away down the drive.

Guy's gaze followed it until it disappeared into the winter darkness. When he turned his mother, her arms wrapped around her body as a shield against the cold, was still beside him.

'I don't understand,' she said, looking up into his face. 'Why did you quarrel? Why ever did you let her leave?'

'Because she came for the wrong reason.'

'But she *did* come. Isn't that the important thing?'

He didn't answer. Not because he didn't know the answer, but because it would be too difficult to explain it to her.

He had found he was having a hard enough time explaining it to himself.

Chapter Nine

'I'm afraid there's not a room to be had, madam, with tonight's coaches cancelled and all.'

The innkeeper's regret seemed less than genuine, but then he had probably repeated this same message to most of those crowded into his public room. There was a roaring fire in its massive fireplace, but the thought of spending another night sitting upright was almost more than Isabella could bear.

Buck up, my girl, William would have told her with a grin. *You've endured much worse than this bit of inconvenience.*

'Thank you,' she said with a smile, but the man had already turned away to handle the next stranded traveller's concerns.

She started towards the public room, which at least offered the promise of sustenance. The vision of the laden tea tray she'd left behind at Woodhall Park flashed into her head, but she banished the memory. A cup of tea and a piece of toast would see her through until morning. Perhaps by then the coaches would be running again.

She glanced towards the doors to the courtyard to assess the snowfall. The agent who had been kind to her earlier was coming through them. He stopped to beat the heavy flakes from his hat.

When he looked up and saw her, his eyes widened. 'You're back.'

'As you see,' she said, managing another smile.

'What happened? His lordship in town?'

'No,' she said succinctly. *We do not suit* was hardly an explanation she could give to a stranger.

Hardly an explanation at all, her heart chided, but she ignored that, too.

It was clear her former benefactor was at a loss. She had convinced him that she and Lord Easton were indeed acquainted. It must seem to him now that she had been turned out into the cold.

'That doesn't seem right,' he said. 'The family has a reputation for hospitality.'

'It was quite my decision, I assure you.'

'To leave? In the middle of a storm?'

She shrugged, unwilling to go into her reasons, and certainly not here in the entryway of one of the busiest coaching inns in the district.

She had already taken a step towards her intended destination when the agent's question stopped her.

'Is his lordship still well, then?'

'Still?' Even as she repeated its salient word, his question echoed in her head. *Is his lordship still well, then?*

'After his trouble. We were assured he'd recovered.'

'What kind of trouble?' Her voice was remarkably calm, considering the clamour in her breast.

'With his eyes. You know he was blind when he came home from the war?'

'I did know.'

'Well… Must have been the end of the summer, I guess. A fever of some kind, maybe. Or something tied to his wounds. I'm not sure I ever heard the reason. All I know is that for a time he was blind again. When I heard he'd regained his sight I drunk a pint in his honour, I can tell you. The family has been good to folk around here, especially when times are hard. Seems his lordship is like to continue their benevolence.'

She had not been misinformed. The gossip that had sent her foolishly rushing here had been true.

And then, almost as those realisations were forming, came the next. Guy had known why she'd come and had allowed her to believe that she'd been mistaken.

Must we be prostrate in order to be attractive to you? Or merely blind?

Her immediate response to his deception was anger. To be fair, however, he hadn't lied to her. He had simply not admitted to the condition that had sent her hurrying to offer him things he no longer wanted from her. Comfort and succour.

I have always needed you.

She had sworn that if she accepted Guy's suit it would be because she loved him as she had loved William. Passionately. Completely. As equal partners.

Why was it wrong, then, for him to desire those same terms for their relationship?

'I shall need the chaise again, I'm afraid,' she said to the agent. 'I'm sorry to give you so much trouble, but I find I must return to Woodhall Park.'

'Now?'

'As soon as possible. I have unfinished business there.'

'But the weather—'

'Yes, I know, but I trust that you have someone who can get through the storm. After all, the distance is not so great.'

'I'm sorry, miss, but there's no one to drive you. They're either on their way to their homes or bedded down already. I can't ask any of those men—' He stopped, seeming to realise that nothing he said was having the desired effect.

'Then if I may hire a horse? Or a pony cart? A wagon. Anything I can drive myself.'

'I can't let you do that, miss. Not fit for man nor beast out there.'

'But I am neither. I shall make it worth your while.' Even as she offered the bribe, she mentally counted the few remaining coins in her purse.

No matter. If the worst came to the worst, she could throw herself on Lady Easton's mercy.

'It ain't a matter of money, miss, believe me—'

'I must return. And tonight. I know that I can't possibly make you understand the urgency—'

In truth, she didn't quite understand it herself. All she knew was that she needed to go back. To confront the man who on one hand claimed to need her and on the other hand sent her away.

'I'll take you,' the agent said. 'It's against company policy, you understand…but seeing as how it's his lordship.'

'Thank you, Mr… I'm sorry. I don't know your name.'

'Simms, miss. My name is Simms.'

'Mr Simms, you have my undying gratitude. And if I have my way, I believe you shall have his lordship's as well.'

'Despite what they say about his lordship's bravery in the face of the enemy, my money's on you, miss. I don't reckon there's been many times when you *didn't* get your own way.'

'It's Mrs, actually,' she corrected with a smile. 'Mrs Stowe. The *widowed* Mrs Stowe,' she clarified when his brows lifted. 'And I can't tell you how delighted I am to have made your acquaintance, Mr Simms.'

There were far fewer lights in the house this time as they rounded the final curve. Isabella's eyes again considered the imposing structure, but without that same sense of trepidation that had afflicted her before.

Now it was simply another obstacle in the course of her impatience. A door to be knocked upon. A servant to be convinced to give her admission, despite the hour.

'Shall I wait for you, Mrs Stowe?' The agent's question as he opened the door of the carriage brought her quickly back to the practical.

'I don't believe that will be necessary.' In the dark interior she poured the contents of her purse into her gloved hand. Too few coins for such a service, but it was all she had. 'Thank you so much. I'll never forget your kindness, Mr Simms.' She held out her hand to him.

'It's Christmas,' he said, folding her fingers over the money on her palm. 'At least I think it is.'

She, too, had lost all sense of time, but surely it was past midnight. 'Take them, please.'

'You say a good word for me to his lordship. Payment enough, I promise you.'

'Are you sure?'

'As the sunrise. Now, let me help you down. It seems the staff has taken advantage. Probably having their own celebrations below stairs. Don't you worry, though,' he continued as he saw her safely to the ground, 'I'll knock 'em up in no time. There's always somebody on duty in these great houses. Even at Christmas.'

His hand firmly under her elbow, they climbed the steps together. When they reached the top, the agent reversed the whip he carried and banged its handle against the door. 'Open up, in there. You've a guest out here in the cold.'

After a moment his demand was answered. Although the servant was not the one who had let her in before, his assessment was as quickly made.

'Madam?'

'I'm here to see Lord Easton. Please tell him Mrs Stowe has come again.'

The servant's brows rose, but something—perhaps the assurance in her tone—made him step aside to allow her entry.

She turned back to smile at Mr Simms. 'You'll never know how much—'

'Are you sure I don't need to wait?'

'Lady Easton invited me to spend the night when I was here before. This time I plan to take advantage of her kind invitation. I'm sure there'll be somewhere here for you to sleep if you wish.' She turned questioning eyes to the footman, who responded with what was clearly a sniff.

'Don't you bother your head about me, miss. There'll be plenty of places back at the inn. Good company,' Simms said, looking pointedly at the haughty servant, 'a pint or two, and it will seem like a party.'

Isabella held out her hand. 'Happy Christmas, Mr Simms. God bless you for your kindness.'

The agent hesitated a moment, before reaching out to take her fingers in his. The thick gloves he wore made the contrast between them even greater. Solemnly he bent, his lips smacking the air just above the black leather.

'And you, Mrs Stowe. May you get what you want for Christmas.'

She smiled at him again as he stepped back. The footman had closed the door even before the agent had turned to return to the chaise.

'If you'll wait in here, madam,' he said, directing her with his hand to the small cold room where she'd been sequestered before.

'Somewhere with a fire, if you please. And a cup of tea would not come amiss.' She smiled at him, too, but there was no mistaking that she had just issued a command.

And, despite the poor quality of the gown she wore and the exhaustion that must be etched in her face, it was rather quickly and efficiently obeyed.

Guy was standing before the fireplace in his office, looking into the flames without seeing them. The only images in his head were of Bella. Her eyes shadowed by fatigue. Her hands scrubbing at tears he had caused. Her too-thin figure disappearing into the frigid darkness of a hired chaise.

When the door opened behind him he assumed someone had come to build up the fire. He automatically looked down at the hearth, realising from the glow of embers exactly how long he'd been standing here.

'A Mrs Stowe to see you, my lord. She's in the drawing room.'

He wasn't sure what Bella's return implied, but despite everything he couldn't be sorry for it. At least she was not out in the night's bitter cold.

'I'll go to her. Did you offer her tea?'

'She sent for it straight away, my lord.' The footman's tone held a trace of admiration. 'It should have arrived by now.'

'Thank you, Trimble.'

He wondered all the way to the room where she waited what he would say. Did the fact that she'd come back signify that something had changed? Or simply that with the storm she'd been unable to complete her journey?

He entered the room to find her comfortably ensconced before the replenished fire, pouring a cup of tea from a silver pot. She looked up immediately, but he could read nothing from her expression.

'Tea?' she asked calmly.

'Are you all right?'

'Slightly chilled, but I expect the tea and the fire will take care of that. And you?'

'I beg your pardon?'

'I understand you've been ill.'

He should have known. Someone had told her what had happened last summer. Her return was merely the inevitable result of that knowledge.

'That was weeks ago.'

'And you saw no point in telling me that what I had been told was in fact true?'

'True no longer. And, since that is the case, I wonder that you're here.'

'A glutton for punishment, perhaps.'

'Punishment?'

'I am concerned for you, and you respond to that concern by deceiving me. But then deception has been your stock in trade from the beginning.'

'Which doesn't answer my question. Indeed, it seems to make your return even more curious.'

'I came back to ask what you meant.'

'What I meant? About what?'

'You said that you had always needed me.'

'I hardly think there is any mystery about that. I *did* ask you to marry me.'

'Yes, I know. But need didn't seem to play a role in your suit. Not as I remember it. It seemed to be much more strongly rooted in desire. Or am I wrong about that?'

'You know I desire you. I made no secret of it.'

'But the fact that you need me…' She paused, her cup halfway to her parted lips, her eyes on his face. 'I think you have been rather more secretive about *that*.'

For a moment the only sound in the room was the cheerful crack and hiss of the newly stoked fire. Finally Isabella lowered her cup, replacing it on the saucer.

'The truth, if you please,' she said softly.

The truth. Whatever her motives in coming here, she deserved at least that.

'You told me once that coping with blindness would require a man of remarkable courage.'

'Did I? I don't remember that. But, as I've admitted, I was apt to say whatever I thought would give comfort or encouragement…' She shook her head, her gaze still on his face.

'I'm not sure I have that kind of courage. Not any more.'

He could almost see her putting the pieces together. Realising, as she had that night so long ago, exactly what he feared.

'Then…you believe there is some danger that what happened last summer might happen again?'

'When I was burned, my right eye was more severely damaged than the left. Even after I regained my sight it was prone to periodic inflammation. In August it became inflamed to such an extent that the infection spread.'

'To the left?'

He nodded, the memory of the morning he'd awoken to that realisation so strong it blocked his throat.

'And you fear that it may happen again?'

'As a result of the infection I have lost what sight remained in the right eye. That vision returned in the left was perhaps another of the miracles you promised. I'm not sure anyone ever gets *three* such miracles.'

'You think that you may one day be blind again?'

'With good reason.'

'A good enough reason to cause you to rescind your proposal?'

'You turned *down* my proposal. I didn't question your reasons.'

'Actually, you did. And quite rightly. They were simply a matter of pride.'

'Believe me, I understand the importance of one's pride. Especially when one has little else to cling to.'

'And what if I hadn't turned down your proposal? What if we had been married when you lost your sight?'

He could only be glad that it was not what had come to pass. 'Perhaps that was *your* miracle.'

'A lucky escape?'

'Whether you believe it or not.'

'Rubbish,' she said feelingly.

'I understand that you think there is something romantic— noble, even—about caring for someone who is unable to care for himself. You proved that in France. You proved it again by coming here as soon as you heard about my blindness.'

'I came because I care a great deal about what happens to you. When I heard that you had lost your sight…' She stopped, seeming to choose her words carefully. 'It made me realise how little the rest mattered. My age. Your title. Even the fact that I might not be able to give you children. Nothing mattered to me then but being with you.'

'To care for me in my hour of need?' His sarcasm was bitter.

'Isn't that what a marriage is supposed to be? Two people caring for one another?'

'Perhaps you are willing to spend the rest of your life leading your husband about by the hand. Forgive me, dear Bella, if I am unwilling to be led.'

'And your reason is as much about pride as were mine.'

'Of course.'

'In the months since you left I have found pride to be a highly inadequate companion.'

It was as close to an admission that she'd been wrong to turn down his proposal as he was likely to get. If she had made it only a few months earlier…

'You believe a blind man would be a more adequate one?'

'What was it you said when I told you I might be barren? If you are blind, then you are blind.' As he had done, she distinctly enunciated each of the last four words. 'Have I not been foolish enough for both of us, my love? Life is so short. You and I have lost too many of those we held dear not to know exactly how fleeting it is. With my pride, I've thrown away months we could have been together. Will you throw away years? Because of something that may not even come to pass?' She held out her hand to him.

A hand that, if he accepted it, might one day have to guide him in his darkness.

And would that not be a blessing? A miracle of the same magnitude as the others he'd already been granted?

In the months since you left I have found pride to be a highly inadequate companion.

What kind of solace would *his* pride be in the coming years?

All he had to do to secure what he had dreamed of through so many lonely nights was reach out and take Bella's hand. And take with it all the joy that would come with his acceptance.

For richer for poorer, in sickness and in health, to love and to cherish… The essence of all the promises inherent in marriage.

Isabella had apparently made peace with the first of those. To secure his right to the last all he must do was accept her assurance that she wanted him, no matter what the future held. And who could ever know what that would be?

'Listen,' Isabella said softly.

And, ears straining in the midnight stillness of the great sleeping house where he had been born, Guy finally heard what she did. By some trick of the wind, or because of the crystalline clarity of the snow-tinged air, the sound of bells drifted upward from the old Norman church in the village below.

Christmas. The season of miracles.

Surely, dear God, I am allowed one more.

Tears blurred his vision, but blindly Guy reached out, his fingers closing around the slender ones that offered him everything. Even, if that day should come, guidance in a darkness that he knew now would never again be empty.

Epilogue

'**S**hh…'

Despite Isabella's warning, Guy continued to advance across the room, his footsteps soundless on the thick Turkish carpet. The moonlight from the window behind them haloed Bella and the baby she held like a Madonna and Child from some medieval masterpiece. He knelt before her chair, reaching out as he did so to caress the fine down of his son's hair.

'Did the night nurse call you?'

'I knew he was awake.' Her fingers found Guy's to bring them to her lips. She pressed a kiss against his hand before she freed it.

'How could you possibly know that?' he asked with a smile.

She shook her head, her gaze returning to the babe. 'I always know.'

'Awake or not, he's well looked after. And you need your sleep.'

'I know, but sometimes… Sometimes I have to hold him, just to make sure it's real.'

'He's very real, my darling. I promise you.'

'Not just him. You. This. All of it.'

He laughed, the sound a breath in the quietness. 'You're like a child—afraid the treat someone has given you will be snatched away.'

'More like a soldier, I think. Determined to savour every moment of every day I live.'

She stirred, and he rose to give her room to stand. He watched as she placed the baby in the elaborate rosewood cradle that had held generations of Wakefield infants. They stood together a moment, watching their son relax again into a depth of sleep only the truly innocent could achieve.

Finally Isabella turned to him, once more holding out her hand. He took it, bringing it to his lips.

His body reacted, as it always did, to the scent she wore. Something exotic, which evoked even in the darkness the image of her beauty.

'Come to bed, my darling,' he whispered.

She nodded, and then, her hand still clasped in his, led him out through the nursery door. The night nurse was standing vigil in the hall.

'He's asleep,' Isabella said to her.

'Very good, my lady. Shall I call you if he wakes again?'

Guy held his breath as his wife's eyes found his in the dimness. When she turned back to the woman, she shook her head.

'I think he'll sleep now. If he does awaken…I'll leave him in your very competent hands, Rose.'

'Thank you, my lady. Goodnight. My lord.' With a quick curtsy in Guy's direction, the nurse slipped back into the nursery, easing its door closed.

'She *is* very competent,' Guy reminded her.

'I'm sure she is. Just as I'm sure he'll sleep until morning.'

'Very prescient, my dear. You never told me you had such remarkable powers.

'Not so remarkable. They didn't forewarn me about you.'

'Did you need warning?'

'That you would sweep me off my feet and lure me to the wilds of Herefordshire? If I had known, I should have been more prepared, I promise you.'

'To resist my advances?' he asked with a smile.

'To succumb to them. If I had, I should have saved myself a great deal of trouble.'

'What did your mother tell you? Folly must always be paid for? And with your most valuable coin? You were *very* foolish to refuse me.'

'Luckily I came to my senses before it was too late.'

'I'm not sure it would ever have been too late. You had only to crook your little finger...' He raised her hand, taking that particular digit to his mouth as they walked. 'And I was yours.'

'Your memory is at fault, my love. I had to work very hard to entice you back into my web.'

He stopped before the door to her bedchamber and, using his free hand, nudged it open. 'Successfully. By the way, your bed is very cold without you in it.'

'And my abigail is scandalised to find you there every morning.'

'Then you need a new abigail.'

He allowed her to precede him inside, closing the door behind them. The same moonlight that had flooded the nursery, ridiculously located on the same hall as their rooms, illuminated the tumbled bed they had shared all the nights of their marriage.

Bella started towards it, but he stopped her by putting his hands on her shoulders. As he slipped off the *robe de chambre* she wore, he bent to place his lips against her neck. She tilted her head, leaning it against his.

Once more the fragrance of her skin sent blood roaring through his veins. He would never get enough of her. Of this.

He allowed her nightgown to fall, the gossamer silk pooling at her feet. His mouth moved down the slender column of her neck and along her shoulder to nuzzle the small depression behind her collarbone.

He felt as well as heard her intake of breath. Her hand found his cheek, caressing. He turned his head to it, pushing a kiss into the centre of her palm.

With that she turned to face him, head tilted, lips parted,

waiting for his mouth to cover hers. As it did, the breath she had taken was released in a sigh.

He bent to slip his arm under her knees. He held her a moment, his lips moving over hers with sweet familiarity, before he laid her on the bed.

He stretched out beside her, propped on his elbow so that he could see the moon-touched beauty of her body. His thumb traced a slow line from her lips downward, following the ridged column of her throat to the centre of her chest. His hand spread over the rounded globe of her breast, catching its already tautened nipple between his fingers.

She gasped, but he knew too well her responses to hesitate. He lowered his head, exchanging his hand's teasing caress for that of his mouth. Her breathing quickened as he began to rim the now-sensitised nub with his tongue.

When he replaced that tantalising stroke with his teeth her fingers locked in his hair, pushing his head downward. Begging for an even closer contact between them.

One he was more than willing to provide.

He eased his body over hers, smiling down into her eyes. Wide and dark, they clung to his as he pushed the fullness of his arousal into the warm, welcoming wetness of her body.

Again and again he thrust, now almost mindless with need and desire. Finally, just when he had begun to believe that this time he might not be able to wait, her eyes drifted shut and the first delicate tremors began to vibrate throughout her frame.

Given permission, he closed his eyes as well, clenching them against a flood of sensation so overpowering this time that for a moment he was lost in it. *Lost in her.*

And after it was over they lay together a long time, unmoving now, his hand covering her breast. Her eyes had once more found his face, and she was content to look at him, it seemed, without speaking. When she finally did, it was nothing he might have expected she would say.

'Do you ever wonder why we have been given this, and so many others…?'

The question trailed, but he knew what she meant. She had

reminded him once before that life was fleeting, meant always to be lived to the fullest.

Too many of those they had loved—her husband, his father, countless comrades too young by far—were all gone, while the two of them...

He shook his head, as always humbled, even a little frightened, to acknowledge the preciousness of the gift they'd been given.

'I don't know,' he said truthfully. 'I try not to think about that.'

A superstitious unwillingness to tempt Fate to snatch it all away? Leaving him in a darkness far greater than any he had known before. A darkness whose depth he literally could not imagine.

'I'm sorry,' she whispered. 'They say having babies makes you maudlin. Apparently they're right.'

'Stop worrying. He's as strong as his mother.' He leaned forward to kiss her forehead.

'His mother?' she asked with a smile. 'Surely—?'

'The indomitable Mrs Stowe. Fate wouldn't dare trick you, my darling. You'd tilt your chin up at him and demand what in the world he was thinking to trouble your happiness.'

'However much I was able to convince you of it, I never felt indomitable, I assure you.'

'And when you are old,' he teased, warming to his theme, 'you'll terrify the servants and tell your grandchildren harrowing tales of when you followed the drum. They will hold you in enormous awe. As does your husband.'

As he whispered the last, his hand trailed lazily across her stomach. And then moved lower still.

Her eyes widened, but not in protest. 'Awe?' she repeated. 'Is that what this is called?'

'*This*, my darling, is called adoration. But I promise you we shall proceed to awe very shortly.'

And, rather spectacularly, they did.

* * * * *

SNOWBOUND AND SEDUCED
Amanda McCabe

Dear Reader,

I was so excited a few years ago when Harlequin asked me to create an anthology with two of my very best writing friends, Deb Marlowe and Diane Gaston! We had so much fun creating the chaotic, fun-loving, passionate Fitzmanning family in *The Diamonds of Welbourne Manor.* I always wanted sisters of my own, and the Fitzmannings let me live that vicariously for a while!

So I also loved the chance to revisit their world in a Christmas novella, which became *Snowbound and Seduced.* When I started writing my Diamonds story, *Charlotte and the Wicked Lord,* I didn't intend for the hero's sister-in-law Mary to have a romance of her own. But I liked her sweetness and kindness, and she seemed so lost and sad. And then out of nowhere, her old flame Dominick showed up! I saw right away the source of that sadness, and I wanted to give Mary and Dominick their Happily Ever After. What better time to rediscover lost love than at Christmas! It's the perfect day for family and romance.

I hope you enjoy their story as much as I loved writing it! (I even cried a bit at the end.) And watch for more Fitzmanning stories in the future….

Amanda

For my grandmother Roberta McCabe,
who loved Christmas so much! I still miss you
every year when I unpack the Santa dolls, Nana…

Prologue

Welbourne Manor, Summer 1820

She should not have come here.

Mary Bassington paced the length of the little *faux*-ancient temple and back again, her footsteps soft on the marble floor. Across the garden, Welbourne Manor shimmered in the night, all its windows lit by a welcoming golden glow. The party still carried on there, a merry game of hide-and-seek still in progress, but she had been able to bear it no longer. The walls had seemed to press in on her, suffocating her, and she'd had to flee.

Not that there was much relief to be found in the little temple. It was a place made for love, for secret meetings and murmured declarations. Little benches were tucked cosily in the shadows, where a marble Cupid laughed down from his pedestal, his arrow at the ready.

Mary glared at him. He had best not point that arrow at *her*—not again!

She stopped at the edge of the stone steps, wrapping her arms tightly around herself as she stared at the house. How very welcoming it had seemed when she'd first arrived, the home of her dear brother-in-law's best friends! How warm and noisy, and full of fun. She had been reluctant to leave her home at Derrington Hall, leave her mourning for William, gone now for many months. She was sure the Fitzmanning family, renowned for their high spirits, would think her nothing but a fusty widow, old before her time at twenty-six.

That was not at all the case. They could not have been more cheerfully welcoming. Especially the youngest lady, Charlotte, who reminded Mary of her own three sisters. She had even begun to enjoy herself. Then...

Then *he* had arrived. Dominick, as handsome as ever. More so, even, for now his face had reached the chiselled perfection his younger visage had promised. Just as charming, too. She'd felt her heart pound inside her as she had watched him laugh with Charlotte at dinner. She'd hardly been able to keep smiling through the interminable meal, to swallow her wine and go on pretending her placid world had not been suddenly upended.

She stared at the house, but she did not really see its pale façade. She saw the past romantic, carefree girl she'd been before she'd married William. She saw a quiet veranda at a ball, the flash of her white dress behind a potted palm. Dominick's teasing smile, the gleam of his guinea-gold hair as he bent his head to kiss her. The gentle, warm touch of his hands on her bare arms

'No!' Mary shook her head, trying to dislodge those memories. She had pressed them down so hard over the years, tried to forget them, and they had almost disappeared. The Bassingtons and Dominick moved in very different circles: the Bassingtons—except for Drew—with staid country families and Dominick with increasingly rakish friends and fast women. The two circles never overlapped. She'd thought her heart healed, her youthful infatuation nothing but a foolish mistake that was long over.

It was not. When she had looked out of that window and seen him today, laughing as he swung down from his horse, she had become that silly girl all over again. It had been as if the years, her respectable marriage, her son, Dominick's scandalous wild ways, didn't exist. All the old excitement had flooded back over her, and she'd had to clap her hand over her mouth to hold back a cry.

But the years *did* exist. She was the widowed Countess of Derrington, with a child and responsibilities, and he was a scandalous rake. The memory of his infamous elopement to France with Lady Newcombe, and that lady's death in childbirth at Calais, was still fresh in Society's mind.

Mary could not afford to be the silly girl she once was. She should leave Welbourne at once. But—but she did not *want* to leave! The thought of plunging back into dark mourning at Derrington Hall, after glimpsing the bright joy of life at Welbourne, filled her with dread.

She kicked out at a marble pillar, forgetting she wore satin evening slippers. 'Ow!' she cried, pain shooting through her foot. 'Blast it all.'

'You shouldn't be out here in the dark,' a deep, rich-rough voice said. 'There are too many obstacles in one's path.'

Mary's heart pounded all over again. She spun around on her good foot to see Dominick coming up the shallow steps. He had not come from the house, but along the pathway leading from the pond, so she had not seen him. And he still moved with the silent grace of a forest cat, deceptively slow and elegant.

His dark evening clothes blended with the night, but the moonlight gleamed on his bright hair. He watched her warily, as if she might kick at him instead of the pillar.

'Are you hurt?' he said.

Mary had quite forgotten about her foot in the shock of seeing him again, but now the pain shot up her leg. 'Only my dignity, I fear.'

Dominick laughed. The old carefree sound was tinged with a new harshness, as if he, like her, found little enough to laugh at in life. 'More than your dignity, I think. You can't even put your weight on that foot.'

'It is quite all right.'

'Nonsense. Here, sit down before you fall over.'

Before she knew what he was about, he took her elbow in a gentle clasp, his long fingers warm through her silk glove. That part of him—the feel of his touch—it was the same. It made her shiver with long-dormant desires.

'You see, you're chilled, too,' he said, helping her sit on one of the marble benches.

Cupid still looked down at her gleefully, as if he had engineered this meeting himself. As if he had summoned Dominick to be alone with her in the night.

'You shouldn't have left the house,' Dominick said, kneeling down beside her.

'I needed some fresh air. As did you, I see,' she said hoarsely.

'I wanted to smoke a cigar by the pond,' he answered. 'And be alone for a moment.'

As had she. But now they were alone together, and his presence seemed to fill up the night, fill up every inch of her consciousness. The warmth of him, kneeling close to her leg, the clean, smoky scent of him, enveloped her senses.

'I suppose you have no need to play hide-and-seek games,' she said. 'The ladies line up in the open for you.'

Oh! Why had she said *that*? Mary bit her lip, wishing the words back.

But Dominick just laughed again. 'Now, why would you think that, Mary?' The sound of her given name in his voice made her shiver again. It had been so long since she had heard it from him, so long since she had been just 'Mary'. 'I see no line forming here, do you?'

He gazed up at her steadily in the moonlit darkness, his eyes that unearthly blue-green she had once thought she could gaze at for ever. 'I see only *you*.'

She was so captured by those eyes she didn't even see him reach for her foot until she felt her slipper slide free. Cool night air rushed over stockinged instep, only to be quickly heated by the even more shocking touch of his hand.

'What are you doing?' she cried. She tried to snatch her foot away, but he held onto her.

'I just want to make sure you didn't break anything,' he said gently, softly, as if he calmed a skittish horse. He'd always been so good with his horses, firm but tender; it was one of the first things she had noticed about him when she was young. She'd used to walk with her sisters in Hyde Park every day, hoping to glimpse him riding there.

'Does this hurt?' he asked, pressing carefully on her toe.

Mary had quite forgotten her injury in the midst of old memories, but a jolt of pain reminded her. 'Ouch! Yes, it does. But only when careless people press on it like that.'

He smiled wryly, carefully rubbing the edge of his thumb over her other toes. The soft touch awakened very different pains inside her, calling up long-suppressed feelings of desire and need. They were feelings she had certainly thought dead—strangled by her husband's discreet fumblings under her nightdress in the marital bed.

But, blast it all, with one soft touch on her foot Dominick had sent that need roaring back into flaming life.

'I would say it is not broken,' he said, gazing down at her foot. The white stocking glowed against his dark coat in the moonlight. 'But you should put a cold compress on it soon, or you won't be able to wear your pretty shoes tomorrow.'

'You have much knowledge of treating injuries, I think,' she murmured, thinking of all the rumours of his fights, his long hours boxing and fencing at Gentleman Jackson's saloon.

'Horses' injuries, perhaps. Not those of fine ladies who insist on kicking innocent stone pillars.' He let go of her foot, but still knelt beside her, leaning slightly against her skirts. He was so near she could reach out and touch his hair, trace the stark, elegant lines of his face. Touch that tiny scar just by his temple.

She tucked her hands firmly in a fold of her skirt, away from temptation.

'It is good to see you again, Mary,' he said. 'You are looking very well.'

'So are you,' she admitted. Better than well, blast him. The years had hardly touched him, whereas she felt so very old sometimes.

'It's been far too long since I saw you.'

Had he thought of her, then? She longed to ask, to know

what he had imagined of her over all this time. But she just laughed. 'Well, I have lived mostly in the country since I married. I hear you cannot often tear yourself away from the pleasures of Town.'

The corner of his mouth quirked. 'Town does offer many distractions. If I was alone too much with my thoughts, I fear I would run mad.'

What were those thoughts, then? She wanted so much to know of his scandalous Town life! A life so different from her own quiet existence. At Derrington Hall there were no distractions at all. 'I do envy you.'

'Do you?' he said. 'You certainly should not.'

For an instant she felt the lightest pressure against her skirt, against her leg, just at the vulnerable bend of her knee. She glanced down, startled, to see he had caught a fold of silk between his fingers, his golden head leaning close, as if he inhaled her perfume.

An ineffable tenderness, a sad longing, swept over her. She remembered all she had once longed for with him, all she had had to give up. She stretched out her hand to touch his cheek, only to draw back in fear.

It had hurt so much to lose him back then, when she was just a silly, romantic girl. She couldn't afford to feel that way again, and she was very much afraid she would. He still had that power over her senses.

'I should go back to the house,' she said hastily. Forgetting her shoe, forgetting her hurt foot, she jumped up and dashed from the temple. She limped as fast as she could along the pathway and up the steps to the terrace, only to be brought up short by the sight of her brother-in-law.

Drew leaned against the stone balustrade, a cheroot between his fingers. For a moment she feared he had seen her with Dominick in the temple, but he said nothing and went on staring out into the night. His handsome young face looked solemn, as if he, too, carried the weight of all the Bassington troubles on his shoulders.

She thought of going to him, of sharing their problems as

they had ever since William had died, but she was too tired and confused. She couldn't tell anyone about Dominick, not even Drew, who had become like her own brother. So she just slipped into the house, avoiding the laughter in the drawing room as she hurried up to her own chamber.

Surely everything would seem much clearer in the morning, and she would feel like herself again. Like sensible, practical, cool-headed Lady Derrington. Silly, romantic, impulsive Mary Smythe was gone.

Dominick leaned against the marble pillar, watching Mary run away from him across the gardens. With her dark hair and deep purple gown she seemed a part of the night, but her pale face glowed.

Mary Smythe—no, Lady Derrington. She was *here*, at Welbourne Manor, surely the last place he would expect to find her. If he had known she was here, would he have refused the invitation—or would he have come much sooner?

He slammed his hand against the cold stone, but nothing could erase the image in his mind of her dark eyes, as startled and delicate as a doe's, when he'd touched her foot. *Mary, Mary.* How hard he had worked to forget her! He'd thought he *had* forgotten her, the sweet memory of their youthful kisses buried in so many other beds, so many card games and fights. What were the innocent smiles of Mary Smythe to all that?

But now he saw he had never really forgotten at all. The reality of her presence, of the beautiful woman she had become, only sharpened those old memories. When he'd touched her, smelled the lavender perfume she still wore, such a fierce longing had swept over him. He'd wanted to lean down, to kiss her foot, caress the warm curve of her leg and make her cry out with need.

He curled his hand into a tight fist. Her parents had once thought him not good enough for her, and they had been quite right. He had been a reckless, romantic young man, full of futile dreams. How much worse would he be for her now, with scandals by the score attached to his name?

The one honourable thing he had ever done in his life was letting Mary Smythe go. He wouldn't ruin that good deed now by pursuing Lady Derrington. No matter how much he still wanted her.

Chapter One

'But I love him! And he loves me. Why can we not be happy? It is so unfair!'

Mary closed her eyes and sighed deeply as she listened to her sister's sobs. Poor Ginny. She very much feared romantic matters would end no better for her sister than they had for her own seventeen-year-old self, when she had been so infatuated with Dominick she hadn't been able to see straight. She also feared she was now turning into their mother.

We must all grow up and be sensible sooner or later, she thought as Ginny cried on. Being sensible wasn't such an entirely bad thing. It saved a woman much grief and vexation if she could just see life as it was, and not as a romantic novel.

So why, then, if she was such a sensible widow now, did she feel so achingly sad?

Ginny gave another frustrated shriek, and Mary opened her eyes to see her sister flop down on a brocade chaise, her pretty face streaked with tears. Poor Ginny. She was the youngest of Mary's three younger sisters, the last one unmarried. Cynthia had married a clergyman with a fine living, Elizabeth a country baronet much like their own father.

But none had wed so well as Mary, to the Earl of Derrington. Now that she was widowed and alone, after the terrible death of her son a year ago, it had seemed a good idea to offer to launch Ginny. Maybe having her sister to live with her in London would distract her from her grief and the sadness that never seemed to end.

Maybe it would even distract her from those memories of meeting Dominick again that summer at Welbourne Manor, of hearing his voice say her name and feeling his touch on her almost bare foot. The feeling of not being so lonely, just for a moment. She just had to forget Dominick again, that was all, and the bustle and noise of launching Ginny into Society had seemed a good way to do that. It had seemed to work at first. Town did offer many diversions for a young lady. Even though the Season was over, there was shopping to be done, plays to be seen, even a few parties to attend. Ginny was very lively company, and Mary had been enjoying getting to know her sister again. Being with family made the ache of loss seem a bit less. All had seemed to be going well enough. They had even looked forward to the bustle of the Christmas holidays.

Until Ginny had fallen in love with young Captain Heelis. Dominick's own cousin. Nothing had been peaceful since.

'It is so unfair,' Ginny wailed again. 'I thought the purpose of my coming to London was to find a husband. So why am I not allowed to marry the man I love?'

Mary folded her hands on top of her desk, taking in a deep breath. 'Because Captain Heelis, though an admirable young man in many ways, does not yet have the income to take care of a wife and family,' she said, for what felt like the twentieth time.

'Income!' Ginny rolled over, burying her face in the cushions so only her rumpled auburn curls, redder and prettier than Mary's own brown ones, were visible. 'Who cares about such trifles when there is *love*?'

Mary pressed her lips together to keep from laughing aloud.

'You will certainly think better of that, dear Ginny, when you find *love* cannot put a roof over your head or food on your table—or buy the pretty gowns you like so much. You will especially think better of it when you have children.'

Children—they changed everything. She well remembered that feeling when she'd held her baby in her arms, and the terrible ache when he was gone. Children changed a woman's life completely.

But Ginny, who had never had to worry about such matters, thanks to Mary's advantageous marriage, seemed most unconvinced. 'Captain Heelis has excellent prospects.'

'Prospects don't put shoes on children's feet,' said Mary, feeling more like her mother every moment. In fact, she was quite sure Jane Smythe had said something very similar when Mary had wanted to marry Dominick, who had not yet inherited the Amesby viscountcy and estate. 'Society will now be open to all your sisters,' her mother had said, when Mary had cried and wanted to refuse Derrington. 'None of us will have to worry again. Would you be selfish enough to turn all that away?'

In the end, Mary had been selfless so her sisters would not have to be. Now she didn't want to marry again, ever. She just wanted to take care of her family the best she could. But that didn't mean Ginny should marry a handsome, penniless officer, even one with connections like Viscount Amesby! Mary's jointure could not support them all.

'Oh, Mary!' Ginny cried, kicking her feet. 'You have become so stodgy and stuffy. You've probably never been in love, so you can't know how I feel.'

Could she not? Mary remembered that terrible, aching longing she had felt as she had looked down at Dominick in the Welbourne moonlight. And further back, all those years ago, the tearing feeling that she would die if she couldn't be with the man she loved. The agony of young love thwarted.

That pain faded, though. It became nothing more than a dull ache, pushed far down in the secret recesses of her heart.

'I do know how you feel,' she said quietly. 'Being in love can be glorious. But sometimes it cannot give you a safe, suitable life.'

'I don't care about *safe*!'

'Not now, perhaps. But when you are older, when you have children, you will. You are so young, Ginny dear, and so is Captain Heelis. You have time to consider your choices.'

'I will never feel any differently about Captain Heelis,' Ginny protested. 'Time will change nothing.'

'Then you will not mind waiting.'

Ginny gave another frustrated scream. She leaped up from the chaise and ran out of the drawing room, slamming the door behind her. The loud bang reverberated through the quiet house.

Mary stared out of the window at the leaden grey evening sky, suddenly so tired. This was not at all how she had pictured her Christmas season! It was her first Christmas in her own pretty townhouse, away from Derrington Hall at last. Her husband and his dour mother had never cared for Christmas, as her own family had, so she hadn't celebrated properly in years. And since little Will had died she hadn't wanted to celebrate anything at all. The world had seemed all black and empty.

For too long there had been no colour or laughter in her life, no merry Christmases, and she found she wanted them again. She daydreamed about greenery and mulled wine, music and feeling just the tiniest bit alive again. But now those wistful dreams were dissolving in quarrels, memories, and cold grey skies.

Mary pushed back from the desk and her unanswered letters, hurrying to the window as she drew her warm Indian shawl closer around her. The street below was nearly deserted, empty but for one carriage rattling past and one maidservant hurrying on her way, laden with packages. Everyone who had not left Town for a country Christmas was wisely huddled indoors, away from the cold wind.

Mary shivered, remembering that Welbourne summer party. The sunny blue skies, the picnics, the laughter. Seeing Dominick again. There, for a few days, things had seemed almost hopeful. She had quite forgotten what *fun* was like, and it was wondrous.

But now she was certainly back to reality, back to being sensible and dutiful.

As she reached for the satin drapery to pull it closed she caught a glimpse of something bright out in the gloom, a flash of red against the endless grey winter. She peered closer, and saw it was Captain Heelis's red coat. He stood out in the wind, staring up at the house with sad longing written on his handsome face.

Mary's heart ached for him, and for her sister. First love could be so terrible. It could rip at the heart and leave a person feeling like nothing but a hollow shell. A human with only a half-life.

She pulled the draperies tight over the pitiful sight, as if she could conceal all her old feelings along with it. Ginny and Captain Heelis would have to learn, just as she had. They all had to learn the terrible taste of loss.

Mary left the drawing room, hurrying up the stairs as the servants came in to light candles against the gathering night. It was good they had already planned a quiet evening at home, as Ginny was obviously in no condition to be among company. Choked sobs echoed from behind her closed door.

She was too tired to talk to her sister again. Ginny never listened anyway, and Mary had begun to feel like a trained parrot, reciting the same words over and over again. She turned on the landing, going up to the nursery on the second floor. She knew she would find no solace there, yet she was drawn to that room. She would just sit there for a few moments, and remember.

The nursery was cold and dark, the air full of the staleness of disuse. Of loneliness and sadness. But the old crib was still there, covered with canvas dustcloths like ghosts. The toys were piled up in the corner, the little clothes carefully folded and packed away in a trunk, even though no small hands would reach for them again.

Mary slowly sat down in the abandoned chair, staring out at the silent, shadowed nursery. Her chest ached with a physical pain that never seemed to really go away. It was duller than the sharp, deathly ache it once had been, but still there. Always there.

And sometimes she was afraid it *would* go away, and take the last vestige of her son with it.

It was over a year since little Will had died, swept away so fast by that fever. So many children in London had been lost to that illness. Surely it should not still hurt so? Her own mother constantly urged her to move forward, to marry again and have more children. Yet how could she? She hadn't been able to protect even one.

Mary stared at the covered crib and remembered Will's tousled dark curls, his plump pink cheeks. The sweet, sleepy way he would call out 'Mama!' and hold his arms to her for a hug. When it was bedtime he had always been exhausted from running as fast as he could all day, trying to embrace all life had to offer. He and Ginny had been so alike in that way—always grabbing for their desires with both hands, heedless of any consequences.

She'd tried to hold them back, to keep them safe. But she had failed. How could she do all this alone, when she was so very tired?

Mary pressed her hands to her eyes, which ached with unshed tears. 'I'm so sorry,' she whispered. She didn't know if she talked to Will, Ginny or herself.

Chapter Two

Ｈow wonderful ancient statues were, Mary thought as she strolled through the British Museum, passing between rows of marble gods and goddesses. They were so beautiful—and so blessedly silent. Not one of them sighed and wept; none of them stormed away from the breakfast table in a fit of high emotion. Perhaps in the old tales the gods had thrown thunderbolts and quarrelled and ruined the lives of mortals, but here in the museum they just stood on their pedestals, gazing down with empty eyes on the passers-by.

Not that there were very many of them today. The cold weather had kept sensible people away, but not Mary. She'd had to escape her house, which was now a vale of tears, for an hour or two. The museum had seemed just the place to do that.

Mary tucked her hands deeper into her fur muff, gazing up at Artemis as she pointed her stone bow into the distance. Surely the virgin goddess of the moon had it right—men and love were nothing but trouble.

'Lady Derrington!' she heard someone call, and turned to see Sir Edward and Lady Quickley hurrying towards her. Their daughter Angelica trailed behind them, looking bored by all the ancient culture around her. She and Ginny had become bosom bows in the last few weeks, and Mary knew for a fact the two of them much preferred fashion papers to art.

'Sir Edward, Lady Quickley,' Mary said. 'I am glad to see I'm not the only one who dares to venture forth on such a dreary day.'

'And they say it's going to get much worse before Christmas!' Sir Edward said cheerfully, as if he relished a good winter storm.

'We're leaving for the country tomorrow,' his wife added. 'Which is why we wanted one more look at the marbles before we left.'

'Very wise of you,' Mary said. 'My sister and I plan to spend our holiday here in Town.'

'Is Ginny with you today?' Angelica asked. 'I do so want to tell her about my new bonnet before I am dragged away to the country!'

'She didn't come with me to the museum, but I'm sure she would enjoy a visit from you this afternoon, Miss Quickley,' said Mary. Perhaps a nice coze with her friend was just what Ginny needed to distract her.

After chatting about Christmas plans for a few more minutes, the Quickleys departed and Mary went on to the next gallery, alone again in the echoing silence.

But not entirely alone, she saw with a shock. Dominick was there, examining a case of antiquities. The dim grey light from the high windows gleamed on his bright hair.

Mary took a step backwards, as if to flee, but he glanced up and saw her there. For an instant an unguarded smile of surprised welcome touched his lips. But it quickly faded into wariness, and he gave her a polite bow.

She looked back longingly over her shoulder, but even as she thought to flee she knew she could not. It would be craven and silly to run away from him again, as she had at Welbourne.

She straightened her shoulders and walked towards him as if it was the most normal thing in the world for them to be face to face. 'Lord Amesby. Such a surprise to see you here.'

'Because you think I do not care for art or history?' he said with a laugh. 'Only horses?'

Horses—and cards, and women. 'I don't know what you care for,' she said, and was surprised at how true that was. It had been so long since she had seen Dominick—years before the Welbourne summer party. She'd heard gossip about him often, yet knew so little of the real man now. And she found she longed to know far more. She wanted it so much it made her heart ache all over again.

'I don't see how anyone could fail to care about something so very beautiful,' he said, gesturing to a small marble statue in the case.

Mary glanced down to see a Grecian lady, her hair carved into perfect curls, her draperies falling around her slim body in fluid lines. She held a basket of flowers balanced delicately on her shoulder, and a small, secret smile curved her lips.

'It's lovely,' she said. 'Who is she?'

'Persephone.'

Persephone—snatched away from her sunlit life by the god of the Underworld. The first elopement. 'Do you have some— affinity with her story?' Mary said carefully, thinking of Lady Newcombe.

'I fear I am no scholar of ancient myths,' Dominick answered. 'I like her because she looks like you.'

'Me?' Mary examined the statue closer. It made her want to laugh and blush like a schoolgirl to think he considered her so pretty. To think that he considered her at all.

'And what of you?' he said. He leaned closer as they both looked at Persephone, not touching but near enough that she could feel his warmth. 'Do you visit a favourite statue today?'

'There are many pieces I love here. But I confess I mostly came for the quiet.'

'The quiet?'

'Yes.' She peeked at him from the corner of her eye to find he watched her very closely. No wonder all the ladies sighed for him—he still had that wondrous gift of making a woman feel herself the only person in the world. The only person he cared about. 'You see, my youngest sister has come to stay with me.'

Dominick laughed. 'Then *quiet* must indeed be in short supply at your house. I, too, have a young relative in residence—my cousin.'

'Captain Heelis.'

His brow arched in question. 'You know him?'

'Sadly, I do.' A thought suddenly struck Mary—perhaps Dominick could help with her Ginny dilemma. He knew about scandal and wild-hearted young people. Perhaps he had some influence with Captain Heelis. It was obvious she had none with Ginny. 'I fear my sister has developed a *tendre* for your cousin, and I have heard little from her but his name these last few weeks.'

His eyes narrowed. 'So it is your sister.'

'What is my sister?'

'He has been spending a great deal of time writing letters and reading volumes of poetry of late,' Dominick said. 'But he has been quite secretive as to the object of his affections. If it comforts you, Mary, I am certain his intentions are most honourable.'

'Oh, I know they are. He has already made an offer. But my parents do not approve.'

'Ah, yes. Surely they would *not* approve of a young man with few prospects courting their daughter.'

Mary remembered all too well that that had once been their objection to *him*. 'I am sure Captain Heelis is an upstanding young man, but—you do see my dilemma? Ginny is in my care now.'

He nodded. 'I will speak to Arthur. Though I fear talking will do little good. Young people in love…'

'Should be committed to Bedlam,' Mary muttered.

Dominick laughed. 'It does often seem so. But such feelings pass—remember?'

Did they? She had once thought that, but just now, caught in the spell of his beautiful eyes, she wasn't sure they *did* pass. Not entirely.

'I just wish they would pass a bit faster,' she said. 'My sister cries and wails at all hours, I fear.'

'At least she does not try to write poetry and then read it to you for a critique,' Dominick answered. 'Byron's literary reputation has nothing to fear from my cousin's work.'

'Thank you for agreeing to speak to him,' she said. 'Even if it does no good now, perhaps it will plant a seed of practicality in his head. I fear I will have to remove Ginny to an entirely new locale soon.'

'You are leaving for Christmas?'

Mary shook her head. 'Not until the New Year. I want to celebrate in my own home—not that it will be very peaceful with Ginny carrying on so!'

'Oh, yes.' Dominick glanced back down at Persephone, an unreadable expression on his face. 'I do remember how you loved Christmas.'

A sudden burst of laughter from just outside the gallery doorway startled her. She had quite forgotten that anyone existed in the world but Dominick and her.

'I must go,' she said quickly. She took one of her hands from her muff, holding it out to him. 'Thank you again for agreeing to talk to Captain Heelis. It has been a weight off my mind just to speak of it all with someone else!'

He folded her gloved hand between his strong, elegant fingers, raising it to his lips. He actually brushed a kiss against her knuckles, his breath soft through the thin leather. 'I'm glad I could be of service.'

Feeling suddenly hot and cold all at once, she snatched her hand back and hurried from the gallery. As she left, she passed a group of two ladies and three gentlemen. One of the ladies, a blonde in a most sophisticated feathered hat and a gown too low-cut for day, called out. 'Dominick! So *this* is where you have been hiding yourself, you naughty man...'

Mary rushed on, even as she longed to look back and see how the 'naughty man' responded to the woman. But, no, she didn't care! She *couldn't* care. Not any more.

* * *

Dominick hurried along the street, not seeing the busy, happy crowds around him as they carried their Christmas packages home. He didn't see the shop windows, brightly decked with greenery and streamers, or the wintry grey sky.

He saw only Mary's chocolate-brown eyes, watching him from beneath her lashes as at last a tentative smile touched his lips. For one brief moment it had seemed as if they were the old Dominick and Mary, bound together in an understanding and an attraction that was natural and magical. And when he'd kissed her hand in the museum…

But then Dorothy and his friends had appeared. Dorothy was an actress who had once briefly been his mistress. He had seen the look on Mary's face as she'd watched Dorothy call out to him. She'd looked so solemn and strangely disappointed.

Well, blast her anyway! She had no right to be disappointed in anything he did. Just as he had no right to feel the way he did—wanting to rush after her, take her in his arms and explain everything. As if he *could* explain his misbegotten life.

A lady suddenly stepped out of a shop door, nearly running into Dominick as she laughed down at the little girl holding her hand.

'Oh, I do beg your pardon!' she cried, peering up at him from beneath her hat. 'Why, Lord Amesby. How do you do?'

He *was* cursed with all things associated with Mary today, he thought. For the lady was none other than Charlotte Fitzmanning—Mary's sister-in-law.

'How delightful to see you again, Miss Fitzmanning,' he said politely, tipping his hat to her. 'Oh, but I must call you Lady Andrew Bassington now.'

'Indeed you must—though it sounds a most fusty title indeed. And I am Lady Derrington now. My husband's poor little nephew died of a fever last year,' she said sadly, the light in her eyes dimming. She put her arm around the little girl, who ducked her face shyly against Charlotte's skirt.

'Died of a…?' Mary's son gone? A cold, stunned sadness washed over Dominick and he could only stare at Charlotte, appalled. *Oh, Mary!* She had always so loved children. How terrible it must have been for her—must still be. How he would have given anything to be there for her. 'I am very sorry,' he said.

'It was quite terrible,' Charlotte answered. 'He was such a dear child, and gone so quickly. Mary was devastated.'

'Is she—how is she now?' he asked. He had to restrain the urge, barely leashed for all the months since they had met at Welbourne, to run to her. She surely would not appreciate his sudden appearance back in her life.

'She does try to be brave, to assure us she feels so much better,' said Charlotte. 'But I see her sadness, hidden underneath. She used to love Christmas so very much, Drew and I, and our daughter Anna here, were hoping to find a way to cheer her up a bit this Christmas. We were just in that shop trying to find a gift for her.'

Dominick glanced past Charlotte's shoulder to the shop window. He could hardly see the sparkling gems for his sadness for Mary and her poor child. 'Did you find something to suit?'

'Anna thought she would like those amethyst earrings,' Charlotte said. 'Purple is Mary's favourite colour. But, alas, she will only wear grey now! I think I must keep on shopping for a way to put colour in her life again.'

Put colour in her life again. If only *he* could do that. But he had forfeited that right long ago. 'I wish you good luck.'

'I am on my way to Hatchards now, to meet my husband. Would you like to accompany us? I remember you are a reader yourself, and I know Drew would like to see you again. It has been too long since we had your company.'

The little girl, Anna, peeked up at him with adorable dark eyes.

'I fear I have urgent errands to finish, Lady Derrington,' he said. 'But please give Drew my greetings.'

Charlotte nodded slowly, her gaze much too perceptive as she watched him. 'We did miss you at our wedding, and at Anna's christening. But perhaps we will meet again soon?'

'I hope so, Lady Derrington.' Dominick watched Charlotte

and the toddling girl hurry away down the street, a package-laden footman rushing to keep up with them. The crowd pressed around him, but he did not notice. All he could see, all he could think of, was Mary. Poor, brave, beautiful Mary and her grief.

Could there be any greater, deeper pain than to lose a child? He had seen such grief before, felt its knife-cut to the soul. It had shown him how unfit he was to be a father, how he could not protect those he loved. And for Mary to suffer so…

Dominick turned away, blindly seeking he knew not what. But his attention was captured by those earrings, sparkling at the centre of the window display. So deep and rich a purple, like the hopeful flash of violets in bleak, cold white snow.

Before he could stop and think better of what he was doing he stepped into the shop.

By the time he made it back to his town house, with the package he would probably never deliver tucked inside his greatcoat, his cousin had gone out for the evening. Their talk about the young Miss Smythe would have to wait.

That was probably for the best, Dominick thought as he locked away the jewel case. He was in no shape to lecture anyone coherently about being responsible. Not when all he could think about was Mary.

Chapter Three

Mary tapped her finger against her chocolate cup, staring at her sister's empty chair across the breakfast table. It appeared Ginny was still sulking; she had even stayed in her room through dinner last night. 'This must cease,' she murmured.

'I beg your pardon, my lady?' said the maid, who was laying out fresh toast.

'Is my sister unwell this morning?' Mary asked.

'I don't know, my lady. I haven't seen Miss Smythe's maid this morning.'

'I will just look in on her, then.' Mary laid her napkin beside her plate and rose from her chair, trying to keep a pleasant smile on her face as she slowly strolled from the breakfast room and up the stairs. The servants surely had enough fodder for gossip, with all Ginny's fits and their quarrels!

Mary marched up to Ginny's door and knocked firmly. 'Ginny, you must eat something! You will make yourself ill.'

Nothing. Only silence. Mary slowly turned the knob, peeking into the chamber as she braced herself for more tears.

But Ginny's room was dark, the draperies still drawn over the windows. Her heart pounding, Mary dashed over to throw them open, spinning around as grey morning light flooded in.

The bed had not been slept in; the dressing table was empty. The wardrobe doors were open to reveal several gowns missing.

For one stunned moment Mary was sure she was imagining things. It had to be some prank on Ginny's part, to pay her back for not supporting Captain Heelis's suit! But then she saw a folded paper propped on the pillows of the bed.

It was a note in Ginny's looping handwriting.

Dearest, dearest Mary,
I am so very sorry to do this, after all your kindness to me, but I fear I have no choice. I love Captain Heelis with all my heart, and we know we must be together. By the time you read this we will be on our way to Gretna Green. Please forgive me, dearest sister, and be happy for us.
All my love, Ginny.

Oh, the foolish, foolish girl. Mary crushed the note in her hand, her mind racing. Their parents would be so furious! Surely they would now cut poor Ginny off without a penny, and blame Mary for being a bad chaperon. It would be such a scandal—on the Smythes *and* the Bassingtons. The Bassingtons, who prided themselves on their good name.

Unless—unless she could stop them before anyone found out. If she could just trace them before they reached Scotland no one would need to know. It could all be hushed up.

And she knew the one person who could help her.

Still clutching the note, she hurried out of the room, closing the door behind her. She had to send for the carriage immediately.

Mary stood on the doorstep of the narrow townhouse, shivering despite her thick wool pelisse and the veil on her velvet bonnet. Was this the right place? She had double-checked the address, but it seemed quite deserted, with all the shutters drawn and no smoke from the chimneys.

She glanced down the street, the sky grey and hazy through that veil. It, too, was quiet, if respectable enough. For a moment she regretted dismissing the carriage and walking here after calling on the Quickleys, but she didn't want anyone to know where she was.

Perhaps it was better no one was here anyway.

But as she turned away the door suddenly swung open. It was no butler or footman who stood there; it was Dominick himself.

She had obviously interrupted him in a private hour, for he wore no coat, just a brocade waistcoat unfastened over his shirt, his cravat loosened. His golden hair was rumpled, a wave of it falling over his brow. His expression looked as stunned as she felt.

'I beg your pardon—' His words were choked off as she raised her veil to reveal her face.

'My sister has run off with your cousin,' she blurted out. 'I need help.'

Dominick's lips pressed together in a tight line, a muscle flexing along his strong jaw. 'You had better come in, then.'

Mary nodded and stepped into the house, her hands clutched inside her sable muff. As he shut the door behind her she had the wild urge to flee, as if by leaving she could outrun all her reawakened confused feelings for him. He was the only one who could help her now, though.

And, if she was honest with herself, she did not really *want* to leave.

'I'm sorry, but I gave my servants the day off,' he said, 'so it's a bit desolate at the moment. Come with me. It's warmer in the library.'

He strode down a narrow corridor, buttoning his waistcoat and smoothing back his hair. The gold signet ring on his finger gleamed in the dim light. *Well,* Mary thought, *in for a penny, in for a pound*—as her nanny had used to say when she was a child. She followed him.

The library was indeed warmer, less stark than the bare foyer and corridor. Warm jewel-green and red carpets were spread across the parquet floor, and there were dark green velvet draperies over the windows, keeping away the cold day. Lamps were lit on the desk and a small fire smouldered in the grate, illuminating the books lining the walls. Crates lay open by the hearth, as if he had just begun to unpack them.

'I have no idea how to make tea,' he said with a rueful laugh. 'There is brandy, but I'm sure you don't care for that.'

'Actually, brandy sounds precisely what is called for today.' Mary laid her muff and gloves on the table, untying her bonnet ribbons.

'Brandy it is, then.' He poured generous measures of the amber liquid into two glasses, handing her one. His hand brushed lightly against hers as she took the drink, warm and strong and strangely reassuring.

Mary took a long swallow, relishing the burn of it in her stomach. It gave her courage, even if it *was* only false bravery. 'Yes, definitely what is called for,' she said.

'Glad I could be of *some* service, then. Here, Mary, sit down by the fire and tell me what has happened. How long has your sister been gone?'

Mary dropped into the chair he held out for her, holding the glass tightly in her hands. His own brandy, she saw, was barely touched as he sat down across from her.

'Since some time last night,' she said, and took another sip. 'She didn't come down to dinner. I thought she was sulking again, but she must have been packing. When was Captain Heelis last here?'

Dominick shook his head. 'I have not seen him since yesterday morning. He was not at home when I returned from the museum, but he often keeps erratic hours.'

'Whenever Ginny can sneak to meet him, I suppose.'

'Do you know anything of her plans?'

Mary stared down wearily into the dregs of her glass. 'Her note said they were headed to Scotland, and that she was sorry. I went to see her bosom bow, Angelica Quickley, before I came here. After much browbeating she admitted Ginny and Captain Heelis plan to follow the Great North Road as closely as possible because of the unpredictable weather. I have tried to keep it quiet, but…'

'But gossip has a way of getting about,' he said tightly. 'Yes, I know that very well.'

'Captain Heelis said nothing at all to you?'

'He keeps his own counsel—aside from that unfortunate poetry. Surely you know I would have alerted you had I any notion of their plans?'

'I—well, you don't seem entirely *averse* to elopements, Dominick,' Mary said, and immediately rued her words. Perhaps brandy was not such a good idea after all.

Dominick's lips tightened again, but he said nothing. He just went to one of the bookshelves, drawing out a thick volume and laying it out on the desk. Mary saw it was a book of maps, and he studied it intently, his palms braced on the desk. That stray lock of hair fell over his brow again, and Mary had the strangest urge to go to him and brush it back, to see if it was as soft as it looked. As soft as she remembered against her skin.

She firmly set aside her glass and folded her hands in her lap.

'They have a considerable head start if they left last night,' he muttered. 'But if they do indeed stay on the main road north, there's a chance they can be found. There's no travelling fast in winter. I will set out immediately.'

'*You* will set out?' Mary said.

'Of course.' He peered up at her, his face solemn and unreadable, cast in chiselled shadows by the lamplight. 'Did you think I would just sit back and let a young couple fall into ruin?'

'I…' In truth, she did not know what she had thought. She had just needed help, and instinctively had turned to him. 'You cannot go alone.'

'Who else would you trust with this tale?'

No one, of course. No one else would understand and not judge, only Dominick. He knew how these matters worked better than anyone. But it pained her to think of him going alone into the winter weather, after *her* foolish sister. And she had to be there to persuade Ginny to come home peacefully.

Even if the thought of travelling with him, being alone with him, made her heart pound all over again.

'She is my sister. She was my responsibility and I failed in that,' she said. 'I will go with you. I'll have to take charge of Ginny once you find them.' Maybe in that way she could atone just a bit for not being able to help her son.

'Mary.' He shook his head firmly. 'It's December, and bitter cold. There's not time for a large carriage.'

'Surely you have something smaller? Faster? I heard you raced a curricle to Brighton last summer.'

Dominick laughed. 'You want to take a curricle out in this weather?'

'I'll hire a brougham, then. You could drive that. Or we can ride; I still have a good enough seat. One way or another, I *am* going.'

'Mary,' he said again. The sound of her name, plain old Mary, in his rich, dark voice, made her toes curl in her boots. 'What if someone saw us together? The respectable widow Lady Derrington with that rake Lord Amesby—what an *on dit* that would make. You haven't thought this through.'

That was true enough—she had not been *thinking* at all ever since she'd found Ginny's note. But she was so tired of always thinking everything through so carefully, so prudently. Of always being so blasted cautious. Being cautious had got her into this mess.

'I have thought about it,' she said. 'I can't sit at home and fret while you go after them. My sister needs me, and I need to make this right.'

'Mary…' he began, a sharp edge to that word now.

'No, Dominick. We must go together. I have made up my mind, and I do not change it.'

'I do remember *that*,' he said. He shut the book, bracing his fists on top of it. 'I have never met a lady so stubborn.'

'I'm no different now.' Mary rose from her chair and moved slowly to his side, as if drawn by the bright beauty of him. 'Dominick. You turned me away before, when we were young. Please don't turn me away now. Help me to help my sister.'

For an instant there was a flash of pain in his eyes, before that unreadable veil fell back into place. He reached out and gently brushed the back of his hand over her cheek. The soft touch left a trail of pure fire along her skin.

'The only honourable thing I ever did was to turn you away back then,' he muttered. 'I can't be so noble twice.'

'Then don't be!' Mary reached up and pressed her hand over his, holding him against her. His fingers curved, cradling her cheek. 'Let me go with you. I promise I am strong. I can face whatever we find.' As long as he was there, she could face it.

He stared down at her, and she felt as if the very air around them crackled with tense awareness. She could see nothing but him. His head tilted, bending towards her. *Was he going to kiss her?* Mary's lips parted, and she found herself leaning infinitesimally towards him, longing to know if he still tasted the same. If his kiss would make her feel as wondrously, burningly alive as it once did.

But then he turned away from her and braced his hands against the desk, his shoulders stiff. Mary drew in a shuddering breath. What a great fool she was, to long so much for a kiss from him! Their youthful romance had been so long ago; they were no longer the same people they once were.

She had come here to enlist his help in finding Ginny. She had to remember that.

'Can you be ready to depart within two hours?' he said roughly.

'I—yes, of course,' she answered. She had no one to answer to now.

'Meet me back here, then. I will see to our transportation. And Mary…?'

'Yes?'

'Charlotte told me about your son. I am so very sorry for your loss.' His words were simple, but his tone was full of understanding and terrible pity.

Mary nodded, even though she knew he could not see her, and rushed from the room as if demons nipped at her heels. She impatiently dashed away the hot tears from her eyes—tears at his simple words of kindness.

If she was so unsettled by being in his company for an hour, what would this journey north, just the two of them, feel like? Would she go mad? Throw herself at him on the carriage seat? Something unfortunate was surely bound to happen.

Yet somehow, despite everything, she almost felt like giving a shout of laughter as she turned towards home.

Dominick strode down the street, ignoring the people who hurried around him on their way home, happy Christmas smiles on their faces. A few of his acquaintances even started to greet him but, seemingly put off by his scowl, soon went on their way.

He had found the livery stable that had rented a vehicle to his cousin, but they had had no idea which direction Arthur Heelis had intended to take. They'd rented Dominick a brougham, though, a little two-seater carriage, and warned him of the harsh weather that was surely on the way.

Damn Arthur for a fool, anyway, Dominick thought, as a puddle of cold water splashed over his boots. Not only had he run off with Ginny Smythe, when he knew he could not properly take care of a wife, but he had headed to *Scotland* in the dead of winter. At least when Dominick had taken Lady Newcombe away they had tried to make it to warmer climes.

Not that it had done poor Eleanor any good in the end. And now he faced the harsh effects of an elopement by Mary's sister.

Mary. Well, if Arthur was a fool so was he, for agreeing to take Mary with him on what was bound to be a long and arduous search. When they were younger he had turned her away because he had feared he could not control himself around her. He still feared he could not.

When she looked at him with her large dark eyes he could deny her nothing. And when she parted her soft pink lips…

He wanted to catch her in his arms, to drag her so close there was not even a breath between them, and kiss her until they were both senseless. To see if she still tasted the same—sweeter and more intoxicating than any wine.

If they were together for days on end, bound by this wild quest to save her sister, would he be able to control himself at all? Or would the old memories be irresistible, bursting free after all their years of restraint and determined forgetfulness?

He would soon find out. But he had kept from ruining her life once; surely he could do it again? He was too old to marry now, too set in his ways and no good for any woman, let alone one as inestimable as Mary. He would find her sister for her and exorcise Mary Smythe from his memory once and for all.

Chapter Four

Perhaps this was not such a good idea after all.

Mary huddled on the carriage seat, wrapped in a pelisse *and* a cloak, the fur-lined hood drawn around her face. Yet still the cold wind bit at her skin. The sky, a purplish-grey bruised colour, seemed to lower around them every minute. The clouds looked ready to unleash a fury of rain at any moment.

When they found Ginny at last she would have to shout at the girl until they were both senseless for putting them through this! Then she would sit by a warm fire the rest of the winter.

She peeked at Dominick, who sat silently at her side. She could barely see him, wrapped as he was in a greatcoat and hat, a scarf muffled around his lower face as he urged the horses onward. He had hardly said a word since they had set out, but every once in a while he would reach out and tug the lap robe closer around her.

She stared out at the road again, at the hedgerows and trees concealed in the mist. They seemed to be the only two people in all the world. Everyone else was sensibly tucked up at home by their fires, leaving them all alone. It felt almost like a fairy story—two people on a magical quest.

Except she did not feel *magical* in the least. She felt cold, tired, and distinctly unsettled to be so near Dominick and yet still so far away.

She shifted on the seat, tucking her hands deeper into her muff. The hot brick at her feet had long gone chilly, but she pressed her feet closer to it anyway.

'Are you all right?' Dominick asked her, his voice muffled.

Mary was startled by the sudden sound in the midst of all that silence. 'Yes. Just cold.'

He nodded. 'It will be nightfall soon. We'll find an inn to stop at for a few hours.'

An inn, where there was sure to be a fire and warm things to drink. It sounded wonderful, but... 'If we stop, they will get even further ahead of us, yes?'

'They can't travel at night, either,' he said sensibly. 'My cousin might be a romantic young puppy, but I'm sure he would never put your sister in danger. Just as I won't put *you* in danger. Besides, we should enquire if they've been seen along here. We'll set out again at first light, and try to make it to my Aunt Beatrice's home by tomorrow night. Perhaps she's heard something of our runaways.'

'Aunt Beatrice?' Mary asked, seeking conversational distraction from the damp cold. 'You have an aunt?'

Dominick laughed. 'I'm not so solitary as all that, Mary. I do have *some* family.'

'I know you do—everyone does.' She had just seldom thought of Dominick in such ordinary terms as having kinsmen and obligations, as she did. When she was young he had seemed like a golden prince, complete in himself. Now she was not sure what she thought of him. 'Tell me about your aunt.'

'She is the Dowager Lady Amesby—the widow of my uncle. Sadly, it was the deaths of her husband and son that made me the heir. My father was her husband's younger brother.'

'And Captain Heelis?'

'He is the son of their younger sister. Unfortunately Aunt Kate was always a flighty sort. She lives in Ireland now, so she can't talk any sense into her son's head.'

Mary laughed. 'I'm sure I should be glad to meet Lady

Amesby, then, especially if her house has lots of fireplaces. My own father's sister, my Aunt Hester, always tried to save on expenses by lighting just one tiny fire in her own sitting room and severely restricting candles. She did not like children to laugh or talk too loudly, either, and had my sisters and I quite terrified of her. We hated to visit her, but our father made us go there every year.'

'No fear of talking too loudly in Aunt Beatrice's house. She is rather deaf. Luckily for me, that means she hasn't heard any of the gossip about me, and thus thinks I am still an upstanding fellow.'

Mary was beginning to think he was not so bad herself. No one with a completely black heart would go with her in the dead of winter to chase after her eloping sister. But she could not forget Lady Newcombe, or the blonde woman at the museum. *Dominick, you naughty man...* The ladies did still flock to Dominick, as they always had. He would never look twice at *her* now.

She shivered, and Dominick shifted the reins to one gloved hand, putting his arm around her shoulders and drawing her close. 'We will stop soon, I promise.'

Mary couldn't help herself. She rested her head on his shoulder, leaning into him as the carriage lurched on through the wind. 'I suppose searching for an inn under inauspicious circumstances *is* appropriate for Christmas.'

'Perhaps so,' he answered. 'But I can think of better ways to celebrate.'

She closed her eyes, relishing the warmth of him through all their layers of wool, linen and fur. 'I can, too. When I was a girl, my sisters and I used to go out and gather greenery. We made wreaths and swags for all the mantels and picture frames, and tied enormous red and gold bows around everything we could find. We didn't have much pin money, but we would save up and buy each other books and drawing pencils and lacy handkerchiefs, and hide them until Christmas Day.'

'And did you have a great feast on the day?'

'Oh, yes.' Mary smiled at the memory. 'Roast goose, baked ham and plum pudding. After church, all my parents' friends would come home with us for dinner. Then there was music and dancing. It was—wonderful.'

His arm tightened around her. 'Did you keep such traditions when you married?'

Mary opened her eyes, suddenly cold again at the reminder of her grown-up Christmases. 'No. My husband and his mother did not care for Christmas. We would just go to church and then spend the day reading or walking. Drew and I would sometimes sneak out and buy each other a small gift, though, and sing a Christmas carol or two when no one was about. When I had my son I tried to make it special for him, but…' She couldn't go on at the thought of those old Christmases.

Dominick said nothing, but Mary thought she felt him gently pat her shoulder through her wraps. 'Christmas is still a few days away. You can be back in time to spend it in Town however you would like…'

'Perhaps.' Somehow she doubted it, though. Finding Ginny was like looking for a star amid the clouds.

They soon found an inn, and its proprietors were shocked to see anyone out in such weather at all.

'Of course you and your wife are most welcome, sir,' the innkeeper's wife said as her husband saw to the carriage. She showed them to a parlour. 'We have plenty of rooms to offer you, and a nice hot venison stew for supper. We didn't expect any travellers in such unholy weather, and so near Christmas.'

'We had some family business to see to at once, or we would not be abroad, either,' Dominick said as Mary removed her damp cloak and bonnet and sat down by the blessedly warm fire. 'We were very grateful to find your establishment before nightfall. But you have seen no one else for a time? Not even another couple?'

'You're the only guests we've had for two days at least,' she answered. 'Only a very few carriages have gone past on the road, even.'

'Of course,' Dominick answered. 'Everyone sensible is at home.'

'If there's nothing else, sir, I will just go and see to the food and have some water heated for washing,' she said, hurrying away and leaving them alone again.

Mary watched as Dominick laid his coat to dry by the fire and sat down beside her. Silently he reached for her hands and slowly peeled the leather gloves from her fingers. She stared down at his touch against her. It made her feel so—so strange. Warm and shivery all at the same time—taken out of herself. Not even the most passionate kisses from her husband—which had never been *very* passionate—had made her feel even a fraction of the way this simple touch did.

And when the landlady had called her Dominick's wife—she definitely did not want to consider the thrill that one word had given her!

That was surely a very dangerous sign indeed. She knew she should pull away from him, but she just couldn't. She loved the way he made her *feel* again, after so long in the frozen dream of sadness.

'Your hands are so cold,' he muttered, gently rubbing at them, bringing her skin to tingling life.

'So are yours,' she whispered.

'You should have let me come on this journey alone. Then you would be tucked up by your own fire at home.'

'And endlessly worrying about Ginny.' And worrying about Dominick, too, on this search all by himself. 'I couldn't bear that. It's much better that I be at least somewhat useful. Besides, this fire is just as cosy.'

He let go of her, and turned to stare into the crackling flames. She wished she knew his thoughts, but he seemed very far away from her.

'Did you have grand plans for Christmas?' she asked. She propped her feet on the hearth, wriggling her toes in her boots as they slowly came back to life.

'Not as grand as roast goose, plum pudding and dancing,' he said. 'My friend Lord Archibald is having a party. Perhaps I would have gone to that.'

'Indeed?' Lord Archibald was a notorious rake. She could just imagine the sort of party *he* would have. There would surely be women like the one Dominick had been with in the museum, just ready to give him a wonderful time. A time full of the fun she had almost forgotten.

Dominick gave her a crooked smile, as if he read her thoughts. 'Or perhaps I would have stayed home and finished unpacking those crates of new books.'

There was no time to ask him anything else, for a line of servants bustled in with their supper and more fuel for the fire. By the time they had finished eating and retired to their adjoining but separate rooms, Mary was deeply tired.

Yet she found she could not sleep. She lay under the quilts, listening to freezing rain beat against the window.

And listening to the sounds of Dominick moving around in the room next door. It seemed her ears were intently sensitive to every noise—the splashing of water as he washed, the creak of floorboards as he walked, the rustle of cloth as he changed clothes. The sigh of the mattress as he laid down.

She closed her eyes tightly, but that did not help. She just saw him in her mind, lying in that bed so very close to her own, listening to the same rain. Did he lie awake, too? What did he think about?

And what did he wear to bed? A nightshirt and cap, as William had? Or—nothing?

Oh, blast it all. Now there was a new image in her mind, an image of his lean, bronzed body bare against white sheets, his golden hair rumpled on the pillows. Surely it was the landlady's assumption that she was Dominick's wife that made her think such things? Made her imagine his touch, his kisses.

She rolled over, pressing her hot face into the bedclothes. *Go away, go away,* she told the images, and slowly they faded away. But she still could not sleep.

Chapter Five

'We shouldn't be out in this, should we?' Mary shouted over the howling wind, the pelting of freezing rain against the carriage. She could barely see three feet of the road ahead of them, and leaned tightly against Dominick's side. The muscles in his arm were taut and hard as he held tightly to the reins.

It had not looked so very bad when they had set out from the inn that morning. The clouds had even cleared a bit, and they had been able to stop and make enquiries at hostelries and villages along the way, tracing rare sightings of Ginny and Captain Heelis. Until this storm had rolled in, like a sudden onslaught to block their quest.

'Of course we should not be out in this,' Dominick shouted back. 'We should be safe in our own homes, as all sane people are.' He tugged hard on the reins as the frightened horse veered off the road.

Mary bit her lip in a sharp pang of conscience. If not for her and her sister Dominick would never be in this situation. He would be enjoying his Christmas season, not mixed up in *her* troubles again.

But then she wouldn't be here with him now…

'We need to find shelter,' he said, slowing the horse to a safer pace.

Mary glanced back the way they had come, ice pellets stinging her cheeks. 'The last village seems as if it was hours ago!'

'It *was* hours ago.'

Really? Somehow the time had gone by fast for her, as they'd talked of books and gossip and places they would travel to if they could. 'Are we near another inn?'

'Not for miles yet.'

But what they did soon find was a farmer's small hay barn, just beyond a low stone wall in the midst of a frosty field. It was a rough structure, with the wind whistling through gaps in the rough plank walls and rain dripping from the rickety roof, but to Mary it seemed a glorious palace of sanctuary.

Dominick spread the lap robe over a thick pile of hay for her, before seeing to the horse. Mary took off her damp cloak and sodden half-boots, digging out a clean pair of stockings from her valise. As she tried to get warm, she surreptitiously watched Dominick calm the frightened animal, talking in a low, deep voice as he stroked its velvety nose.

She almost cried at his gentleness, at the calm, firm way he took control of the situation and kept cold panic at bay. She had the terrible feeling that, if not for him, she too would be running into the storm shrieking! But instead she felt—safe. She also felt all would work out in the end, even though the true likelihood of that was very small indeed.

How very strange that the same man who so disrupted her hard-won peace of mind, who made her feel so confused, could also make her feel so much better.

He turned from the now quiet horse, shrugging off his great-coat, and Mary looked hastily away. She covered her flustered feelings, her overly warm cheeks, by digging a hairbrush out of the valise. Her hair was a tangled, damp mess, and she was sure the curls she tried so hard to keep smooth were now a frizzy rats' nest.

'Are you hungry?' Dominick asked, sitting down beside her on the hay. He held a hamper from the carriage. 'We still have the food the innkeepers gave us before we left this morning. Meat pies, pickles, cheese, and—oh, yes—some wine.'

Wine—she should definitely *not* have that with him! Who knew what she would say under its influence? 'I'm not hungry yet. I fear my stomach is still unsettled from our wild ride.'

'Hopefully the storm will pass by in a few hours and we can go more peacefully on our way.'

He lay back on their makeshift chaise, his hands under his head as he looked up at the slanted roof. His eyes were shadowed by purplish stains, as if he too had not slept last night. She wondered what *his* thoughts had been as he lay on the other side of the inn wall. So close, yet so far.

He kicked his booted foot against the hay. 'A barn—it's all a bit *too* authentically Christmas-like, don't you think?'

Mary laughed. 'At least we are not here to pay our taxes, as Mary and Joseph were. And I did not have to ride here on a donkey.' There was no baby, either. No sweet infant with Dominick's blue eyes to coo and reach for her with tiny hands. She had dreamed of that when she was younger…the beautiful children they would have.

And that thought made her feel the sadness of loss all over again. The loss of her children, real and imagined.

To cover her sudden rush of wistfulness she yanked the brush through her tangled curls. At least her stinging scalp would excuse the prickle of hot tears in her eyes.

'Here, you're going to tear your hair out,' Dominick said. He sat up beside her and took the brush from her hand. His touch was gentle as he worked the bristles through her hair, so soft she could barely feel it. No wonder the horse had been soothed to sleep by him.

Her eyes drifted closed and she leaned back into him. She could not resist.

'You're very good at that,' she murmured, trying not to think of the other women whose hair he had brushed. They didn't matter at that moment, when she and Dominick were alone in their strange little shelter with the storm raging outside. This was a time apart from real life, the real world of responsibility and obligation. Soon enough all that would intrude again—but not yet.

'My mother had curling hair,' he answered quietly. 'But it was blond, not dark like yours. She used to get terrible headaches, and when I was a child I learned how to soothe them by brushing her hair.'

'You had a mother?'

'Of course I did. Did you think I sprang from the Underworld fully formed?' he said, laughter in his voice.

'I'm not sure what I thought. You've never spoken of her.' But then, when they were young their meetings had been secret, full of desperate kisses. They had spoken of nothing at all since then, and she was surprised and delighted by his small confidences now.

'She died in childbirth when I was eleven, and my father sent me to school,' he said, the stroke of the brush never faltering in its slow, sensual rhythm.

'I'm so sorry,' she whispered.

'That was one thing I always envied about you, Mary. Your family, and how much you all loved each other. The way you *still* love each other—even your wayward sister.'

'I *do* love them, even when I don't agree with them—which is often,' Mary admitted. 'But once I did hate my parents for keeping us apart.'

The brush stilled for a barely perceptible second before moving again. 'They only wanted what was right for you. And it was all for the best.'

Mary frowned, remembering things she had hoped were forgotten. In the end it had not been her parents who had kept them apart, but Dominick himself. When she had wanted to run away, as Ginny had, he'd turned her away. Rejected her. And, humiliated and heartbroken, she had married William.

'I suppose it *was* for the best,' she said. 'I had a secure life, and once…' Once she had had her son. That had made it seem worthwhile. 'But I did always wonder about you, and what you were doing.'

'I always thought of you, too.' Dominick laid the brush aside and twisted her now smooth hair into a loose braid. Slowly, gently, he swept it over her shoulder, leaning close to the curve of her neck. He drew in a deep breath—and she could not breathe at all. She felt the warmth of him, his very essence, soak into her skin, wrapping all around her.

'You smell of rain,' he whispered. 'And lavender.'

Mary spun to face him, reaching up to frame his face in her cold hands. She traced his cheekbones with the edge of her thumbs, and rubbed over the pulse beating in his temple. His hair tangled over her fingers and he stared at her, as if greedy for the sight of her. As if she was water, and he had been wandering in the desert for years.

'Oh, Dominick,' she said, her throat tight. She could say nothing more. After all that time, all those lost chances, what was there *to* say?

He seemed to feel the same way, for his arms wrapped around her waist, pulling her close until they were pressed against each other. His head lowered towards hers, slowly, as if he waited for her protest.

She made no sound except a small moan of longing, and his lips claimed hers. It was *not* a gentle kiss. It was hungry, desperate, his tongue delving into her mouth to taste her. Mary met him with equal passion, revelling in the scent and taste and feel of him, the sense of jumping out into blank space and somehow landing where she had always belonged.

It was just as she remembered it. That blurry, hot *need* engulfed her as they kissed. And yet it was even better. They were older now, more experienced—or at least *he* was. His kisses and caresses were more skilled, his hands sure as they swept down the curve of her body, pressing, lingering, at just the right places to make her groan. She wished she had more to offer him, too, but all she had was her passion, which had slumbered inside her for too long.

Her hands twisted in the damp linen folds of his shirt, luxuriating in the hot feel of his skin underneath. Through the cloth she traced the lean, muscled planes of his chest, his hard shoulders.

He moaned against her mouth, his lips tearing from hers to trace the curve of her jaw, the line of her throat as her head fell back. Her hands clutched at him, as if she would drown if she let go.

How *alive* she felt! She had been asleep for so long, it seemed, resting in a cocoon of comfortable silence and stillness. Now that enveloping shelter had cracked wide open, spilling her out into a world of colour and noise and wild sensation. Her long years of careful restraint were burned away and she felt young again. Young and free.

She wasn't really, of course. There was still her family, still Ginny out there somewhere. But for the moment she pushed all that away and held onto Dominick with all her might.

He held onto her, too, his strong hands at her back, her hips, as he pulled her tight against him. She felt every angle of his lean body, every shift of his muscles, and it heightened her awareness to a perfect, exquisite clarity.

He pushed away the high collar of her dress to kiss the pulse that beat at the base of her throat, fast and frantic as that hot life rushed through her. He nipped at it, soothing the little sting with the tip of his tongue.

'Dominick,' she whispered hoarsely. She shoved his shirt away from his shoulders to trace the naked skin, savouring the warm, satiny feel of him, the sheer power of his body.

He carried her down to their makeshift bed, both of them sinking deep into the hay. The furore and cold of the storm seemed completely gone even as it still raged over their heads. The whole world had narrowed down to only the two of them.

Dominick kissed her lips again, frantic and hard, and she felt his palm slide over her ribs, along her hip and down the curve of her leg. He dragged up her heavy skirt, and for a second she felt cold air through her stocking, chilling her. But that burned away under his touch.

Mary couldn't breathe. She wrapped her leg around his waist, drawing him into the curve of her body. She felt his erection through their clothes, iron-hard—he wanted her. Had he missed her, too, all these years? That seemed impossible, but it was enough that he needed her now. That they had this one moment.

She trailed her fingertips over the groove of his spine, the taut muscles of his back, and skimmed over his backside. She pressed him even closer, wrapping both her legs around him as she kissed him, putting all her desire and need, all the dreams she'd once had, into that kiss.

How wonderful it felt to be wanton! No wonder William had always held her back—he must have sensed her terrible capacity to be a loose woman. But Dominick did not hold her back. He sank deep into the cradle of her legs, his caress hard and needful as he traced the curve of her breasts through her gown. The wool and linen chafed deliciously.

Still revelling in that wantonness, Mary slid her hand down his chest, damp against the shirt, and covered his penis. She traced her fingers down that thick, hard length, arching up into him.

Dominick raised his head, staring down at her with narrowed eyes. His hair fell in golden waves over his brow, his skin flushed. 'Mary—are you sure?'

Her throat was too tight to speak. She just nodded. Tomorrow she would probably not be *sure* at all. But right now she could not live for another minute without him.

He buried his face in the curve of her shoulder, reaching down between them to unfasten his breeches. Her skirts fell around them in a froth of wool, linen and lace as he eased himself inside her, slowly, carefully, inch by delicious inch.

Mary's head fell back, her eyes tightly closed. She loved the hot friction of him as he slid deeper, the strange feeling of being exactly where she was meant to be. She buried her fingers in the rumpled silk of his hair, holding him close to her.

He drew back and plunged deep again, the two of them finding their primitive rhythm together, faster and faster, ever more frantic, as something built deep inside of her. She had never felt anything like it before, and she reached out for it desperately.

It grew and grew, expanding over all her senses, a pleasure so pure, so hot and wondrous. A golden light emanated from him, flooding along her body until she was utterly consumed by it.

'Dominick!' she cried out. The force of her feelings frightened her with their hot intensity. Would she burn up inside them?

'Mary, Mary,' he whispered hoarsely. 'Just let it happen. You're safe here with me.'

And those words freed her. She let her heart open, let all those sensations rush into her like the red roar of a bonfire. She fell into the flames and never, ever wanted to escape their all-consuming touch.

Dominick cried out above her, his body taut as he found his own release. With one last thrust he gasped her name, and in that instant Mary knew she would never again be so close to another person. Her heart, so guarded for so long, had been set free—and it longed for *his* heart.

Not that his heart could ever be hers, she feared. Too much time, too much experience separated them, and in the morning they would be Lady Derrington and Lord Amesby again. But now she was just Mary—the girl who had been so in love with Dominick she hadn't been able to see straight.

He collapsed beside her on their straw bed, his arm heavy over her waist. The harsh sound of his breath, the frantic beat of her heart, blended with the pattering icy rain on the roof. A warm languor stole over her, and she closed her eyes as she pressed her hand over his arm, holding him with her as if he might fly away like a dream.

'Mary…' he said, his voice harsh and rough. Did he have regrets already?

But she wanted to hold regrets—hers *and* his—at bay until morning. She wanted to forget her life, and the desperate errand that awaited them out in that storm.

'Shh,' she whispered, stroking her fingers lightly up his arm. She felt the tickle of the hairs over his warm skin and it made her smile. How very *masculine* he was, her handsome Dominick. 'Don't talk now. I'm tired.'

For a moment she thought he might argue, might insist on saying something. Insist on—*oh, no*—apologising. She wanted none of that. Not now.

Finally he just rolled closer to her, resting his head on her shoulder. For the first time in so very long she felt warm and safe. Far away from the griefs of the world, from painful memories. Dominick had given her that—a very precious gift.

Yet even he could not keep the real world at bay for ever. Even as she lay in his arms she remembered. Her lost little boy, poor Ginny out there in the storm—her failure to protect them all.

She turned her face away from Dominick and wept silent hot tears for all she hadn't done, all she had lost, all she could never have, no matter how hard she wished.

Chapter Six

So now he had the answer to the question he had asked himself back in London. He was not, in fact, able to control himself with Mary. He thought of her tears, the tears she had wept silently so he would not hear. But he had heard. He was so perfectly attuned to her now, and those tears had made his heart ache like nothing else ever could.

Dominick rolled onto his side, propping his head on his hand to watch her as she slept. She had drawn her clothes around her against the chill, but her dark curls were still wild around her face. Her cheeks glowed pink with the aftermath of lovemaking, her parted lips cherry-red. She looked wanton and sweet, and he longed to kiss her awake, to hold her in his arms again and feel her passion stir to life. Her passion for *him*.

A strange, fierce possessiveness swept over him like a rainstorm. He had made love to *Mary*, to the woman he had once wanted above all others—the one woman who couldn't be his. He had kissed her, felt her cry his name against his lips, felt the fierceness of her desire as she wrapped her legs around him and he drove inside her.

That passion had seemed to startle her, too. He remembered the look of surprise and delight that had spread across her face, the gasp of pleasure she had been unable to contain. He held tightly to that memory; it was an image he would always carry with him now.

Gently, so as not to wake her, he brushed the back of his hand over her cheek. Her skin was soft as rose petals. She sighed in her sleep, turning her face towards him as if to follow that touch. But she did not wake.

Dominick lay back down on their straw bed, drawing her against his side. She murmured softly, burrowing into his warmth. He was tired, too, his body relaxed as it had not been in such a very long time. Usually a terrible restlessness overtook him after sex—a pounding need to escape. But now he just wanted to hold onto Mary, to drift down into sleep with her.

But he kept himself awake and alert. Their time together was very short, this second chance, and when it was gone it would never come back again. He could offer her more than when they were young—a title, though one less than the title she already bore, and a house—more than one if she wanted them—sexual passion—they obviously had *that*.

But he still could not give her the respectable life her husband had. He could not give her an untainted name. She had not cared about such things once, or had claimed not to. She was older now, though, and would think of their children as well as herself. Could he ever be a fit father? Once, when he'd first met pretty young Mary Smythe, he had dreamed of a family, a home. But the years had shown him he was unfit for such a life. Could he change now?

Mary sighed in her sleep, her breath cool and soft against his neck. He gently kissed her temple. This night *was* his second chance. He would never forget it. But once their little adventure was over, once her errant sister was found and they went back to their own lives, he would have to let her go—for ever this time. His soul was not entirely blackened.

Only partially black, he thought as she threw her leg over his, curling her body around him. His manhood hardened in response, and he was ready to leap on her all over again.

'Mmm,' she murmured, her eyes fluttering open. A lazy, sensual smile curled her lips. 'So it was not a dream.'

Dominick couldn't resist kissing her, but he held himself firmly in check and didn't deepen the caress as he longed to do. He didn't jump on her and rip her gown off.

'It's only a dream if you want it to be,' he said.

Mary's smile widened. She curled her hands into his rumpled shirt, pulling him back for another kiss. 'No—I want to remember every single *real* second.' No matter what happened to them tomorrow, she wanted to keep this. She needed to keep it.

He traced her parted lips with his fingertip, the bruised softness of them. She bit at him lightly. 'I think the rain has ceased,' he managed to say.

She tilted her head to the side, as if to listen to the silence outside their rough shelter. 'So it has.'

Dominick forced himself to ease away from her, to rise to his feet and reach for the rest of his clothes. 'We should leave while the weather is still clear. I'd like to make it to my aunt's house today—perhaps she has had word of Arthur and your sister.'

'Oh, yes. Ginny.' She sounded a bit startled. Had she, too, forgotten their errand in the firestorm of last night? Yet another sign they should not be together—good sense flew away when they touched. 'I hope they have found shelter.'

'I know it does not seem like it, but my cousin is a sensible enough man. He won't let your sister suffer.'

Mary reached for her boots, tugging them over her feet. 'I know. He is a military man, after all. I just…' Her words trailed away into heavy silence.

Dominick knew how she felt. What words could there possibly be for them now? What could erase the past, make it all right again?

She struggled to fasten the stiffened leather of the boots, a frustrated sigh escaping her lips.

'Here, let me,' Dominick said. He knelt beside her, taking her foot onto his lap.

Mary watched solemnly as he worked at the fastenings. 'First you put right my tangled hair, now my shoes. You *do* know what a lady needs.'

He automatically gave her a flirtatious smile. 'Ah, well, I aim to please, my lady.'

'And you are very good at it.'

He finished fastening her other boot, but somehow could not quite let her go. He smoothed a gentle touch over her ankle, the water-stained white stocking, along the soft curve of her calf. Her breath caught and she went very still. Dominick bent his head and pressed a kiss to her leg.

She touched the top of his head, one fleeting caress as quick as the brush of a butterfly's wing. Then it was gone, and he lowered her foot back to the floor.

'We should go, then,' she said, 'if we want to reach your aunt's today.'

Chapter Seven

Rose Cottage. Mary peered past the pretty sign on the neat stone wall to the house just down the tree-lined lane, half-shrouded in grey mist. It didn't look much like a cottage, more like a substantial redbrick manor, and of course there were no roses in evidence at all. It looked a quiet, respectable, austere place, and she had never been so glad to see a house in her life.

The long, silent day, sitting close to Dominick on the carriage seat, only speaking in short, polite sentences such as 'Are you too cold?' and 'I'm quite well, thank you,' had made her want to scream.

It was as if the passion of the night before had in truth been only a dream. She had no idea what to say to him, or what last night had really meant. She only knew that she felt completely different deep down inside. The passion and the tears had done that. A part of her she had put away when she had married William, pressed down until it was nearly invisible even to herself, was peeking forth again. Its bright warmth, faint and tentative as it was, had melted the edges of the ice she had lived in for so long.

Dominick didn't seem touched by that light, though. His forehead was creased as if he was deep in worry—or regret. Regrets?

For a man of his reputation? It planted a tiny seed of hope deep inside her. Maybe her old love, her Dominick, was still there after all.

'Is this your aunt's house?' she said as he turned down the lane. The frosty hardened mud crunched under the horse's hooves, while the cold wind rattled the branches overhead.

'It is,' he answered. 'I only hope she is at home.'

If she was not they would have the whole large house to themselves, Mary thought with what felt strangely like wicked pleasure. Wouldn't that be terribly unfortunate…?

Alas, a few days alone with Dominick was not to be. No quiet evenings by the fire to get him to talk to her at last; no long nights in big bedchambers. No sooner had he stopped the carriage by the front steps than the door opened. An elderly butler appeared there, followed by a flurry of maids and footmen, squinting against the cold grey glare.

'My lord!' the butler cried. 'We certainly did not expect you in this weather.'

'No, Makepeace, staying home would be too sensible for the likes of me,' Dominick said. He swung down from the carriage, hurrying round to help Mary alight. His gloved fingers tightened on hers for an instant, and then his touch was gone.

Somehow Mary felt even colder than before.

'There was no time to send word ahead,' Dominick said to the butler. His hand moved to her elbow, helping her up the icy-looking stone steps, but it was a brief, polite touch now. 'Is Lady Amesby at home?'

'Of course, my lord,' Makepeace said. 'Her ladyship always spends Christmas at Rose Cottage. She will be very happy to see you.' His glance fluttered over Mary, a flash of curiosity in his eyes. But he was too professional to let any speculative gleam remain.

Did Dominick bring his ladies here? Mary wondered with a sad pang. Had he brought Lady Newcombe?

'This is Lady Derrington,' Dominick said. 'I hope my aunt will have a guest chamber for her, as well?'

'Certainly, my lord. You know how Lady Amesby enjoys company.'

'Even of the unexpected variety?' Dominick said with a laugh.

As the servants bustled around the carriage, unloading their meagre luggage, he led Mary into the house.

The contrast of the warm, cosy space with the bleak, wintry world outside was immediate. The foyer was painted a lovely deep blue, trimmed in white plasterwork like clouds in a summer sky. A few sunny Italian landscapes hung from the picture rail, and wreaths of holly and evergreen were twined along the staircase banister. Their crisp scent was sweet in the warm air. From behind one of the closed doors Mary could hear the strains of a pianoforte. Someone played 'Greensleeves.'

'What a lovely home,' she murmured, untying her bonnet and letting a maid take away her damp cloak.

Dominick gave her a half-smile. 'This is only the foyer.'

'Oh, I know. But I have a feeling for houses. They have their own souls, and this is a kind one.' Unlike Derrington, which had frozen her heart the first time she had set foot in it as a bride.

'A port in the icy storm,' Dominick said.

The door flew open, letting out that flow of music along with a tall lady clad in fur-trimmed brown velvet and a brown satin turban. A few silvery curls escaped to frame her rosy cheeks and sparkling hazel eyes. Eyes which seemed to miss nothing as they swept over Mary and Dominick.

'Dominick! You beautiful, impulsive man—dashing through such wretched weather just to spend Christmas with your old auntie,' she said merrily. She hurried forth to seize Dominick in her arms, kissing him on both cheeks. 'You are quite frozen through, and so must your friend be.' Lady Amesby turned that sharp, sparkling gaze onto Mary. 'And so pretty she is. Have you turned respectable at last, my boy?'

Dominick laughed ruefully, and Mary thought she saw a hint of red beneath the bronze of his cheeks. *Shocking.* 'Aunt Beatrice, may I present Lady Derrington? She is an old friend, and I fear we are on something of an urgent errand—'

A piercing shriek interrupted him. The music ended abruptly, and a flash of red and white came flying out through the door behind Lady Amesby.

'Mary!' Ginny screamed, and threw herself into Mary's arms.

Mary stumbled back against the wall, too shocked to brace herself for the impact of her sister's embrace. Ginny clung to her, sobbing.

'Ginny…' Mary murmured. 'Is it really you?'

'Oh, Mary! I longed for you so much, and here you are. It's a miracle.'

All Mary's fear and anger towards her sister faded in one great rush of relief. Ginny was *safe*. She was here, out of the cold storm, warm and fed and healthy. And—Mary peeked at the hand against her shoulder for any sign of a ring. And not married.

'Ginny, you foolish girl,' she said, wrapping her arms tightly around her sister. 'What were you thinking about to run off like that?'

Ginny just shook her head. 'I fear I was not thinking at all. It was so cold, and Arthur got lost, and there was this horrid inn with drunken people…'

'Drunken people?' Mary cried in alarm. 'Did they hurt you?'

'Oh, no, we left there right away, after Arthur had a fight with one of them. But it was dark and snowing! I thought my nose would freeze off.'

'Just as your sister's nose will, Miss Smythe, if you don't let her sit down by the fire,' Lady Amesby said. She sounded amused by the little scene, as if she sat in Drury Lane watching a farce.

'Oh, Mary, I am so sorry! You *do* seem cold. Come—sit down and tell me how you found me,' Ginny said. She tugged on Mary's hand, leading her into the drawing room.

Mary hadn't even realised how very tired she was until she dropped into a soft armchair set in front of the roaring fire. She sank back against the cushions, weary of the travel, her worry over Ginny, the sudden relief at seeing her again—and especially her confusion over Dominick and her feelings for him. Or his feelings for her, if he possessed any at all.

Ginny plopped down on a stool at her feet, burying her face in Mary's skirts as if she were a child. Mary almost laughed aloud at the thought that *this* was the same young lady who had insisted so stoutly that she was ready to marry.

'Where is our young knight in shining armour?' Dominick asked Lady Amesby, his neutral tone giving away no hint of anger or any other emotion. He was hidden from her again.

'I do not think Arthur is the only knight in shining armour here,' Lady Amesby said. 'But of course you will want to have a little chat with him. He is in the library. I'll send for some tea while you young people all become—reacquainted.'

Mary laid her hand gently on Ginny's shining auburn hair, studying Dominick over her sister's head. He watched them solemnly. 'Oh, Ginny,' she murmured as he turned away. 'You dear, silly girl.'

'Mary, I am truly sorry,' Ginny sobbed. 'Eloping is not nearly as much fun as I imagined it would be.'

'No,' Mary murmured, thinking of Dominick and his flight with Lady Newcombe, which had ended so badly. Thinking of last night in the hay, and how Ginny was not the only foolish Smythe woman. 'I would imagine it is not.'

But now she had to cease being foolish and be responsible. Just for a moment. Mary held Ginny's trembling hands tightly in hers and said sternly, 'Ginny, you must see how bad this is.'

'Oh, Mary! I never—'

'No, dear. Just listen to me. To be so disregarding of your reputation, of the family's name, was bad enough. It could have ruined you for your whole life! You would have had to go and live in the country with Aunt Frances for ever.'

Ginny's eyes widened with horror. Their mother's sister lived in the depths of Devon, with ten dogs and a monkey in a smelly little cottage. 'I never thought of *that*!'

'Exactly. You did not think. And worse than Aunt Frances was running off into a terrible winter storm and putting your life in danger. I do not know what I would have done if I had lost you. I can't bear to lose anyone else.'

'Oh, Mary.' Ginny's eyes filled with tears again. 'I never want to make you sad. I will think from now on. I promise.'

'I hope so.' Mary took her sister in her arms and held onto her very tightly. 'I do so hope so, my dear.'

'They arrived here yesterday evening,' Beatrice said as she led Dominick along the corridor to the library. 'Frozen through, and the girl half hysterical.'

'I'm relieved they found their way here, then,' Dominick answered.

'It's quite a miracle. They're a pair of complete babes in the wood, and I shudder to think what the future would hold for them if they *did* manage to marry.' She gave him a questioning glance. 'Unlike the sister. *She* seems to have plenty of spirit.'

Dominick laughed ruefully, remembering Mary's fierce insistence that she should go with him on this journey no matter what. Her stoic tolerance of the cold and damp. The passion of their lovemaking. 'She certainly does.'

'And a *lady*, too. I do remember hearing what a dry stick Lord Derrington was—quite elderly before his time. That couldn't have been much fun for her.' She stopped next to the closed library door. 'Do be kind to the lad, Dominick. He's utterly guilt-stricken at putting his lady-love through such a trial. I'm sure he will never do such a bacon-brained thing again.'

'It's my task to make sure of that, isn't it?' he said grimly. 'If he truly loves Miss Smythe, how could he do such a thing?'

'Dear Dominick. Everyone thinks you so wicked, but in truth you are the most honourable man I know. You are so protective of those you care for.'

Honourable? Him? No, he was the most selfish of men, taking his pleasures where and when he wanted them. Even with Mary in the midst of a winter storm. 'I fear you are the only one who thinks that, Aunt Beatrice.'

She tilted her head quizzically to one side as she watched him. 'Am I? No, I don't think so. In fact, I am quite certain the

Smythe sisters would agree with me. Especially if they knew the truth about Lady Newcombe...'

Dominick frowned. 'Aunt Beatrice...'

'Oh, do not worry. I promised you I would say nothing and I won't. Besides, it's a tale Lady Derrington should hear from *you*.' She gently patted his arm. 'Now, I will go and make sure the guest chambers are properly prepared and leave you to your scolding.'

He watched her walk away, half wishing she would not leave him alone. Scolding was certainly not one of his favourite tasks! But he had to convince Arthur that if he loved Ginny Smythe he had to win her properly, with the consent of her family, or there would be no peace in their marriage. Dominick knew that sad fact better than anyone.

But when he pushed open the door and saw Arthur sitting there Dominick knew nothing could make his cousin more miserable than he already was. Arthur sat slumped over in a chair by the fire, his hair and clothes a rumpled mess, his hands covering his face.

'Well,' Dominick said, slamming the door behind him to startle his cousin from his stupor, 'it's a fine mess you've got us all into, Arthur Heelis.'

'Dominick!' He leaped up from his seat. 'Whatever are you doing here?'

Dominick crossed his arms sternly across his chest, leaning back against the door as if to block any escape. Not that Arthur looked in any shape to be escaping. He was pale and haunted-looking, his jaw shadowed with beard and his hair tangled. A bruise darkened one cheek—probably from that inn fight Ginny had mentioned. 'I am here to find you, of course. Why else would I leave my warm house in the middle of December?'

'I—how did you know we were here?'

'I didn't. Lady Derrington and I merely sought shelter from the storm with Aunt Beatrice, hoping she might have had word of you. Finding Miss Smythe playing the pianoforte in the drawing room was a rare stroke of luck. At least you showed *some* good sense in bringing her here.'

'Lady Derrington is with you?' Arthur groaned, sinking back into the chair.

'Of course. She is terribly concerned about her sister's welfare—unlike other people I could name.'

'That is not fair, Dominick! I *love* Ginny. She is everything to me.'

'So because you love her you asked her to elope with you? To risk losing her family, her reputation, her very life?' Dominick shook his head. 'That does not sound like love, Arthur.'

Arthur rubbed his hands sullenly over his face. 'It was her idea to run away. I could not argue with her.'

Oh, the tale just got better and better, Dominick thought sarcastically. Arthur was not just a bacon-brain, as Beatrice had put it, but a weakling who had refused to put Ginny's welfare ahead of his own.

It was going to be a long evening indeed.

Chapter Eight

Mary took a slow bite of her dried-apple tart, surreptitiously studying Dominick across the dining table. Lady Amesby had kept up a bright, steady stream of chatter throughout the meal, asking after her friends in London and imparting all the neighbourhood gossip. Even Ginny had managed to become more cheerful, joining in the talk as her suitor sat beside her in chastened silence.

But Dominick, even though he smiled at his aunt and answered her questions, seemed preoccupied. It was as if although he sat with them in the warm, candlelit dining room his thoughts were very far away. What she would not give to know what those thoughts were! Perhaps he was missing the pleasures of Town, left behind to help her with this wild chase. Perhaps he regretted the flash of chivalry that had made him come with her.

'Well, I know the circumstances are not all that could be desired,' Lady Amesby said, 'but I must say how happy I am to have both my nephews with me for Christmas. And Lady Derrington and Miss Smythe, too! It will be a very merry time.'

Mary gave her a smile. In only the short time they had been at Rose Cottage she had come to like Dominick's aunt so much. Her warm welcome and cheerful conversation kept away even the cold outside. 'It is very kind of you to take us in, Lady Amesby. But surely Christmas should be for family? It seems the storm is abating. Ginny and I could leave for London in the morning.'

'Leave?' cried Lady Amesby. 'Certainly not. Christmas is to share with everyone, and I love having so much company. My cook has prepared far too much food for me to consume myself. Unless there is someone in Town awaiting your return, Lady Derrington?'

'Only my brother-in-law and his wife, who are such dears,' Mary answered. She felt a pang as she thought of her son, who was *not* there. But it did not have quite the terrible sharpness it once had. 'I sent them a message as soon as we arrived here, saying I am quite safe.'

'Then you must stay,' Lady Amesby insisted. 'It is still very cold outside.'

Mary glanced again at Dominick, who watched her with that unreadable expression on his face. The candlelight gilded his skin and hair, his jewel-like blue eyes, making him glisten like a pagan idol. She could not quite catch her breath. 'You are very kind, Lady Amesby.'

Ginny clapped her hands happily. 'Oh, it will be so much fun! Just like when we were children, Mary. Shall I play some Christmas carols after dinner?'

Mary smiled at her sister, glad to see that Ginny had ceased weeping and sulking to find some joy in the Christmas holiday. She did not remind her that when Ginny had been a child she, Mary, had been grown and married. She did not want to feel old—not tonight. Not when Dominick was there.

'Ginny is the finest musician I know,' Captain Heelis said— the first time he had spoken since the fish course. Ginny gave him a shy smile, strange after all the two of them had got into together.

'Christmas carols will be most welcome,' Lady Amesby said. 'My poor pianoforte has become quite rusty with disuse, I fear.'

'Oh, no, Lady Amesby! It is a lovely instrument,' Ginny said. 'So much finer than mine at home.'

And when they all gathered in the drawing room after the meal she demonstrated that fineness for them. With Captain Heelis to turn the pages, she launched into song. "'I saw three ships come sailing in, on Christmas Day, on Christmas Day. I saw three ships come sailing in, on Christmas Day in the morning!'"

Mary leaned against the pianoforte, sipping at a glass of warm spiced wine as she listened to her sister's sweet, clear voice. With the music, the firelight and the wine, she felt the cold tension of the journey finally slide away from her and the first soft, bright feelings of Christmas slip into its place. Her sister was safe, and Mary had a little more time with Dominick. They were all cosy against the cold outside, the cold that waited in her real life.

I will enjoy this, she thought fiercely. And then she would have to put this moment of contentment away as a precious little memory.

Ginny finished her song, and smiled at their hostess. 'Lady Amesby, what is your very favourite carol?'

Lady Amesby laughed, gesturing to the footmen to bring more wine. 'My mother used to sing "The Holly and the Ivy". It always makes me think of her.'

Ginny nodded, striking the first chords of the old song. "'The holly and the ivy, when they are both full grown, of all the trees that are in the wood the holly bears the crown…'"

By the end they were all singing, even Dominick.

"'The rising of the sun and the running of the deer, the playing of the merry organ, sweet singing in the choir!'"

'You have a beautiful voice, Mary,' Ginny said as the last note faded away. 'And yet I never hear you sing!'

Mary laughed. 'That is because only my sister would say my voice is *beautiful*.'

'No, Miss Smythe is quite right,' Dominick said quietly. 'You do have a beautiful voice.'

Ginny gave him a searching glance, her eyes wide. 'You see, Mary, I have confirmation. Won't you sing something for us?'

Mary shook her head, still laughing. 'I fear I don't remember any carols well enough to sing alone.'

'Nonsense,' Ginny said. 'What was that song you used to sing to me when I was a child? No one else knew it.'

'I remember. It was something my old Cornish nursemaid used to sing when *I* was a child.'

'Then you must teach it to us,' Lady Amesby said. 'I insist.'

'Please, Lady Derrington,' Dominick added. He smiled at her, and she could not resist.

'Very well. But do not blame me if that pretty looking glass over there shatters, Lady Amesby!'

Mary took Ginny's place on the piano bench, her fingertips poised over the keys as she tried to recall the whole song. It had been so long, and yet the tune was still there, buried deep inside her.

'"Tomorrow shall be my dancing day,"' she sang. '"I would my true love did so chance to see the legend of my play, to call my true love to my dance."'

She looked up to meet Dominick's gaze, so dark and mysterious in the night.

'"Sing oh my love, oh my love, my love, my love. This have I done for my true love…"'

She sang what she remembered of the song, then rested her hands on the edge of the keys. A sweet sadness washed over her, warm as the wine, as a long-concealed realisation revealed itself in that song. She had only ever had one true love, and that was Dominick.

And she loved him still. No matter what he had done in the years since they had parted. No matter that she felt his own true love must be the poor, lost Lady Newcombe. He must never know, and she would have to forget. But now she fought back her tears.

She folded her hands in her lap, smiling at her sister. Tears shone in Ginny's eyes, too. 'Was that the one you remembered, Ginny?'

'Oh, yes,' Ginny said. 'That is exactly it.'

'That was indeed beautiful, Lady Derrington,' said Lady Amesby. 'Will you sing another?'

'I fear I am quite tired,' Mary answered. 'I think I will retire now—if you will excuse me, Lady Amesby?'

'I will show you to your chamber,' Dominick offered.

Lady Amesby quirked her brow but said nothing; this hardly seemed a gathering for strict propriety.

He was the last person Mary wanted to be alone with, not when she was feeling so suddenly vulnerable and sad. But she was too tired to argue, and she had to admit still too desirous of his company.

'Thank you, Lord Amesby,' she said, rising from the bench to accept his outstretched arm. He felt so warm and strong under her touch. 'Goodnight, everyone.'

'Goodnight, Lady Derrington,' Lady Amesby said. 'Be sure and get some rest. We must plan our festivities tomorrow!'

Dominick led her up the evergreen-bedecked stairs and along a long dim corridor. The soft carpet runner muffled their footsteps, the only sound the occasional soft hiss of the candles in their wall sconces. They were alone in the dark quiet.

'Here we are,' Dominick said, stopping in front of the chamber door.

'Thank you,' she answered, slowly sliding her hand from his sleeve. 'For everything, Dominick. You have been a good friend to my sister and me.'

He shook his head. 'Mary, I have not been a good friend at all. There are things I need to tell you—things you must know if I am to prove myself your friend in truth.'

Confidences? Whatever could they be? She did not think she was yet strong enough to hear truths about his life and loves. 'You need not…'

'Yes, I *do* need to,' he said. 'Please, Mary. I need to tell you the truth. You deserve that from me, at least.'

She was now thoroughly confused. 'Do you want to talk now? Here?'

He glanced down the deserted corridor. They could hear the faint echo of the others, talking and laughing, the strains of the pianoforte. 'Can I come to you later? When the house is quiet?'

And with those few words all her resolve to stay sensible and forget about Dominick and their night together flew away on snowy wings. Her stomach fluttered with trepidation, excitement, and a foolish hope. What did he want to say to her? Was it good—or ill? What *good* could there be in their situation? And yet—yet there *was* that hope. A hope she'd thought long-dead.

She studied his face, cast in flickering shadows, but she still could not read anything there. His eyes were full of caution as he watched her—as if he, too, felt that uncertainty. Felt that sense of standing atop a cliff: one push and they would tumble down into a life they didn't even recognise.

She should send him away, once and for all. But she could not. 'Yes,' she whispered. 'Come to me later.'

He nodded, and his hand slid past her waist. She thought he would touch her, curl his hand around her and pull her close again, and she shivered, imagining it. Yet he just turned the knob and opened the door. 'Thank you, Mary,' he said, and then he was gone, vanishing into the darkness of the corridor.

She slipped into her room, closing the door behind her before she collapsed to the floor. She covered her face with trembling hands and felt as young as Ginny. All the years between tonight and her first meeting with Dominick might never have passed at all.

Yet they had. Time had certainly passed, and so much had happened to both of them. She felt the marks of her life on her body and her soul—and especially on her heart. She would never, ever forget her son and her great love for him. But maybe she could let go of the terrible grief and keep only the sweetness of his life in her heart. Could she? Was it even possible?

She caught a glimpse of herself in the large looking glass across the chamber. Her brown curls were pinned back in an austere knot, revealing the dark shadows of sleeplessness under her eyes, the tiny lines around her lips that had *not* been there when she had first met Dominick. She wore one of the few gowns she had packed, a sensible grey silk, with a high neckline and matronly elbow-length sleeves.

Whatever Dominick had to tell her, whatever was meant to

happen between them tonight, she couldn't see him while she looked like a frump. She scrambled to her feet and hurried over to the wardrobe. She had to remind him—remind them both—of how things had once been...

Dominick stood outside Mary's door, listening to the silence of the house. His aunt, along with the young lovers, had retired at last, and most of the lights in the corridor were now extinguished, leaving only one sconce near the stairs to chase away the winter gloom. The storm outside had ceased; no sleet battered at the windows, no wind howled. Only the cold remained.

He should go back to his own chamber, leave Mary alone. She had the life she was always meant for—a life of position and respectability which her kind heart and devotion to her family deserved. The flame that obviously still burned between them should not take that away—*he* should not take that away.

But she deserved to know the truth. He could not keep it from her any longer. He knocked on the door.

After a moment, a moment that seemed to last an hour, there was a rustle and the click of the lock being drawn back. The door swung open and Mary stood there, outlined in the golden glow of dozens of candles. Her hair flowed over her shoulders, a dark, soft cloud, and she wore a pale pink dressing gown trimmed in fluffy white fur. She looked so young and bright and warm, a spirit of sunrise mornings and summer days. She smiled at him, and all he wanted to say, all his honourable intentions to leave her, were worth nothing.

His body obviously agreed, as he felt an erection stir to life at the sight of her smile. He remembered their night in the hay barn, the hot need between them, the way her skin had felt against his and the sound of her cry as she'd climaxed. It took all his strength not to grab her, to carry her down to the floor and make love to her again, just as rough and fast and desperate as before.

'I thought you had changed your mind,' she said. She reached out and took his hand, drawing him into the chamber.

He kicked the door shut behind him.

'Or that maybe you had forgot,' Mary said. Her hand trailed

lightly up his arm, her fingers drifting over his linen shirtsleeve, along his shoulder, before she toyed with the edge of his open collar. Everywhere she touched she left little drops of pure fire.

'How could I forget?' he said hoarsely.

With the very tip of her finger she traced his throat, the taut line of his jaw. She gently cupped his cheek, studying his face as if she had never seen it before. 'I'm glad you're here now.'

He reached up to catch her hand. He could not think at all when she touched him like that! 'Mary, I have to tell you…'

'I think—I think I would like a kiss first, Dominick,' she murmured.

She tried to give a seductive smile, but her lips trembled and her eyes were wide with uncertainty. That only made him want her more, his sweet Mary. There was no artifice about her, as there was in all the other parts of his life.

'I would never want to disoblige a lady,' he said. He slid his hands around her waist, slender and warm, unencumbered by any stays. Was she *naked* under her robe? Her bare skin covered only by pink silk? The alluring image made him grow even harder, but he kept his touch gentle, his movements slow, as he drew her close to him.

She held onto his shoulders, going up on tiptoe and leaning into him. Her cheeks were flushed, her lips parted as she stared up at him. He traced the supple curve of her back, tangling his hands in her hair. This was *Mary* he held, Dominick thought in disbelief. Mary who stood only a breath away from him, when for so long he had thought her lost to him for ever.

'I should never have let you go,' he muttered, and covered her mouth with his kiss.

It was soft at first, as he savoured the taste of her, the way her body moved against his. He wanted to go slowly this time, to enjoy every single moment with her. But that resolve was sorely tested when she moaned against his lips, her hand drifting over his chest. She caught the hem of his shirt, bunching it in her fist as she dragged it up to touch his bare skin.

His stomach muscles tightened at the lightning-hot shock of

pleasure. He parted her lips with his tongue, tasting her deeply. He untied the sash of her gown, pushing the soft fabric away from her shoulders. She stepped back, letting it fall to the floor, and he opened his eyes to see that she was indeed naked.

For an instant her eyes shifted away from his in uncertain shyness. But then she straightened her shoulders, shook her hair back, and smiled at him. 'Well? What do you think?'

Think? He could not think at all—not one single coherent thought. The tantalising glimpses he had had of her as they had tumbled through the hay had only fuelled his imagination, but the reality was so much more beautiful.

She was pale and slender, her waist a narrow line above a stomach still flat after her child, an alluring triangle of dark curls. Her breasts were upturned, delicate, crowned with enticingly lush pink nipples. She was—perfect.

Her hands fluttered, as if she would cover herself with them, and he caught them in his fingers. 'You are so very beautiful, Mary.'

'So are you,' she whispered.

He could bear it no longer. He swung her up in his arms, carrying her to the waiting bed. He laid her gently amid the soft sheets, lowering himself to her side. 'A real bed this time,' he said with a hoarse laugh.

'Is it?' She fell back into the pillows, her hair swirling around her. 'I hadn't noticed. I fear all I can see is you.'

He kissed her again, bracing himself above her as they both sank deeper into the feather mattress. She wrapped her legs around his hips, tugging him closer into the curve of her body.

'And I fear you are much too overdressed for the occasion, Lord Amesby,' she said. She laughed, too, a gloriously carefree sound, like silver chimes in a warm breeze.

'As I said—I always try to oblige a lady.' He went up on his knees, dragging his shirt over his head, and Mary watched him avidly, lolling among her pillows like a sultana waiting for her pleasure.

Dominick certainly did not want to keep her waiting. He

unfastened his breeches, and she reached out to help him pull them over his hips. He could do no more as she wrapped her legs around him again and urged him close for another kiss.

'Mary, Mary,' he whispered, trailing his lips over her cheek, her throat. He leaned his face into the curve of her shoulder, where her hair fell in a riot of curls, inhaling deeply of her very essence. She smelled of lavender soap and the salty, intoxicating musk of desire. A sharp longing swept over him. He had never known anything like this sheer, desperate *need*.

He felt her kiss the top of his head, felt the stroke of her caress through his hair. 'Dominick,' she whispered, and he knew what that longing was. His whole life, ever since he had seen Mary Smythe at that ball so long ago, had been leading him here. To this moment in her arms.

He traced the tip of his tongue over the soft swell of her breast. She even tasted of summer, of lavender and sun, and green, vital growing things. She tasted of the light that burned away the ice around his heart.

Mary sighed, and he felt the powerful beat of her heart against his mouth. Maybe she felt it, too, this surge of life and fate and wonder. He softly licked the very tip of that pink nipple, blowing across it as he watched it harden in desire.

'Dominick!' she sobbed, and he took her into his mouth, suckling her until she moaned.

He touched her low on her stomach as he kissed her, combing his fingers through her damp curls. Her legs fell open, urging him closer, closer, until at last he touched her *there*. His finger slid inside her, touching the velvety warmth of her, and she cried out as he found that one tiny spot…

'Dominick!' she cried again, and he pressed his mouth over hers to hold back the sound. It was all he could do not to shout out himself, not to give a warrior cry at the glory of being with her. The whole house would be down on them in an instant, and *Mary* would be the one compromised, rather than her runaway sister!

'Please,' she whispered. 'Please, now.'

And they were joined at last, his body plunging into hers as she arched up to meet him. For the first time he truly understood the phrase *Two shall become one*. He did not know where he ended and she began, and he feared his heart would never know the difference again.

Chapter Nine

'Dominick?' Mary whispered. 'Are you awake?'

'Yes,' he said roughly. His hand drifted lightly over her back as she rested against him, draped over his chest. 'Are you?'

She laughed, snuggling closer. Most of the candles had gone out, and the bedclothes were kicked to the floor, leaving them drifting in warm darkness, wrapped around each other. It was still black beyond her window, and she wished the night would never end. That these precious hours would last for ever.

She kissed the hollow of his throat, tasting a single salty drop of his sweat. 'That was…'

'Extraordinary?'

'Yes.' Though she feared she did not have much to compare it to. She had never been entirely naked with William, let alone draped wantonly over his bare body like this. It had frightened her at first, to let go of her clothes in front of Dominick, but now it felt like the most natural thing in the world.

'*You* were certainly extraordinary, my lady,' he said, his arm tightening around her waist.

'Was I? I *am* glad. I've never really tried anything like that.'

'Not at all?' he said, his tone surprised. 'Not bad for a beginner.'

Mary sighed and rolled off him, lying back in the pillows at his side. 'Before I married my mother said I should just lie still and think of fat, pretty babies, that it would soon be over. Someone obviously gave William the same advice—that it would soon be over.'

Dominick propped himself on his elbow, staring down at her in the dying light. 'That poor devil. How much he missed.'

Mary stared at the hard muscles of his chest, the smooth skin gilded by pale hair. She traced a caress over it, mesmerised. 'How much *I* missed,' she murmured. 'Is it always like that?'

He caught her hand in his, kissing her palm. 'Almost never.'

She rolled onto her side facing away from him, curling into him as he wrapped his arm over her waist. *Almost never.* How ridiculous it was, the warm glow that flowed over her at those two words. She was special. *They* were special. It was enough—at least for the moment. Especially when he kissed her shoulder like that…

'You said you wanted to talk to me?' she said, pressing her hand over his where it lay against her waist.

Dominick chuckled, kissing her shoulder again. Their legs tangled together, their entwined bodies keeping the cold night away—without those lost blankets. 'Did I? I don't remember thinking about *talking* at all—not when you greeted me wearing only that pretty robe.'

'It was a good idea, wasn't it? I didn't want you to think I was an old frump.'

He gave a snort. 'No one could ever think that, Mary.'

'*I* think it,' she admitted. 'Sometimes I feel so old and tired. But not tonight. Tonight it felt like when we first met.'

'Yes—it did,' he said.

Mary turned her head to look at him. With his hair tousled like that, the sputtering candlelight sparkling over him, he looked no older than he had at that ball. 'Do you remember, too? Lady Ingram's ball?'

'Of course I remember. Your mother didn't want you to dance with me.'

'So we sat in the corner and talked instead. I was the great envy of all the other young ladies.'

'And then we just happened to meet in the park the next day…'

'By complete coincidence, of course.'

He grinned at her, kissing her hand. 'Of course.'

'And you kissed me on the terrace at the Harlington ball.'

'Behind the potted palms.'

'I had never felt so very alive before.' Until tonight, she thought. She finally did feel alive again—felt the warm tingle of it deep down to her toes. She had thought it could never happen again but here it was. 'I didn't even know a person could feel like that at all.'

'Neither did I.'

Mary stared at their joined hands, thinking how very right it felt to be held by him like this. What would her life have been like if her parents had not objected to Dominick? Would she have married him back then and lived every night since like this? Or had they had to live their lives apart, learn their separate lessons, in order to appreciate this moment?

She could not regret what had happened, because she had had her beloved son—even if only for a while. But still she wondered. What would have happened if Dominick had not sent her away when she'd asked him to run away with her?

'I did want to talk to you, Mary,' he said, suddenly solemn again. 'I need you to know certain things.'

'Oh, dear. I suddenly feel quite *under*dressed for the occasion.' Mary sat up, reaching for the sheets tangled on the floor. She propped the pillows behind her, wrapping the bedclothes over her nakedness.

Dominick, too, leaned against the pillows, close to her but not touching. He wound the sheet over his lean hips, frowning as if he were considering how to begin.

Mary thought she might prefer it if he did not begin at all. She wanted nothing to mar the shimmering fabric of the night, the memory she would take away from it. Yet she could see he had to say whatever it was that burdened him, and she would listen, no matter how it hurt. She might even have a few things to say herself.

'When you asked me to help you find your sister, you said "Don't turn me away now."'

'I—yes, I suppose I did say that,' she answered in surprise. 'I should not have said such a thing. I was desperate.'

'No, you were right. I *did* turn you away back then. I left what we might have been.' He reached out and took her hand again, holding it lightly as he stared down at her fingers. 'But leaving you then was the only honourable, unselfish thing I ever did in my life.'

Mary's throat felt dry and tight, and she swallowed hard as she forced herself to remember those long-ago days. The stunned pain that had seemed to freeze her heart, leaving her unable to eat or sleep or move about in the world at all. Her mother had taken her off to Brighton, in hopes of reviving her spirits in the sea air. William had followed them there, and she, no longer caring who she married at all, had accepted him.

It had hurt more than anything in her life until the tragedy of her son's loss. 'Your letter said I was too young and too lacking in fortune, that our union could never work,' she said. She had thrown that hurtful missive into the fire after she had read it, yet the words were still there. 'When I went to your lodgings, the servants said you had left London.'

His hand tightened over hers, and he gazed at her searchingly with those blue eyes. 'And you believed that letter?'

Mary shook her head, just as she tried to shake away her young, wounded self. 'I could not believe you would suddenly leave me because of my meagre dowry. I knew you too well by then to believe you cared so much about fortune. But something had driven you away, made you change your mind about us. Another woman, maybe? Or I feared you were tired of me and my young, lovestruck ways.' She stared down at their hands. 'What was it, Dominick?'

'I had a visitor.'

'A visitor?'

'Your father came to see me.'

'My father?' Mary cried. She had not expected that. Her father had always been such a quiet man, always escaping to his library to get away from the clamour of four daughters. Back then she hadn't even been sure he knew what was going on. It had usually been her mother who lectured. 'What did he want?'

'To talk about you, of course. He told me how close your family was, how much you loved your sisters and wanted to take care of them. He told me Derrington wanted to marry you, and spoke of everything an earl could offer and I could not. The life you would lead as Lady Derrington.'

'And you—you decided I would be better off with William?' she whispered.

'He was rich and titled, and he had a reputation as a good and steady man. I knew that if I loved you I had to forget my own selfish desires and do what was best for *you*. And was I wrong? Look what my life has been, and look at your own. Derrington gave you all I could not.'

Mary took back her hand, inexplicably angry. Yes, look at what her life had been—dull and colourless, with a husband who had never understood her, never seen her as anything but a possession, an ornament. And now Dominick told her he had left her to be *noble*. To do what was best for *her*. Yet he had never asked her what that might be, what she would choose if given the chance. He, her father and William had decided her fate.

But no more! She was free of them now, and she would make her own choices from now on. Would she choose Dominick again? She did not know. If she did, it would be entirely on her own terms.

'Your life doesn't appear to have been so very bad,' she said, tugging the sheets higher over her shoulders. 'Gambling and carousing, having fun.'

He gave a bitter-sounding laugh. 'That has all been decidedly exaggerated.'

'Indeed? And what of the women? What of the lady I saw at

the museum? Or Lady Newcombe? It was said you and she were the great love story of the age.'

'Mary...' he said tightly, shaking his head.

'If we are sharing confidences, you might as well tell me. Did you love her?'

'I did love Eleanor,' he admitted. He lay down on his back, his arms braced under his head as he stared up at the canopy. 'But not in the way everyone says. Not in the way I loved you.'

He had loved her? Mary's anger slowly faded, replaced by a tired, bittersweet sadness. *Loved*—past tense. 'How did you love her?'

'She was my friend. I met her at Hatchards, you see, and we talked about books. We both loved horses and the theatre, and we enjoyed each other's company very much. We understood each other.'

'Just—company?'

A wry smile quirked the edge of his mouth. 'She was older than me, and her husband was a very jealous man. We would just meet at the bookshop or walk the quiet pathways of the park. Then one evening she came to my lodgings, wearing a veil just as you did.'

'And did she want you to help find a runaway relative?'

'Not at all. She wanted me to help *her* run away.'

'She *what*?' Mary gasped. This, then, was the infamous elopement?

'Yes. I said her husband was jealous. When his suspicions were aroused he became violent. Someone had seen Eleanor talking to me, and he had confronted her about it. He—well, he beat her, Mary. Her back and shoulders were a mass of bruises.'

'Oh.' Mary pressed her hand to her mouth, feeling cold and sick. 'That poor lady.'

'What was worse, she was pregnant. She had miscarried several times since she'd married, and she did not want to lose this child. She said I was her only real friend, and begged me to help her run away somewhere to have the baby in peace.'

'And so you did.' Mary shook her head, inexpressibly sad for that poor, lost woman who had only wanted to protect her child, even against terrible odds. She *did* know how that felt. And Dominick helping her like that—Mary wished she had been able to turn to him when Will had died.

'Of course I did. No one else would help her. The monster was her husband. So we left for France together, and waited at Calais for the birth.'

'While everyone here gossiped about the terrible outrage, and Lord Newcombe stamped around threatening to kill you.'

He gave her a surprised glance. 'You knew about all that?'

'An *on dit* of such magnitude spread even to Derrington.' And she had gone out for a walk to cry alone. That was when she had truly known she must let go of her old dreams of Dominick. He had a new life, a new love. A love he would run away with— unlike her. She had been sure he had not loved her after all.

'Eleanor had a very difficult time with the birth,' he said quietly. 'It was a long one, and she was so weak. The child lived only an hour—a handsome little boy. She followed soon after. I stayed abroad for many months, trying to forget. And by the time I came back to England, alone, her brute of a husband had married someone else—a poor little sixteen-year-old. He married her only weeks after poor Eleanor died.'

'And your reputation was ruined.' Of course it was. Even Mary had half believed the stories about him. She felt horrible about that now—horrible that she had ever doubted him at all. Her noble, loving Dominick.

'My reputation? Even before Eleanor I had no reputation to speak of, which was one reason your parents so rightly objected to me. But I had to help Eleanor, Mary. She had no one else, and she wanted that child so very much.'

'Oh, Dominick.' She reached out and gently touched his cheek. Cold numbness was spreading through her until she thought she would smother under its weight. 'What a chivalrous white knight you are. You give away so much to help people like me, like Lady Newcombe and even Ginny. Do you never think of yourself?'

He smiled at her, a whisper of his usual flirtatious grin, and turned his face into her palm. 'I certainly thought of myself tonight, my dear.'

She shook her head. 'Yet you are willing to let everyone think you a careless rake?'

'What do I care what they think?' He suddenly seized her by her waist, rolling her back down to the bed as he braced himself above her. 'I only care what *you* think. Are you still angry with me for leaving you?'

Mary stared up into his eyes. Angry? How could she be, when he looked at her like that? She could hardly think at all. And yet he had told her so much tonight—told her things that changed the way she saw her whole life, the world around her. Changed the way she saw *him*. Her white knight in black armour.

'I do not know,' she said, winding her arms around his neck. 'I shall have to think about it.'

'Is there nothing I can do to make you forgive me?' He kissed her shoulder, the soft curve of her breast. 'Nothing at all?'

She felt the rough velvet of his tongue over her sensitive nipple, and she gasped. 'Well, perhaps you could try.'

Chapter Ten

Mary carefully cut a sprig of holly, the berries a bright blood-red against the glossy dark green leaves, and tucked it into her basket. Beside her, Ginny did the same, inspecting the branches for the prettiest leaves, while Captain Heelis climbed a rickety ladder in an attempt to find mistletoe. Though he and Ginny cast uncertain glances toward each other, they seldom spoke.

What a silly, romantic tangle this Christmas was, Mary thought. Ginny's young, wild almost-marriage was thwarted, and she and Dominick—well, she simply had no idea *what* was happening with them. Whenever she thought of him, and of last night, she wanted to laugh out loud with the joy of it all. Yet still at the back of her mind a doubtful voice whispered to her.

Dominick made her feel young and carefree again, but the truth was things were not entirely as they had been back when she had first met him. She was a widow now, not a green girl. She twirled the bit of holly in her gloved fingers, watching the whirl of red and green. Yet that did not mean she could not enjoy her Christmas—which was turning into a bright one indeed.

'You seem in a good mood today, Mary,' Ginny said.

'I am. The rain has stopped, and it's a lovely morning.' Mary dropped the branch in with all the others—a tangle of greenery to replenish the boughs on Lady Amesby's banister.

'But it's still cold,' Ginny said, shivering in her pelisse.

'It's Christmas time—it's supposed to be cold,' Mary said with a laugh. 'Lady Amesby will have warm cider for us when we return to the house.'

Ginny glanced at Captain Heelis from the corner of her eye. He tottered on his ladder, dropping drifts of mistletoe to the ground. 'Perhaps we could make a kissing bough, like when we were children! That was always fun.'

'I think your Captain Heelis is collecting enough mistletoe for twenty kissing boughs,' said Mary.

'Oh!' Ginny's cheeks turned a brilliant pink, which had nothing to do with the chilly wind. 'I don't think he is *my* Captain Heelis, Mary. Not any more.'

'Really?' Mary carefully laid another holly branch in her basket, keeping her tone neutral. Ginny had a skittish air about her, as if she would dash away if pressed for confidences. 'I would think someone who wants to marry you enough to make a dash for Scotland is assuredly *yours*. If you still want him.'

'I'm not sure,' Ginny said quietly. 'I acted like such a ninny on our journey. The cold, the fight at that terrible inn—I couldn't stop crying. I was sure I had made a terrible mistake, just as you warned me.'

Mary reached out to squeeze her sister's hand. 'Do you mean you no longer care for Captain Heelis in that way, Ginny?'

'I *do* care for Arthur! And he cares for me, too, I'm sure. He was so kind when I cried. He felt terrible. But I did realise something.'

'What is that?'

Ginny rubbed her toe along the frosty ground, staring down at the line like a child about to be scolded. 'Well, I realised that you were quite right.'

'What?' Mary cried. 'Good heavens, has the world ended? That can surely be the only explanation for you declaring I was *right*.'

'Oh, Mary, don't tease,' Ginny protested, but she did laugh.

'You were right that I could not be happy without my family and friends, without a proper home. I want to marry Arthur, but only if things are as they should be.'

'Oh, Ginny, dearest. How very grown-up that sounds.' Mary kissed her sister's pink cheek. 'You are young—you have time to make sure things are just right before you make any decisions.'

'But you were my age when you married.'

'That was different.'

'Oh, I know,' said Ginny. 'You had to take care of us all.'

Mary was surprised by Ginny yet again. She had been just a child when Mary had wed William; surely she had not known the truth of their circumstances then? 'I was hardly a maiden in a fairytale, sacrificing herself to save the village from a dragon.'

'No. Lord Derrington was not a dragon,' Ginny said, turning away to cut more holly. 'But he was not much fun, either. I'm not sure someone who does not care for music can be entirely trusted.'

Music was only one of the things William had not cared for, Mary thought sadly. But... 'He was a good man.'

'I am sure he was.' Ginny dropped a handful of leaves into the basket, waving at the Captain. He nearly fell from his ladder, waving back. 'Lord Amesby is very handsome. Charming, too.'

'Yes, he is.'

'Just as handsome as he was when you were my age?'

Before Mary could even begin to answer Ginny skipped away to meet Captain Heelis as he climbed down. They gathered up the branches of mistletoe, then turned back to the house. Mary was left alone with only the holly to hear her thoughts. At least it seemed Ginny had decided to be sensible. Could she do the same? Could she be brave enough to dare to start life over again? To hope again?

She looped the handles of the basket over her arm and followed the young couple to the house. As she neared the gravelled drive she heard the pounding of hooves and turned to see Dominick galloping towards her.

Her breath caught as she watched him. He was so beautiful, so powerful. He had always been a good horseman; now he seemed one with the horse, moving so elegantly. His head was uncovered, his hair gleaming like old gold in the greyish light, tousled over his brow. He laughed as the horse wheeled around—a sound full of pure, joyful freedom.

It made Mary laugh, too. She hurried near him as he reined in the restive horse.

'So that is where you disappeared to this morning—off for a ride,' Mary said. 'I should have known.'

Dominick patted the horse's glossy neck, and the beast pawed happily at the ground. 'Aunt Beatrice said he hadn't been properly exercised in a while, poor thing. I took him for a gallop into the village.'

And Dominick was certainly good at properly exercising— as Mary well knew. To cover her sudden blush, she reached up to stroke the horse's velvety nose. 'Are you sure you weren't just trying to get out of collecting holly for your aunt's decorations?'

He laughed, swinging down from the saddle to stand close to her. She smelled the warmth of him in the cold air, the heady scent of soap and leather and clean, masculine sweat. 'I had very important errands, I would have you know. And it seems you have done a good job of holly-collecting all on your own.'

'I did have some assistance from Ginny and your cousin, I admit.'

He took the heavy basket from her arm, giving over the horse's reins to a groom. 'And how *are* the young runaways?'

'Thinking better of their actions, I'm glad to say. Ginny still cares for Captain Heelis, but she does see that their situation must improve before they are ready to marry.'

'Well, I am sure their situation will soon be not as hopeless as everyone fears.'

Mary gave him a puzzled glance. 'You are up to something, Dominick?'

'Of course I'm not. I'm innocent as a newborn lamb, and quite hurt you would think me up to some scheme.'

'Ha! You, Lord Amesby, are the least innocent person I know.'

Dominick suddenly caught her by the arm with his free hand, tugging her with him around the corner of the house. He dropped the basket and took her into his arms, his lips coming down on hers in a hot, desperate kiss.

That shimmering haze of desire swept over her, her heart pounding louder than the horse's hoofbeats. She went up on her toes, burying her hands in his tousled hair as she met him passion for raw passion.

'You didn't seem to mind my deficiency of innocence last night,' he muttered, his mouth tracing her jaw, the soft, sensitive spot just below her ear. He licked at the pulse pounding there.

'Oh, do be quiet and kiss me again,' she answered, curling her hands into his coat to pull him to her. She knew the answer to her earlier doubts now—she *did* dare to start again. To believe again. With him.

Dominick laughed roughly. 'Whatever her ladyship commands.'

Dominick lay beside Mary as she slept, listening to her soft breath, the silence of the house. Soon that silence would be broken, the household would stir for Christmas, and he would have to leave her. But he had these precious moments to hold on to.

When she had greeted him so warmly on his return from his errand, kissing him so joyfully, his heart had soared. He'd felt things he'd been sure were gone for ever—hope, joy. Love. A true Christmas spirit. Even the thought that maybe he *could* have a family, that he could be a good husband, even a father.

Just maybe...

Mary sighed in her sleep and cuddled closer to him. She trusted him again; could he trust himself?

He pressed a kiss to her soft tousled hair and smiled. Maybe, just maybe, he could.

Chapter Eleven

Some mischief was definitely afoot down there.

Mary leaned over the banister to peer at the foyer below. The drawing room door kept opening and closing, and servants were scurrying back and forth with mysterious covered baskets and boxes. From beyond that door came occasional bursts of laughter or the sounds of hammering. But every time she tried to go downstairs and investigate someone appeared and urged her to go and write letters in her room, or maybe have a walk.

'It is such a glorious afternoon out there, my dear,' Lady Amesby had said. 'Perhaps you could gather more greenery?' Then she had dashed back into the drawing room, closing the door before Mary could catch even a glimpse of what was in there.

She sighed in frustration. It was as if she were a child again, shut out of grown-up doings. She was accustomed to being the grown-up herself now, running her own household.

Plus, being left with nothing useful to do just gave her more time to remember last night, and kissing Dominick behind the house. Every touch, every exploring caress—the way he kissed her *down there*, as she had never imagined could be done before—she remembered everything.

Mary fanned herself with her hand, suddenly quite warm despite the cold day. Maybe she *would* go for that walk after all.

Once she was bundled in her cloak and boots she set off down the drive towards the woods where they had gathered the holly. A few fat white snowflakes swirled around her, sparkling and magical against the pearl-grey sky.

They melted away as they touched the ground, and Mary found herself wishing they would not. That they would pile up into towering drifts, mountains of white, that locked them into Rose Cottage so they could not leave for days and days.

She glanced back at the house, its stark redbrick lines softened by the falling snow. The drawing room draperies were drawn tight, to prevent any glimpse of whatever mischief was going on there, but silvery smoke curled welcomingly from the chimneys. Someone had hung a wreath of holly, ivy and red ribbon on the door.

It did not look like an enchanted house, Mary thought, yet it surely was. She had found things she'd thought long-lost within its walls—laughter, healing, even love. And even herself, the Mary she had feared lost behind the sturdy gates of respectable Lady Derrington. She didn't know what would happen once they went back to London, if she would even see Dominick again there. But she would take away what she had gained here in these few wonderful days and she would never lose them again, not in her heart. She felt alive again, at long last, and that was a precious gift.

That was no small thing. Yet the thought of never seeing Dominick again, never kissing him or laughing with him, made her feel so terribly hollow.

She turned her face up to the falling snow, letting the soft flakes melt on her cheeks. They were cold and gentle, unlike tears. She had had quite enough of tears. Today was Christmas Day! A new beginning.

She tugged the folds of her cloak closer around her shoulders, looking back at the house again. The drawing room also had windows along the side wall, she remembered. Perhaps she could try peeking in there.

Feeling like the naughty child she had so deplored being treated as earlier, Mary ran round to the side of the house. The walls were lined with flowerbeds, sleeping now for the winter under frost-hardened earth. She stepped through them lightly, on tiptoe, catching hold of the stone window ledge to pull herself up. It was still too high.

From beyond the glass and velvet she heard a loud burst of laughter, and it made her even more determined to see what was happening. She wedged the toe of her boot on a brick outcropping and hauled herself up to the very bottom of the window.

The draperies were parted a mere inch or two, and Mary glimpsed a flash of red and green, her sister dashing past with a basket in her hands. But she did not see anything else. Holding on tight to the ledge, she tried to turn her head.

Her fingers started to slip on the cold stone, and to her horror she felt herself falling backwards towards the ground, several frightening feet away.

'Oh, blast!' she cried, scrambling for a foothold.

The wall seemed determined to get away from her. Yet she never hit the hard, frozen ground. A pair of strong arms closed around her waist, snatching her in mid-air.

'Whatever are you doing?' Dominick said, his voice deep against her ear. He didn't put her down, just held her tightly against him, as easily as if she were as light as one of those snowflakes. He rested his chin atop her head, as if he was in no hurry to let her go.

Mary tried to gather her dignity—which was no easy task when one had been caught spying—and was then dangled off the ground. 'I merely wanted to see if you needed any assistance in the drawing room.'

'And you could not knock on the door and enquire?'

'Your aunt sent me out for a walk.'

Dominick laughed, his breath stirring her hair. 'Then that should give you your answer. I have everything quite well in hand there.'

Mary laughed, too, kicking her feet. She didn't really want him to put her down, though. Not just yet. 'Just as you did last night?'

He twirled her around in his arms, still holding her high above the ground as she clung to his shoulders. 'My performance *was* rather good last night, if I do say so myself.'

'And you are modest, too, I see?' Mary teased.

'Truthfulness is more important than modesty,' he said, gently kissing her lips. 'And the truth is this—last night was the best night of my life.'

Mary kissed him back slowly, lingeringly, so she could memorise the exact way he felt and tasted, the softness of his breath on her skin. The cold wind swirled all around them, but she was wrapped in heat and light. 'Mine, too. I have missed you so much, Dominick.'

'As I have missed you.' He slowly lowered her to her feet, and she leaned her forehead against his shirtfront. She heard the steady, strong beat of his heart. 'Nothing was ever right without you, Mary.'

Nor for her without him. All those years she had been walking around with only half of herself and she had not even known it. When they parted this time, once Christmas was over and they returned home to London, she would feel it most acutely. Would the wound ever heal then?

Well, she would just have to make the very most of what they had—of this Christmas. 'Dominick, dearest?' she whispered.

'Yes, Mary?'

'What are you doing in the drawing room?'

He laughed, letting her go. Without his arms around her she felt the cold again and shivered. 'You are chilled. Come, let's go back in the house.'

'And into the drawing room?'

'Not until tonight!'

'Here, hold onto me, Mary!' Ginny said. 'I'll help you.'

Mary could see nothing at all through the scarf tied over her eyes, and it made her feel dizzy. She heard her sister fluttering excitedly around her, like a butterfly that had drunk too much chocolate and had an excess of energy. The air smelled of fresh evergreen, wax candles and cinnamon. Exactly as Christmas should smell.

Mary held out her hand, letting Ginny lead her carefully down the stairs. 'Not so quickly, Ginny, or I am sure to fall.'

'I won't let you. Here—now step down.'

Mary used her free hand to hold up the hem of her gown, so she would not tread on it and send herself pitching headfirst to the ground. She wished it was not the grey silk again; it seemed a most un-Christmassy garment. At least Ginny had helped her sew a new red ribbon trim to the bodice and sleeves, and Lady Amesby had given her a beautiful old black lace shawl. She had also twisted up her hair with red ribbons and sprigs of greenery, and felt quite festive.

Her stomach fluttered with excitement as she felt the stone of the foyer floor under her slippers. 'Ginny, this is quite ridiculous! Why must I be blindfolded?'

'So you won't spoil the surprise, of course,' Ginny answered. 'Wait here for a moment. I have to fetch something.'

'Ginny!' Mary cried. But she heard the drawing room door open and close, and she was alone. Not being able to see even a ray of light was quite disconcerting. She could not tell which way was which, and she held tight to the carved newel post to keep from falling. 'This is the strangest Christmas ever.'

'But I hope it will be a good one,' Dominick said. She heard the rustle of woollen fabric, a footstep, and smelled his soap. 'You look beautiful, Mary.'

She turned her head in the direction of his voice, sensing when he came close. 'I'm sure you do, too—though I should dearly love to see for myself.'

He chuckled, raising her gloved hands to his lips for a lingering kiss. 'All in good time.'

'You and my sister are full of mischief today,' Mary said. 'And your aunt, too. I'm surprised she encourages you like this.'

'She loves Christmas, just as you do, and is glad of the activity.'

'I hope so. Yet I think she will be most glad to have her house to herself again.'

'I'm not so sure about that.'

The door opened again, and Captain Heelis called out, 'Ready!'

Dominick's hand tightened on hers. 'Ready, then, Mary?'

'Ready for what?' she murmured. But she went with him, letting him lead her into the drawing room. That smell of evergreen and cinnamon was stronger there, along with a sugary smell and the sharpness of woodsmoke. For a moment she heard only the crackle of a fire, and then music.

'"We wish you a merry Christmas, we wish you a merry Christmas, we wish you a merry Christmas, and a happy New Year!"' Ginny sang, along with a tenor that had to be Captain Heelis's and Lady Amesby's quavering alto. '"Good tidings we bring to you and your kin! We wish you a merry Christmas and a happy New Year."'

The scarf slid away from Mary's eyes, revealing a marvellous scene—a scene straight out of all her dreams of Christmas. Swags of greenery tied with enormous bright red bows decked every picture frame, table, and curlicue of plasterwork. A kissing bough of mistletoe and ivy, bedecked with white and gold streamers, hung above the open doors to the dining room. Through there Mary could see the mahogany table held a plum pudding, a roast goose festooned with apples, and a crystal bowl full of claret punch.

A huge log—a Yule log—sparked in the grate, keeping every bit of cold winter darkness at bay. Next to the fireplace a table draped in green damask held a towering pile of brightly wrapped gifts.

Dominick held onto her hand as the others kept on singing, so loudly and out-of-key she was sure they must have been sampling the punch beforehand! '"We wish you a merry Christmas and a happy New Year!"'

'What do you think, Mary?' Dominick whispered in her ear. He sounded strangely anxious, as if he was not sure she would be pleased.

Yet how could she not be pleased? How could she not be completely overwhelmed by joy? Here were the people she loved, who loved her in return. Here was life. 'It is perfect,' she said. Her voice was thick with tears, and she dashed them away. 'It's everything Christmas should be.'

She bit her lip, remembering all those quiet, grey Christmases at Derrington, where she would sit by her lonely fire and dream up just such a scene. Greenery, Yule logs, punch, music—people she loved near her. And now here it was, a dream come to colourful, vivid life.

And it was Dominick who had given it to her. Who had made that dream and so very many others come true. It was Dominick who had made her feel alive and hopeful again.

'Then why are you crying?' he asked.

'Because I have never been so happy.' She went up on her toes to kiss his cheek, cupping his face in her hand. His blue eyes were shining so brightly—did he cry, too? Or was it merely the sheen of the Yule log reflected there? 'Thank you, Dominick. It is the loveliest Christmas I have ever seen.'

'Every Christmas should be this way for you, Mary,' he said. He turned his face to kiss her palm, his lips soft through the kid of her glove. 'Everything should always be just as you dream.'

Ginny finished her song, leaping up from the pianoforte bench to run to the presents table, just as when she was an eager child. 'What do you think, Mary? Isn't it a most wonderful surprise?'

'Most wonderful,' Mary said.

'And we managed to keep it all a surprise,' said Ginny. 'Even the gifts! Come and see what we have. I wrapped most of them myself.'

Dominick tucked Mary's hand into the crook of his elbow and led her over to where Ginny excitedly sorted parcels wrapped in scraps of velvet and satin and tied with ribbons. 'This one is from me,' Ginny said, holding up a long, flat box. 'I didn't have much time, I fear, but I do hope you like it.'

'I'm sure I will,' Mary answered as she untied the gold bows. Inside the box were lavender sachets embroidered with a flourishing M in Ginny's neat pretty stitches, along with lace-edged handkerchiefs. 'They are beautiful, Ginny. No one is such a good needlewoman as you.'

'I know how you like lavender, and Lady Amesby let me take some from her stillroom.' Ginny suddenly seized Mary in a fierce hug. 'I am *so* sorry to give you so much trouble, Mary dearest! I hope we never, ever quarrel again.'

Mary feared that was a hope that would go unfulfilled, as Ginny was surely as spirited as ever despite her misadventures, but they would always have their love to carry them to the other side of arguments. 'I can't be angry with you, Ginny. Because of you we have this wonderful Christmas.'

Ginny gave her a smile as brilliant as the Yule log. 'Then open this one, too! And this one.'

Later, once the gifts were opened and the feast consumed, reels danced in the drawing room and the Yule log burned down to embers, Mary sat by the window, listening to Ginny play more carols at the pianoforte. Beyond the glass snow came down in fat white flakes, piling up on the garden in soft drifts just as she had wished they would. Perhaps they would not be able to return to London tomorrow after all. Perhaps they would even be able to stay at Rose Cottage to see in the New Year.

But they would still have to go back eventually.

Mary took a sip of tea, smiling as she listened to Ginny play 'Oh, Little Sweet One.' No matter what, it *had* been a perfect Christmas. And it was about to get even more perfect, she thought as she glimpsed Dominick's reflection in the glass. He walked towards her, his bright hair tousled from the after-dinner dancing, his cravat loosened.

He sat down in the chair across from hers, reaching for her hand. She had discarded her gloves, and their bare skin touched. He took away the teacup, setting it on the table and replacing it with a small ribbon-tied box.

'You missed one of your gifts,' he said, with a smile that quite melted her heart.

'You have already given me the book of poetry,' she said. 'And I fear I have nothing for you at all.'

'Oh, Mary, believe me—you have given me a multitude of gifts this Christmas.' He folded her fingers over the box. 'Open it.'

She carefully untied the bow, lifting the lid. There, on a bed of black velvet, was a pair of amethyst earrings. Drops of the deepest, richest purple, suspended from two perfect, creamy-white pearls. They were the loveliest jewels she had ever seen. 'I—Dominick, they are beautiful.'

'I did hear purple was your favourite colour.'

'Yes, it is,' she said with a laugh. 'Where did you hear that?'

'I ran into Charlotte and her little daughter outside a jeweller's shop just before we left London so precipitately, and she told me. And these were in the window, just waiting for you. I wasn't sure then how I would ever give them to you, but somehow they seemed meant for you.'

'And you carried them with you all this way?' Mary asked. She traced the facets of the stones with the tip of her finger and seemed to feel their purple fire on her skin. Just like the fire that burned, hotter and brighter than ever, between her and Dominick. 'It is the most beautiful gift I have ever been given.'

'I know it is not a ring,' he said. 'But until I can return to Town and buy one, could these be a betrothal gift?'

Betrothal? Mary suddenly could not breathe, could not believe the moment was really happening. After all this time, all the broken dreams and new hopes…

'Are you making me an offer, Lord Amesby?' she whispered. She stared into his eyes, hoping to read all his true thoughts there. And his gaze was open to her, blue as the sky, filled with all the fear, hope, excitement and love she carried in her own heart.

'I am asking you if you would be my wife,' he said. 'I am no better a match than I was when we were young. I'm a rake and a careless rogue, or so they say. But I love you, Mary Smythe, with everything I am. I'm sorry I left you before. Won't you please let me spend the rest of my life making that up to you? Let me be your husband. Let me try to earn your love again.'

Mary looked back down at the jewels. The tears she tried so

hard to hold back fell from her eyes, splashing onto the beautiful amethysts. 'You don't have to earn anything from me, Dominick. I could not possibly love you any more than I already do. You are my white knight, and I have been waiting for you for so, so long.'

Dominick seized her hands in his, the box tumbling to her lap. 'Then you will marry me?'

And she said the words that had been hidden in her heart for years, waiting to be said. 'Yes, Dominick. I will most definitely marry you.'

She could say nothing more, for he was kissing her, and she kissed him back as if she would never, ever stop.

Epilogue

Christmas, One Year Later

'What a fine, handsome husband you have, Mary,' Charlotte said. 'Not as handsome as mine, of course, but definitely second-best.'

Mary laughed, and left her gift-wrapping to join Charlotte at the morning room window. They gazed down at the wintry garden of Mary's new country house, where Drew and Dominick were teaching Charlotte's daughter Anna how to ride her Christmas pony. It looked as if it was a merry start to the Christmas holiday as they laughed and called encouragement to Anna and her little face glowed.

Mary lifted her own baby daughter, Genevieve, from her cradle, so she could watch the happy scene. She gurgled and smiled, reaching out with her tiny hand to grab for Mary's new amethyst necklace.

Mary laughed, and kissed Genevieve's precious tiny fingers. 'That is very kind of you, Charlotte, but I fear I must disagree. My husband is surely the most handsome man in all of England.'

'And the best father, too?' Charlotte said. She softly smoothed the fluff of the baby's flyaway dark hair. 'Next to Drew, of course.'

'Oh, yes.' Mary held Genevieve close and remembered the night of her birth. There had been a terrible storm, and the doctor had been late in coming. Her pains had grown closer and more intense, the servants had been scurrying about madly, but she had not been afraid. Dominick had been with her every moment, holding onto her, keeping her fear at bay even as she saw his own hidden worries in his eyes. The old, terrible memories.

But just at the dawn Genevieve had been born, safe and whole, shrieking at the top of her lungs. And the look on Dominick's face as he had held his newborn daughter, so full of unutterable joy, had been perfect. They were a family, and nothing could ever part them again.

And now it was Christmas again—the best part of the entire year. And Genevieve's first. Mary's heart seemed full to bursting.

'Oh, yes,' she whispered. 'The best of fathers.'

'In a few years Genevieve will be ready for her own Christmas pony. If she's anything like Anna she will be a bruising horse-woman, and—oh!' Charlotte's eyes widened, and she pressed her hand to the bump of her belly under her muslin gown. The next family equestrian grew there. 'And this one, too. He kicks like the very devil.'

Mary laughed and bounced Genevieve lightly in her arms. 'My mother would say it is a boy, then. When I was pregnant with Will…'

Her voice trailed away as her heart gave a sweet-sad pang. Will, her dear little boy. She would never, ever forget him.

'He kicked, too,' she said softly. 'While Genevieve was sweet and quiet even then.'

Charlotte gently touched Mary's arm, her eyes full of concern. 'Oh, Mary, my dear.'

'No, Charlotte, I am not sad. Not now. He seems so close at this time of year, as if he watches over us and his little sister. Your children have a part of him, too.'

'Yes, they do,' Charlotte said. 'The mischievous part!'

Mary kissed Charlotte's cheek, making her smile again, and disentangled Genevieve's hand from her necklace once more. 'No tears, Charlotte! Especially now. Christmas is the time for wonders and all manner of happy things, is it not?'

Charlotte laughed. 'Indeed it is. Speaking of which, when are your sisters arriving?'

'At any moment—so we must finish wrapping all the gifts.' Holding Genevieve against her shoulder, Mary went back to the table piled high with packages and ribbons. Toys and sweets were scattered in an enticing, colourful display. She held up a doll meant for her sister Cynthia's daughter. 'Not that these pretty wrappings will last long. Cyn's brood is a wild one—my mother is always quite appalled when they trample through her house. It's fortunate Elizabeth's twins are such models of good behaviour. I'm hoping Genevieve chooses to emulate *those* cousins, but I fear naughtiness is so much more alluring.'

Charlotte gave her a teasing grin. 'As we well know. Look at our husbands, after all.'

Mary laughed, thinking about last night in their bedchamber, when everyone else had been fast asleep. 'I know. Dreadful, isn't it?'

'Appalling.' Charlotte tied off a fluffy bow atop one of the boxes. 'What of Ginny, then?'

'She is busy planning her wedding now that Captain Heelis has a commission in a regiment leaving for India soon and they can finally marry. I fear we will hear of nothing but wedding clothes and cake from her this Christmas!' Mary held out the box of embroidered linens meant for Ginny's trousseau chest. 'But I will miss her so much when she is gone to Bombay, and so will her goddaughter.'

'It won't be for long, I'm sure.' There was a sudden clatter on the stairs, a shout of laughter. 'It sounds as if the riding lesson has finished.'

Mary laughed, and hurried over to swing open the morning room door. Even after months of marriage, the prospect of seeing her husband filled her with a rush of warm excitement and joy.

Dominick was running up the stairs, Anna holding tight to his hand.

'Auntie Mary!' Anna cried, and dashed over to throw her arms around her aunt's waist. 'Did you see me from the window? I was riding all by myself. Papa says he has never seen anyone learn so fast.'

'I did see, darling.' Mary kissed the top of Anna's head, smoothing her tousled brown hair so like Charlotte's. How fast she grew—and Genevieve, too! Soon they would not be little baby girls any more, but young ladies. 'You did marvellously well.'

'I'll be ready for a horse just like Papa's soon.'

'Well, let's just stay with ponies for the moment, yes?' Charlotte said, taking her daughter's hand and leading her to the fireside, so she could warm up from the chilly day outside.

Mary went to her husband, wrapping her arm around his shoulders as she went up on tiptoe to meet his kiss. His skin was cold from the winter wind, but his lips were deliciously warm. Their baby laughed and kicked between them, their little family complete.

'Merry Christmas, Lady Amesby,' he whispered, holding her close.

And it was indeed. She had her family, her home, and her true love at last and for ever. She had thought last year's Christmas was the best, but, no—*this* was the merriest Christmas ever. And next year's would be even better.

* * * * *

CHRISTMAS AT
MULBERRY HALL
Carole Mortimer

Dear Reader,

Christmas is always a magical time of year for me, a time for family and friends, and writing a Christmas story set in Regency England was especially enjoyable. I could almost feel the coldness of the snow and smell the mistletoe and holly!

I have given Lord Gideon Grayson—Gray, a minor character in several books in the The Notorious St. Claires quartet—his own story, as he meets and falls in love with the woman destined only for him. You will also have a chance to catch a glimpse of the St. Claire family as Gray and the woman he loves join the family at ducal Mulberry Hall for the Christmas holiday.

I hope you enjoy reading Gray's story as much as I enjoyed writing about him!

A happy and peaceful Christmas to you all.

Carole

To all those readers who have come along with me on this wonderful journey as the members of the St. Claire family and their friends find true love and happiness.
This one is for you

Chapter One

December, 1817. Steadley Manor, Bedfordshire.

'A<small>S</small> I am holding a pistol, sir, and it is pointed directly at your heart, I advise you to stop exactly where you are!'

Gray stopped. But not because he was in the least daunted by the threat of having a pistol pointed at him. The cavernous entrance hall in which he was standing was in darkness, and the ghostly white figure at the top of the wide staircase was shadowy at best. Ergo, if Gray could not see the woman with any degree of clarity—a youngish woman by the youthful sound of her voice—then he very much doubted she could see him, either—let alone have a pistol pointed directly at his heart, as she claimed so dramatically. Which was not to say the chit was not in possession of a pistol, only that her aim, if she should choose to pull the trigger, would be far from accurate.

Having spent all day in his curricle, travelling from London to Steadley Manor, his estate in Bedfordshire—something he had realised, as it had begun snowing several hours ago, had not been the wisest of decisions for mid-December!—night had completely drawn in by the time Gray finally arrived. He had been less than pleased at being unable to find either groom or

stableboy to attend to his weary horses. Nor, having seen to the
stabling of his horses himself, a butler or footman to greet him
once he had ascended the dozen steps up to the oak door fronting
the house. Neither had he found candle and tinder on the table
just inside that door once he had let himself in, leaving him no
choice but to try to find his way in the semi-darkness.

Travelling to his estate in Bedfordshire had been something
that Gray had been avoiding since he had come into its inheri-
tance on the death of his older brother Perry some two and a
half years ago, but to now arrive and find himself held at pistol-
point—an event far too reminiscent of one that had occurred
several weeks earlier, and in which a man had died—was beyond
irritating. It was infuriating!

Too infuriating, after such a long and unpleasant day of travelling, to be borne a moment longer!

'I told you to stop, sir!' Amelia warned desperately, as after
the briefest of pauses the man below began to stride purposefully—ominously!—across the hallway and began ascending the
staircase towards her. 'I will be forced to shoot you if you do not
stop, sir.' Her voice rose as the man did not so much as hesitate
but continued to take the stairs two at a time. Each step bringing
him ever closer to where Amelia stood at the top of that wide
staircase.

White teeth gleamed up at her in the darkness in a parody of
a grin. 'A word of advice, sweeting—never threaten a man with
a loaded pistol unless you fully intend to pull the trigger!'

This man was actually mocking her!

He had broken into the house, no doubt with robbery or worse
in mind, and now he had the unmitigated gall to laugh at Amelia's
efforts to defend herself.

Amelia had come to live at Steadley Manor some three years
ago, on the marriage of her mother to Lord Perry Grayson. Only
to have her mother die only months after the marriage, followed
several months later by the death of her stepfather. Their deaths
had left Amelia to the guardianship of her stepfather's younger
brother, Lord Gideon Grayson. A man who had not troubled

himself to visit her once during the past two and a half years. Being left to live here alone, apart from a paid companion, had been unbearable, but to now find herself the source of amusement for a burglar was intolerable!

Too much so for Amelia to allow that amusement to go unpunished...

Her heart thundered in her chest as her back stiffened with both indignation and purpose. Eyes narrowing, she straightened her arms out in front of her, her hands tightly gripping the pistol as she carefully aimed and fired.

'Why, you little—!'

Strong fingers reached out to wrest the smoking gun from Amelia's hands. At the same time she was knocked off balance by the recoil of the pistol and deafened by the force of the blast as it reverberated around the cavernous entrance hall. She landed on her bottom. Painfully. Humiliatingly. She looked up to find the man looming over her in the darkness, giving all the appearance of an avenging angel, the pistol now held securely in his much larger hands.

Amelia was sure a weaker woman might have fainted. That even a strong woman, such as she considered herself to be, might have done so in an effort to escape the obvious wrath of the man who now towered over her so threateningly. Amelia was made of sterner stuff, however, and as such she had no intention of showing any sign of weakness to the man who had broken into the house in the middle of the night.

'It will do you no good to point that pistol at me, sir, when it has already been fired,' she told him with satisfaction, and she gathered herself up to stand unsteadily upon her slippered feet.

Gray wasn't sure whether to beat this woman for her recklessness in accosting a man she obviously believed to be a burglar, or to remonstrate with her for her impudence. After brief consideration, he decided to do neither of those things...

His eyesight had now adjusted to the gloomy, moonlit hallway, allowing him to see that the woman now facing him, with all the courage of an indignant bantam hen, in reality barely reached the height of his broad shoulders. She was in possession of an abundance of what looked to be either gold or silver-coloured hair, framing a small and pale heart-shaped face before it fell in soft curls down the length of her spine to what, if Gray was not mistaken, was a very shapely little bottom.

Although he could not actually see the colour of her eyes, the challenging glitter in them as she continued to glare up at him was unmistakable. A challenge that no red-blooded man—even one who had been travelling for most of the day—could have withstood!

'I— What are you doing, sir?' The little hellion's tone was slightly panicked as Gray dropped the empty pistol on the table beside them before pulling her effortlessly into his arms.

He grinned down at her wolfishly as he held her easily. 'I would have thought my intent was obvious, madam!'

It was more than obvious, Amelia acknowledged as her slender and virtually naked body was pressed—moulded—against a much harder one. And she realised that her sense of outrage was edged with trembling excitement…!

The man who held her so tightly was incredibly tall. With a lean and muscled body that Amelia defied any woman—even one who had been scared half out of her wits only minutes ago—not to be completely aware of. He smelt of a light cologne and horse leather. Not the unpleasant smell it should have been, either, but somehow terribly male. Nerve-tinglingly so!

'Release me at once, sir!' Amelia was aware, as must this man be, that her protest was completely lacking in conviction.

Gray looked down at her mockingly. 'I would, sweet—if I thought you really meant it!'

Her eyes stared up at him angrily as the woman struggled in his embrace. 'But of course I mean it!'

He gave a slow shake of his head as the woman's squirms only succeeded in pressing those lush and tender curves even more intimately against his own. 'I think not.'

'You are impertinent, sir!'

Gray found he had fixed his gaze upon her full and delicious lips rather than actually listening to what those lips were saying, and his arms were unyielding about the woman's waist as he moulded her soft body into his own. One of his hands moved lower still to curve about the full roundness of her bottom as Gray pulled her into the hard throb of his arousal, the grinding of his thighs against hers easing a little of his hunger.

Amelia was filled with a strange, heady delight as she felt the hard press of this man against her; her breasts tingled, and her whole body was filled with a hot and burning ache…a yearning she had never known before.

A yearning that made her question her own sanity!

This man had broken into the house in the middle of the night. Had mocked her attempt to shoot him before holding her against him in this intimate manner. It was madness on Amelia's part—sheer madness—to even consider allowing him further liberties. To allow herself to enjoy being held in his arms…!

Amelia glared up at him as she pushed against the hardness of his chest, and was able to distance herself, to feel the chill of the air against her heated body, as his arms fell back to his sides and he stepped lightly away from her. 'I advise you to leave now, sir!'

'You do?'

'I do!' Amelia took exception to the hard mockery she detected in his tone. 'Before my—my husband appears and decides to beat you within an inch of your life!'

The man's gaze became hooded. 'Your husband, madam?'

Amelia, having impulsively made the claim, now felt slightly flustered. In her determination to best this man she had decided that a husband sounded much more threatening than a guardian—especially as her guardian was very much absent! So absent, in fact, that Amelia had never so much as set eyes upon Lord Gideon Grayson! Even so, her claim of being married might have been a little rash on her part.

Her chin rose challengingly. 'You have broken into this house with the intention, no doubt, of stealing anything of value, you have—have taken liberties with me, and you are not even aware of whose house it is you have broken into!' she accused impatiently.

This young woman looked magnificent in her anger, Gray

acknowledged ruefully. Her eyes were glittering, her cheeks flushed from those 'liberties' he had taken.

A pity, then, that she was also a liar…!

Gray's mouth tightened. 'Is it necessary that I should know a man's name in order to rob him?'

'I would have thought it would have been something that interested you, yes!'

Gray shrugged. 'Then perhaps you would care to enlighten me, sweeting?'

'I am not your sweeting,' the haughty little miss informed him agitatedly. 'And Steadley Manor is owned by Lord Gideon Grayson, of course.'

A fact that Gray—the Lord Gideon Grayson in question—was all too aware of. As he was also aware that he did not possess a wife! 'The man to whom you claim you are married…?'

'To whom I *am* married, sir,' Amelia confirmed firmly, only to frown once again as her claim was met with what could only be called a loaded silence. A silence Amelia found she did not much care for. 'No doubt you have heard the tales of my—my husband's gambling and womanising whilst he is in Town, but do not be fooled by his rakish reputation, sir. I assure you he is an excellent shot. Nor will he take kindly to the fact that you have—have taken liberties with his wife!'

'Indeed?' the intruder drawled dryly. 'Your…husband would also appear to be something of a heavy sleeper…'

Having been rudely awoken herself only minutes ago, by the sound of footsteps crunching outside on the gravel driveway, Amelia had barely had time to locate the pistol she kept on her bedside table and pull on her robe over her night-rail before hurrying out into the hallway to confront this man. She was certainly in no mood to be trifled with. To be mocked. Especially by a man whose only weapon appeared to be her own no longer primed pistol.

Of course he could have a pistol of his own secreted somewhere about his person—indeed could be hiding several weapons under the many folds of his greatcoat. But as he had not produced any so far, Amelia did not believe he would do so this late in their encounter.

'I assure you, sir, you will not find this situation so amusing if my husband appears, or one of the servants should decide to loose the dogs on you!'

'My, my—a sleeping husband who, when awake, is nevertheless an excellent shot. And several dogs—fierce ones, no doubt?—who might also be loosed upon me,' the infuriating man taunted mockingly. 'Be assured I am quaking in my boots, madam!'

The devil sounded more amused than chastened, as Amelia had intended that he should. 'You are insolent, sir!'

'And you, madam—amongst other things—are a liar!' he assured her grimly.

Amelia's hands bunched into fists at her sides. 'How dare you?'

'Oh, I believe, if our acquaintance continues for any length of time—'

'Which I sincerely hope it will not!'

'—that you will find that I dare a lot of things, dear lady,' he continued undaunted.

'I am not your—'

'But first—' the man harshly overrode her protest '—I must dispute your claim of being mistress of this house. I have it on good authority that Lord Gideon Grayson is not, nor has he ever been, in possession of a wife!'

'You have…? Then you have been sadly misinformed, sir,' Amelia blustered as she faced him down defiantly.

'I have?'

He spoke mildly. Too mildly for Amelia's comfort. 'You have,' she insisted firmly. 'Lord Grayson and I were married in the church here in the village but six months ago,' Amelia assured him haughtily. 'A quiet ceremony, attended only by family and close friends,' she added hastily—just on the off-chance this man did actually have 'good authority' with which to consult on the matter.

Not just a liar but a bare-faced one at that, Gray allowed

exasperatedly, as the lies continued to trip so smoothly off this woman's little pink tongue.

But, considering *he* was Lord Gideon Grayson—Gray to those close friends this woman talked of so knowledgeably, the same close friends, no doubt, with whom, when he was in Town he gambled and womanised—Gray knew exactly where he had been six months ago.

And it had certainly not been anywhere near Bedfordshire or this village, and certainly not in a church marrying this impudent chit of a woman…!

Chapter Two

$\mathcal{A}$ll of which posed an interesting question—who the devil was she?

As far as Gray was aware, apart from his household servants—of which there had so far been neither sight nor sound—there were only two people currently in residence at the estate he had inherited on his brother's death two and a half years ago: his young ward, Amelia, and her companion—a Miss Dorothy Little.

Although that name aptly suited the petite young woman standing before him, Gray considered her behaviour in confronting a man with a pistol in the middle of the night, whilst wearing nothing more than her nightclothes, to be reckless. Considering that Gray had 'taken liberties', as she called it, it had been reckless in the extreme!

As for this woman's outrageous claim of being his wife...

Gray's mouth tightened grimly. 'I propose, madam, that we see to the lighting of a candle and begin this conversation anew.'

Amelia was completely nonplussed by the suggestion. This man should have turned tail and run the moment she'd confronted him with a loaded pistol. He certainly should not have mocked her or taken her in his arms, only to then remain completely undaunted by her warning concerning her husband's prowess with a pistol and the threat of having the dogs loosed upon him.

The way he had spoken to her just now, and his proposal of lighting a candle before they recommenced their conversation, did not give Amelia the impression that he had been, or indeed *was*, any of those things!

She searched his face, her eyesight having adjusted slightly to the bathe of moonlight shining in through the windowed cupola high above them, and was able to see now that the man was possibly aged thirty, maybe a little younger, with dark hair that curled about a hard and roguishly handsome face. His light eyes were narrowed—the moonlight was still not sufficient for Amelia to see their exact colour—and glittering down at her.

The covering of the many-caped greatcoat he wore—the reason, no doubt, why he'd given every appearance of being an avenging angel towering over Amelia a few minutes ago—revealed only that he wore snowy-white linen at his throat, a dark tailored superfine, and pale pantaloons above black Hessians.

He looked, in fact, more like an arrogantly confident man of fashion than the burglar Amelia had initially assumed him to be. 'Who are you, sir?' She eyed him warily.

'Should that not have been the first question you asked rather than the last?' he said tautly.

Amelia allowed that, in view of this man's unmistakable air of confidence and wealth, perhaps it should. However... 'Before or after you had broken into Steadley Manor in the middle of the night?'

'I arrived in the middle of the night, madam, because it has taken me all day, travelling in the cold and the snow, in which to get here,' he informed her harshly.

That dark and wondrously curling hair *did* look a trifle damp...

'And I did not break in,' the man continued disgustedly. 'The lock on the front door was already broken, and for some inexplicable reason has not been mended!'

The reason for that was not inexplicable at all; the lock on the front door had remained broken because there was no one left at Steadley Manor, nor the money, to see to its repair. 'That is beside the point—'

'No, madam, that is *precisely* the point.' Gray was fast coming to the state of losing his temper. Something he rarely, if ever, did. As the eligible Lord Gideon Grayson, a man spoilt and fêted by the ton, both for his wealth and his unmarried status, he found there were very few occasions upon which his will was thwarted. Something that this reckless companion of his young ward must be made aware of. 'I require a candle be lit immediately, if you please,' he repeated grimly.

'But—'

'If you please, madam!'

'I am sure there is no need to shout—'

'And I assure you I have not even *begun* to shout.' Gray glowered down at her darkly. 'The candle, madam!'

Deciding that it would perhaps be imprudent on her part to incite this man's displeasure any further, Amelia turned obediently to where she kept an unlit candle in readiness on the table that fitted so neatly into the niche at the top of the stairs, her hand shaking slightly as she struck the tinder and lit the taper before holding it over the wick. She drew in a deep, steadying breath before lifting the candle in its holder and turning back to face the man whose forceful arrogance was rapidly giving her the impression that he might just have a perfect right to have entered Steadley Manor so confidently in the dead of night after all...

One look at that handsome but harshly hewn face, dominated by piercing grey eyes, and Amelia knew he did indeed have that right. No one more so, in fact, when his likeness to Lord Peregrine Grayson, the previous owner of the Steadley estate and Amelia's own deceased stepfather, was so blatantly obvious.

'Lord Gideon Grayson...?' Amelia prompted with a sinking heart, even as she made an elegant curtsey. Something not easily achieved in one's nightgown and robe!

'Ma'am,' he confirmed with a terse bow.

Oh, dear! Amelia inwardly cringed as she realised—acknowledged—that she had not, as she had assumed, fired her pistol at a burglar, but at the man who had inherited the title and Steadley

Manor on his older brother's death some two and a half years previously!

Those grey eyes continued to glower down at her. 'Not your husband, after all…?'

Amelia felt the colour burn her cheeks. 'I only said that because I thought it would—well, that a husband would be more of a deterrent.'

'A deterrent to my taking further "liberties", no doubt?' he drawled.

'Yes!'

'Hmm.' Lord Grayson scowled darkly. 'Now that we have dispensed with the formalities, perhaps you would care to tell me why there appear to be no grooms in my stables and no servants in my house?'

Amelia was more than happy to have the conversation directed elsewhere other than her impetuous claim of being married to this man! 'There are but two servants left on the whole of the estate, My Lord,' she informed him ruefully. 'Mrs Burdock, the cook, has been here for so many years now that she has assured me she is too old to find new employment. And Ned the gardener refuses to be parted from his prize roses.' Her tone softened with affection as she spoke of the elderly gardener.

Gray eyed the young woman disapprovingly, more than ever convinced, now that he could see her clearly, that she could not be a suitable companion for his ward.

Her hair was indeed the rich, deep colour of gold, and fell in gloriously thick waves over and down her shoulders and spine above the thin white robe that was all she wore over her night-gown. The eyes that looked up at him so curiously were the deep blue of the Mediterranean Sea on a clear summer's day, her complexion as white and unblemished as alabaster, and her lips a full bow, as red and inviting as the ripest of berries.

The robe—a flimsy and totally inappropriate garment for a paid companion to wear!—was draped over her nightgown, but not fastened, and revealed the full and deliciously tempting swell of those pert and creamy breasts that had been pressed against Gray's own chest only minutes ago.

Circumstances being what they were, Gray had not as yet had the pleasure of meeting his young ward, but he could see at a glance that the woman standing before him was too seductively beautiful to be the paid companion of any young and no doubt impressionable girl.

In fact, after having enjoyed the lush curves of her body being pressed intimately against his, Gray believed her to be far more suited to being the paid 'companion' of any male member of the ton who might be on the hunt for a new mistress!

Considering that Gray's older brother Perry had been married but a few months before he died, and by all accounts happily so, Gray could not help but wonder what his brother could have been about, hiring someone so young and so seductively feminine as companion to the young stepdaughter he had acquired upon his short but sweet marriage.

Gray's mouth thinned as he looked down at the woman from between narrowed lids. 'You have forgotten to list yourself in that number.'

Those blue eyes widened, before a frown of consternation appeared between those fine eyes. 'Oh. Yes. I am here, too, of course.'

Gray nodded tersely. 'Of course.'

Amelia worried her bottom lip between her teeth as she pondered how best to extract herself from this disastrous situation. Especially as the man in front of her did not look like a man capable of losing even one ounce of that arrogant pride that fitted him as perfectly as his impeccably tailored clothing!

An arrogant and wickedly handsome man who had held her in his arms only minutes ago…

Amelia moistened her lips before speaking. 'I am unsure as to whether your bedchamber is suitable for habitation, My Lord. It is so long since anyone last slept in that particular bedchamber that I am afraid that even if the bed is made the sheets upon it are sure to be damp—'

'I will see to my own sleeping arrangements shortly, thank you, madam.' His pale eyes shimmered down at her in the candle-light. 'At this moment I am more interested in why there should be only yourself and two other servants remaining on the Stead-ley estate?'

Amelia blinked her surprise at what was surely an unneces-sary question. 'Because they have all departed...'

'Why?'

'Because, My Lord, they had not been paid in six months or more...'

'What?' Lord Grayson glared down at her ominously.

She shook her head. 'Mr Sanders had not been able to pay either the household staff or the gardeners and grooms for many months before he was forced to depart for greener pastures him-self only days ago.'

Gray recalled that Sanders had been the name of his estate manager he had written to the previous week, informing him of his intention of arriving at Steadley Manor today...

Having deliberately stayed away from Steadley Manor these past two and a half years, Gray had never met the estate manager who had replaced Mr Davies upon the latter's retirement a year ago. He had, in fact, put all the dealings of the estate, including the hiring of a new estate manager, into the capable hands of Worthington, his lawyer.

Because Gray had not wanted Steadley Manor, nor the estate, nor any of the other responsibilities—such as Perry's recently acquired stepdaughter—that had been left in his charge when his brother had died. The only thing Gray had wanted was his brother back safe and well from the Battle of Waterloo. Something that was never going to happen now Perry had been left broken and dead on the battlefield.

Steadley Manor, the estate, even Perry's dratted stepdaugh-ter, were all just reminders to Gray that he would never see his beloved brother again. Easier by far, then, to ignore them all and simply continue to live his own life in London.

Until, that was, Gray had received a letter a fortnight ago, delivered to his London home one morning, from Daniel Wycliffe, the Earl of Stanford. The Earl's estate was but twenty miles from Steadley Manor, and Daniel had been a childhood friend of Gray's brother Perry. The fact that the other man had written to Gray at all had been cause for surprise, but the content of the letter had been even more so.

The Earl had heard rumours, he had written, that all was not well at Steadley Manor. That livestock was being sold and not replaced. The fields were left untended. The estate cottages were falling into a state of disrepair. The Earl had concluded with the statement that it was not for him to say whether or not these rumours were true, only that he felt he should bring them to Gray's attention.

Gray had read through the letter several times, and each time he'd done so his annoyance had deepened at the Earl having had the audacity to write to him at all. He had no doubt as to why the other man had chosen to interfere—as a friend of Perry's the Earl had decided it was high time that Gray saw to his responsibilities at Steadley Manor. It was an interference that Gray had deeply resented.

So much so that once he had finished his breakfast Gray had sat down and written the other man a terse reply, along the lines that he was perfectly capable of dealing with his own affairs, thank you very much!

Except…

The letter from the Earl of Stanford had arrived at a time when Gray, after years of working secretly as an agent of the crown, had been reflecting on what he should do with the rest of that life, recent events having left him feeling strangely restless and dissatisfied. After a further week of contemplation, of finding no answers to that restlessness, Gray had finally come to the conclusion that perhaps he should travel into Bedfordshire to see if his future lay there after all.

As much as Gray had had no real desire to travel to flat and uninteresting Bedfordshire at this cold and unwelcoming time of year, he'd also known that there was no more perfect a time for him to leave London, now that the majority of the ton had returned to their country estates in anticipation of the Christmas holiday in one week's time.

He *would* visit his estate in Bedfordshire, Gray had decided, and see if there really was any basis for the rumours the Earl claimed to have heard, before travelling on to Gloucestershire in response to an invitation he had received from Hawk, Duke of Stourbridge, to spend Christmas there with the St Claire family.

Gray had not realised when he'd made those arrangements quite how serious the problems at Steadley Manor were. Servants not being paid. The departure of almost all those servants, both inside the house and out of it. How his young ward had been living alone here all this time—apart from the company of a woman Gray already considered totally unsuitable as companion to a young and impressionable girl.

All of them were things, Gray was now only too aware, that he would most certainly have known about—might have prevented from happening—if he had taken the slightest bit of interest in the running of his own estate since his brother died...

Gray scowled. Damn it all, he'd had other responsibilities—his duties to the crown to fulfil—without having to worry about something that should have been ably taken care of by the two men he had paid so generously to do it in his stead.

Which begged the question: if the money had not been paid into the hands of the household and the estate workers, then whose purse had it ended up in? Only his lawyer, Worthington, and the estate manager Sanders had handled the money before it was suitably dispersed to the men and women employed on the estate. As Gray had seen and spoken to Worthington only days ago—the older man had been delighted that Gray was at last taking some interest in his estate—it would appear that only Sanders, the man to whom Gray had written a week ago to inform him of his intention of arriving at the estate some time today, was no longer here to answer any of Gray's questions...

His mouth firmed. 'You did not feel the same need to absent yourself because of the non-payment of your own wages?'

'I, My Lord?' The woman blinked up at him innocently, instantly drawing attention to the long length of the dark lashes that surrounded those huge blue eyes.

Deliberately so?

Gray could not be sure. Nor did he wish to be! From what he

had recently learnt he would have more than enough problems to deal with during the next few days, without having to concern himself with the flirtations of a young woman he did not consider fit to take care of one of his horses, let alone the development of his young ward.

He nodded tersely. 'You, ma'am.'

Amelia looked up at him with a frown. She had to admit that Lord Gideon Grayson, with that stylish dark hair and those enigmatic grey eyes set in a face as masculine and perfect as a sketch she had once seen of one of Michelangelo's sculptures, was one of the most handsome men she had ever set eyes upon.

Unfortunately, having now met him, Amelia realised he was also the most arrogantly forceful man she had ever encountered, too!

She gave a slight shake of her head. 'I do not understand, My Lord…?'

He eyed her impatiently. 'I am asking if you love your work here so much that you have been happy to do it all these months without payment?'

'No, My Lord…'

Really—was Gray to add stupidity to the list of this woman's character defects? It would be a pity if that were the case; even a woman as beautiful as she would do better in the world if she possessed at least some intelligence. 'No, you do *not* love your work here? Or, no, you have *not* been happy to do it without receiving payment?'

She gave a tinklingly dismissive laugh, revealing tiny and perfectly straight white teeth between those plump red lips. 'No, I do not work here at all, My Lord.'

'You—?' Gray gave an irritated frown. 'Explain yourself, if you please!'

'I am Amelia, My Lord—Amelia Ashford,' she added lightly as Gray continued to stare down at her uncomprehendingly. 'Your step-niece and ward.'

Gray was too startled—shocked!—by the revelation to even attempt to hide it, and he openly goggled down at her.

This beautiful and seductively lovely woman—a woman any

man would relish taking to his bed—was the daughter of the genteel but impoverished widow his brother Perry had been married to for only months before her death, soon followed by Perry's own death at Waterloo?

Chapter Three

It could not be!

There had to be an error of some sort. Amelia Ashford was a child—only seventeen years of age—whereas this young woman was—

Perry's stepdaughter had been 'only seventeen' two and a half years ago…

Which would now make her in her twentieth year, not her eighteenth!

Circumstances beyond Gray's control had meant that he had never met Perry's wife Celia, nor her daughter Amelia. Perry had written to Gray at the time of his marriage, of course, assuring him of his joy in his wife, and of his delight in becoming stepfather to such a delightful child as Amelia.

There had not been time for Gray—nor opportunity—to visit the new family at their estate in Bedfordshire before Perry had written to Gray a second time, shortly before he'd had to depart for Waterloo, informing him of his complete devastation at the sudden death of his wife from influenza.

When the news had reached Gray, only weeks later, of his brother's own demise during that last bloody battle he had felt absolutely no desire to visit the estate he had just inherited—to be at or see the place where he would be made aware of his brother's absence the most.

Instead Gray had put the financial running of the estate into the hands of his lawyer, while concentrating his own energies on his duties in London. His only dealings with Steadley Manor during that time had been the twice-yearly meetings Worthington had insisted upon, so that the lawyer might present Gray with an account of estate business.

Never in all that time, Gray now realised uncomfortably, had he given even a thought to how Amelia Ashford had dealt with the sudden death of her mother, quickly followed by that of her stepfather. Let alone considered the loneliness of the life she must have led all this time, secluded away in rural Bedfordshire.

Gray studied her from between narrowed lids now, as he attempted to reconcile his previous image of a young girl on the brink of womanhood with the reality of the beautiful and seductive young woman who stood before him, wearing only her nightclothes. A young and tempting woman, who conjured up images of bedchambers and lithe and naked bodies intimately entwined amongst tangled sheets—

Damn it, Amelia Ashford was under Gray's protection, and as such she was the last woman on earth that he should find himself having such intimate imaginings about! The last woman he should have held in his arms.

'What is your companion Miss Little about,' he rasped harshly, 'that she allows you to run about the house at night dressed only in your nightclothes and brandishing a loaded pistol in order to challenge a man whom you believe to be a thief?'

Whatever Lord Grayson had been thinking during those last few minutes of silence, they had not been pleasant thoughts, Amelia decided ruefully as she heard the hardness of his tone. 'I am afraid Dotty Little was amongst the first to leave your household.'

And although Dotty had been employed to be Amelia's companion when she'd first come to live at Steadley Manor, she could not say she had been sorry when the fussy little woman had departed in a huff some months ago. It had become very tiresome to constantly be told, 'No, that is not ladylike, Amelia,' or, 'No, a lady does not behave in that way, Amelia,' or, even worse, 'No, a lady does not look at a gentleman in that way, Amelia,' if she should happen to glance admiringly at one of the handsome young men who attended the church services on a Sunday.

No, in spite of the occasional loneliness Amelia had suffered in the months since Dotty's departure, it had been pleasant to be free of the constant restraint previously placed upon both her behaviour and thoughts.

Although she could tell by the thunderous scowl upon Lord Grayson's brow that the knowledge of Dotty's departure did not meet the same favour in his eyes.

'When did Miss Little leave?'

'Some weeks ago,' Amelia dismissed uninterestedly. 'You must be cold and hungry after your journey, My Lord, allow me to go down to the kitchen and prepare you a light repa—'

'How many weeks ago?'

'I am sure that there will be some of the thick stew and freshly baked bread left over from my own supper—'

'How many weeks ago, Amelia?'

She looked up at him through the curtain of her long lashes. 'There really is no need for you to raise your voice, My Lord,' she reproved softly.

His young ward was, Gray realised, attempting to be everything that was sweetly innocent. Attempting—because after her earlier behaviour he was not fooled for a moment! Believing her to be other than who she was, Gray might have made a mistake in taking her in his arms, but there had been no doubting Amelia's warm response!

'Perhaps if you were to answer my question I would not feel the need to do so?' he came back mildly—and just as insincerely! 'Perhaps,' he continued grimly, 'if you had written to me at the time of Miss Little's departure the situation here would not have become quite so dire as it is!'

Her eyes widened indignantly. 'I trust you do not consider *me* to blame for the servants having departed?'

'No,' Gray allowed. 'Only for choosing not to inform me of it.'

He was fully aware of who was to blame for the state of things at Steadley Manor. As he was also aware of the debt of gratitude he owed to Daniel Wycliffe for bringing those problems to his attention. Gray knew he owed the other man an apology at the earliest opportunity…

'I did not—My Lord, there is blood upon the sleeve of your greatcoat!' his ward gasped, her hand rising to her mouth in alarm, and a look of fascinated horror in those wide and incredulous blue eyes as she stared at his left arm.

Gray glanced down uninterestedly at the blood-soaked sleeve. 'That is what usually happens when one has been shot, Amelia.'

Cheeks that were already smooth and pale as alabaster became even paler still as all the colour drained from his ward's beautiful heart-shaped face. 'I— You— Are you saying that I—that I aimed true…?' Her breasts rapidly rose and fell as she breathed deeply and erratically.

Gray's mouth twisted ruefully as Amelia reached out blindly to rest a steadying hand upon the banister. 'You did not shoot me through the heart, as you threatened to do, but I do believe I have received a flesh wound upon my left arm that may need some attention. I trust you are not about to swoon, Amelia?' He frowned darkly as he noticed the way his ward had begun to sway on her slippered feet.

Amelia was very much afraid she was about to do exactly that!

Except…

The look of impatient disgust she detected on Lord Grayson's rakishly handsome face as he scowled down at her was enough to bring her back to her full senses.

For Amelia to pinch herself at the realisation that Lord Gideon Grayson was actually here, at Steadley Manor, at last.

Wonderful as her sense of freedom had been after Dotty's departure, Amelia had recently begun to grow a little tired of languishing alone here in Bedfordshire. Now that Lord Grayson was here she certainly did not intend behaving like a complete ninny by fainting at his feet. Bad enough, surely, that after all the years of waiting for this moment she had actually *shot* Lord Grayson within minutes of first meeting him!

'Certainly not, My Lord,' Amelia assured him briskly. 'I was merely overcome for a moment, that is all. We will go to my bedchamber—'

'For what purpose, might I ask?' He lowered dark and reproving brows.

She gave him a frowning glance. 'Only because there is a fire alight in there to warm you and to ensure that you do not suffer from shock as well as loss of blood.'

The only shock that Gray was suffering was in finding that this seductive young woman—and she *was* most certainly a woman, and not a child!—was his ward. A woman he had held in his arms only minutes ago. Intimately.

'The water remaining in the jug following my own ablutions should still be tepid, at least.' She ignored Gray's scowl as she moved to his side and placed his uninjured arm across her shoulders before picking up the candle to light their way.

Amelia Ashford was definitely a plucky little thing, Gray acknowledged with reluctance. Not that it had ever been in any doubt, after the way she had faced him down with a pistol earlier—and actually succeeded in pinking his arm, too!

Gray had been vaguely aware, following the retort of the pistol, of a little discomfort in his left arm, but as it had only been slight—like the stinging of an angry bee—he had as quickly dismissed it. It was, however, starting to hurt like the very devil now that he had been reminded of it!

Damn it, if any of Gray's male acquaintances in the ton— heaven forbid any of his friends amongst the St Claire family!— ever learnt that he had been shot and wounded by his delicate slip of a ward, he would never live it down. Would find himself the butt of their jokes for years to come.

He attempted to extract his arm from about those slender shoulders. 'I assure you it is only a flesh wound, Amelia—'

'A flesh wound that needs to be bathed and bandaged.' She continued to doggedly guide his progress along the shadowy hallway.

'I am perfectly capable of walking unaided,' Gray snapped in his irritation with the idea that Amelia seemed to have acquired that he in any way needed her questionable assistance.

Damn it, he was only eight and twenty—in the prime of his life—not some decrepit old man incapable of walking simply because he had received a graze upon his arm from a pistol shot. Besides, he had received and as quickly recovered from wounds that had been much more serious than this one…

'I am sure that you are, Lord Grayson,' that honeyed voice soothed patronisingly. 'I am merely endeavouring, as you do not know the way, to guide you to my bedchamber.'

Good God, after holding her in his arms earlier, the last thing Gray wanted was to go to this young woman's bedchamber! The marriage between her mother and Gray's brother might have been of short duration, and the couple now both passed away, but Amelia had still been Perry's stepdaughter. And, with no other relatives alive to care for her after her mother and stepfather had died, Gray had become—still was—her guardian.

A guardian who was only too aware of her beauty and her powers of seduction!

And Gray was only too aware now, as he attempted to distance himself, of the soft delicacy of her flesh beneath his arm and hand, the warmth of her body pressed so close alongside his own…!

'This really will not do, Amelia—'

'We have arrived now, My Lord.' She raised no further protest as Gray at last managed to wrest his uninjured arm from across her supporting shoulders, and instead reached out to push open the door to her bedchamber.

A room Gray could not resist glancing into as he found himself filled with a curiosity to know if Amelia's bedchamber would be as feminine as the woman herself.

It was.

Curtains of golden velvet hung at the two long windows, the furniture was of a pale cream and delicate in design, and the matching four-poster bed was draped in white satin and lace, with half a dozen matching pillows plumped up at its head. Pillows which Gray instantly knew would be a perfect foil for the spread of Amelia's loosened gold hair—

Gray drew himself up sharply. 'It is simply not done, Amelia, to invite a gentleman into your bedchamber!'

Her eyes widened at his cold vehemence, before those long dark lashes once again lowered to conceal the expression in the depths of those blue eyes. 'I have invited my guardian into my bedchamber,' she corrected huskily. 'And surely if that man is a gentleman, and intends behaving as such, then there can be nothing wrong in a woman inviting him into her bedchamber...?'

Gray could not think of one gentleman of his acquaintance—several of them married!—who would be capable of *behaving* the gentleman if the lush and kissable Amelia were to invite them into her bedchamber!

'Besides, My Lord, you are injured,' she continued practically.

Injured, yes. Incapable of feeling male desire, no!

'Suffering from a wound that *I* inflicted,' she added with a pained grimace.

There was that, Gray accepted slowly, and he found himself unable to resist the appeal of those sea-blue eyes as she looked up at him so prettily. 'Very well, Amelia.' He sighed. 'But I will remain only long enough for you to bathe and dress my wound.'

'You are very forgiving, My Lord,' she told him.

Forgiving or not—ward or not—Gray was still very aware that apart from the cook, Mrs Burdock, he was apparently completely alone in the house with Amelia Ashford. Completely alone in her bedchamber with the beautiful and seductive Amelia. A woman who had already caused his arousal to throb and ache once this evening...

Despite her earlier protestations, Amelia was less sure as to the correctness of Lord Grayson being in her bedchamber once he had removed his ruined greatcoat—Amelia doubted that amount of blood could ever be removed!—his superfine, his waistcoat, and finally his shirt, before then sitting down upon the side of her bed so that she might tend to the deep graze on his arm.

She had never seen a man unclothed before, but even so Amelia was certain that Lord Gideon Grayson was a very fine specimen indeed. She had already guessed as much, of course, when he had held her in his arms earlier, but she could be left in no doubt now, when confronted with this much naked male flesh…!

Hard and lightly tanned flesh that showed the evidence of several scars.

'Have you fought many duels, My Lord?' Amelia allowed the tips of her fingers to move lightly across the scars on his back and chest, and a puckered and circular blemish on his shoulder that looked as if it might have been caused by a bullet wound. There were several more vicious scars across his back and torso that might have been inflicted by a sword.

Lord Grayson shot her an irritated glance. 'Why should you assume I have fought any?'

Because Amelia knew that Gideon Grayson, rather than join-ing the army, as a second son might be expected to do, had instead allowed his older brother to take up arms in defence of the family name, whilst *he* continued to live the life of the rake in London. Becoming involved in such exploits and scandals there that tales of his many mistresses and excessive gambling had even reached them here in the wilds of Bedfordshire.

Surprising, then, how tanned his skin was. How broad and powerful his shoulders. How the muscles of the bareness of his back, chest and stomach were so perfectly defined they rippled every time he moved. How that chest was covered in a light dusting of hair as dark and curling as that upon his head…

He smelled divine, too—like the outdoors. Earthy, and some-how untamed. And something else. Something indefinable. Something Amelia found wildly—deliciously—alluring.

Amelia met his gaze boldly. 'Perhaps my assumption is based on the fact that you did not hesitate to take an unknown woman into your arms earlier—'

'I believe you have cleansed my wound enough, Amelia!' Lord Grayson scowled his displeasure as he shifted sharply away from her.

Amelia gave a guilty start as she realised that she had ceased bathing his arm long ago, and had instead been running her fingertips lightly over his scarred torso. Fascinated, simply enjoying the sensation, and watching as the muscles rippled beneath that tanned and taut skin each time she did so.

She turned away to wipe her hands upon the towel. 'I will need to go downstairs and collect clean bandages.' Her cheeks were flushed, her gaze lowered to avoiding meeting his piercing grey one as she turned away to place the soiled cloth into the bowl of water before carrying it back to the washstand.

Giving Gray a perfect view of the outline of her voluptuous breasts, her slender waist, and curvaceous hips and thighs, as the light from the candle placed upon the dresser was reflected through the thin material of her nightgown and robe.

The last ten minutes of being tended by his ward had been torture such as Gray had never experienced in his life before. Minutes when he'd had to sit on the side of her bed, completely unmoving, as Amelia stood so close to him that he had been aware of everything about her.

Her breath had been a warm and scented caress against his sensitive flesh. Her long and silky hair like spun gold as it hung loosely about her shoulders and down the length of her spine, on one memorable occasion caressing the bareness of his own shoulders and back as she'd tilted her head the better to tend the graze upon his arm.

And he had been all too aware of her complete nakedness beneath the nightgown and robe as she ran her fingers lightly across his back and chest. His breath had caught in his throat as the firm and creamy swell of her breasts had moved repeatedly within his line of vision, allowing him to discern the size and shape of them. Once again he had been aware of the stirring, hardening, of his own body, and had found himself unable to look away from the tips of those breasts as they'd pressed against the diaphanous material. Tiny twin buds, as tempting and dark as ripe berries—berries that would be sweet and juicy against his lips—

Gray stood up abruptly. 'I will see to bandaging my own arm.'

His voice was a harsh rasp as he glowered across the room at her. 'I believe, Amelia, that you have caused me enough discomfort for one evening!' And in ways Gray did not even wish to even think about. If he did then he might decide not to leave her bed-chamber at all tonight!

She blinked at his vehemence. 'I doubt you will be able to manage alone—'

'I have managed alone for eight and twenty years, Amelia. I believe I will be able to do so one more night, at least!'

'But—'

'I advise you to go to bed and sleep, Amelia,' Gray instructed her coldly, even as he gathered up his blood-sodden clothes from the back of the chair where she had placed them earlier, to hold them firmly in front of the revealing bulge of his arousal. 'No doubt the two of us will have much to discuss come morning.'

Amelia could only stand and watch as Lord Grayson strode from her bedchamber without sparing her so much as a second glance, his roguishly handsome face set into cold and forbidding lines as he closed the door decisively behind him.

Chapter Four

'By all that is—! What on earth are you about now, Amelia?'

Amelia was startled into turning her head sharply towards where her guardian stood in the doorway of the breakfast parlour as she knelt in front of the hearth, careful to keep her coal-blackened hands well away from her pale lemon gown as she sat back upon her slippered heels.

Lord Grayson appeared very large and imposing as he completely filled the parlour doorway. And, although there had been no mention the evening before of his valet having accompanied him, the white linen he wore was impeccable beneath his super-fine, with a silver and black waistcoat beneath, and his legs long and muscular in buff-coloured breeches.

As so often happened in the cold month of December, despite it being a crisp and icily cold day outside, the sun was shining on the snow that lay several inches thick upon the ground. The brightness of that sun now shone through the parlour windows, and allowed Amelia to see Gideon Grayson in the clear light of day.

And to see that he was even more incredibly handsome today than he had appeared the previous night!

The darkness of his hair fell in soft and fashionable waves onto his forehead and against the hardness of his cheeks, and those chilling grey eyes returned her gaze piercingly from beneath lowered dark brows. His sculptured mouth appeared both firm and sensual above a grimly arrogant jaw.

Lord Grayson was not just handsome, Amelia decided. He was wickedly, magnificently so!

'Are you quite well this morning, My Lord?' Amelia's voice sounded as huskily breathless as she felt.

Gray supposed he was as well as any man could be when he had been shot in the arm the evening before, had proceeded to hold in his arms the one woman in the world he should not have so much as touched, and then spent a sleepless and uncomfortable night in a bedchamber that had not only been cold, because the fire he'd tried to light had refused to draw, but in which the bedlinen had also been as damp as Amelia had predicted it might be.

His arm also hurt like hell this morning. A dull and painful throb not unlike the discomfort he had suffered because of his inappropriate arousal the night before!

Damn it, Gray had promised himself he would *not* think again of the way he had held Amelia the previous evening—or of the time he had spent in her bedchamber, of how sensually alluring she had appeared to him as she'd tended to his arm. Of the light and enjoyable caress of her delicate fingers against his flesh. Of how his arousal had throbbed as he gazed upon her body through the thin material of her nightgown and robe.

He especially did not want to remember how his arousal had continued to throb and ache long after he had climbed between those damp and deuced uncomfortable sheets upon his bed...!

'I asked you a question, Amelia,' he reminded her brusquely.

'I thought I would light the fire in here so that the room would be tolerably warm by the time you came down for your breakfast, My Lord.' A questioning Amelia pushed up from her knees to stand before him, a slight and delicate figure in a woollen gown of the palest lemon.

She had confined that golden hair into a riot of gleaming curls this morning, but she looked no less beautiful because of it, as several of those wispy curls fell across her creamy brow, her lightly flushed cheeks, and her long and elegant nape.

It was a delicacy of appearance completely at odds with the feisty woman who had confronted Gray with a pistol yesterday evening before claiming to be his wife!

Gray's mouth twisted mockingly. 'How solicitous of you, my dear.'

'I thought so, too, My Lord.' Sparkling blue eyes returned his gaze impishly.

Gray's gaze narrowed he strode into the parlour, his frown of irritation deepening as he took in the irrefutable evidence that Amelia had obviously become accustomed to lighting her own fires in Steadley Manor—these past few weeks, at least. 'Why did you not write to me weeks—no, months—ago, Amelia, and tell me of the conditions under which you have been living at Steadley Manor?'

But Gray already knew the answer to that question. Knew exactly why this young woman—a woman so totally different from the young girl he had been expecting—had not written to him concerning happenings at his estate.

It had to be because she'd had no faith, no belief, that Gray would be in the least concerned. Either by her own plight or that of Steadley Manor. How could she have thought any other, when Gray had shown his uninterest so markedly?

Amelia took her time answering as she moved to the breakfast table to pick up a napkin and slowly wipe the coal dust from hands that had begun to tremble slightly after she had once again gazed upon Gideon Grayson's arrogantly handsome countenance.

She had expected, after so many years of debauchery, that there would be signs of it upon his face and in his appearance that she had surely missed the evening before. A cynicism, perhaps, etched upon that wickedly handsome face? A sagging, a thickening of his body from imbibing too much alcohol and eating excessive amounts of rich food whilst taking no exercise but that which he found in the bedchamber.

There was none of those things. Instead of cynicism there was a confident arrogance and a shrewdness, an intelligence in those piercing grey eyes when he looked at her.

And she already knew that he possessed a strong and muscled body that had filled her with lustful thoughts the evening before as she'd bathed the wound upon his arm…!

Amelia replaced the napkin carefully on the table before turning back to face him. 'You wish me to answer truthfully, My Lord?'

He grimaced. 'I expect no less!'

She shrugged slender shoulders. 'Then, My Lord, to put it simply, the freedom of no longer having to constantly answer to Miss Little for my every action was affording me too much pleasure for me to wish to bring it to an end.'

Exactly the answer Gray had not wished to hear! 'In what ways, exactly, have you been enjoying this unexpected freedom…?'

Amelia wrinkled her nose. 'I have walked. And ridden. Painted when the weather permitted. And eaten when I wished. Gone to bed when I wished.'

'And have you—did you do all of these things completely alone?' Gray found himself scowling as he waited for her answer. As he considered all the weeks this beautiful young woman had remained here unchaperoned. And vulnerable. So vulnerable that she had been taken advantage of by the first man—at least, Gray *hoped* he had been the first man!—to arrive at Steadley Manor.

'I have already said that I— My Lord?' Her gaze sharpened indignantly. 'I trust you do not think— That you are not implying that because you—'

'I was not implying anything,' Gray assured her hastily, not wishing to dwell on the liberties he had taken with this woman the evening before. 'But surely you must see how utterly foolish it was of you to have remained here so completely without protection?' Once again he glared his disapproval of her behaviour.

Her little chin rose in challenge. 'I did not see that I had any choice in the matter when my guardian had shown absolutely no interest in my wellbeing!'

It was, Gray knew, an accusation he well deserved. One he was also heartily ashamed of.

Just as he had been sickened earlier this morning, as he'd made an inventory of the house and the stables and seen the deplorable condition of both Steadley Manor itself and the surrounding estate. Perry, Gray knew, would be horrified if he could see how uncared for and derelict his former home had become.

How his beloved stepdaughter had been equally neglected…

Gray clasped his hands tightly behind his back as he straightened determinedly. 'I assure you that all of that is now going to change, Amelia.'

She eyed him uncertainly. 'It is…?'

'It is.' Gray nodded tersely. 'I have already been outside and spoken to Ned this morning, and he has assured me that several of the servants and estate workers still living in the village have been unable to find other employment, and should be only too pleased to return to their previous positions here. Including the previous estate manager, Mr Davies, who is not in the least enjoying his retirement,' he added with grim satisfaction.

'I— But— Do you now have the money with which to pay the servants' wages, My Lord…?'

Gray's mouth firmed. 'I have always had the money, Amelia.'

'But—'

'How well did you know Mr Sanders, Amelia?'

'Mr Sanders…?' She frowned her puzzlement. 'Not terribly well. Though I did not like him very much—found him to be a dour and taciturn man whenever I chanced to speak with him. I am sure that my stepfather would never have employed him to replace Mr Davies— Oh!' She looked up at Gray guiltily. 'I apologise, My Lord. I did not mean to sound as if I were criticising—'

'Criticise all you wish, Amelia; in this case it is as deserved as your earlier remonstrations concerning your own wellbeing.' Gray's expression remained grim as he began to pace the room restlessly. 'Perhaps more so.'

Gray had risen from his bed at six o'clock that morning—he had seen no point in lingering any longer when sleep had eluded him for most of the night—to go to the study in search of the estate ledgers. Estate ledgers that completely matched the ones submitted to Worthington. *Falsified* ledgers in view of the fact that half—almost all!—the servants supposedly employed in the house and on the estate, just as supposedly collecting their wages, had left some time ago.

A fact that had no doubt—once Sanders had received Gray's letter informing him to expect his arrival at the estate—caused the other man's immediate and hurried departure!

'The man was a thief,' Gray revealed flatly, having every intention of hunting the man down and making him pay for his crime. 'A thief and a liar. In fact, Amelia—' once again his mouth tightened grimly '—if the man were still here, then I might feel inclined to load your pistol myself and let you loose in a room with him!'

Amelia felt the colour warm her cheeks at this reference to her less than ladylike behaviour of the evening before. At this reminder that Gideon Grayson himself had been the one to suffer the last time she'd held a pistol in her hands. 'I had assumed—believed that—'

'That I am such a reprobate that I must have squandered away the family fortune—including the money to pay the servants' wages and for the upkeep of my estate—on gambling and womanising?' Lord Grayson raised dark brows.

Amelia's cheeks felt as if they were actually on fire as she recalled the circumstances under which she had made that particular comment. Of being held in this man's arms. Of how, in defending herself, she had also laid claim to being this man's wife…!

She knew by the mocking speculation in those shrewd grey eyes that Lord Grayson was thinking of at least one of those events as he allowed his gaze to move slowly over each of her features—and then lower still to the column of her throat and the pulse that beat so erratically there, the now rapid rise and fall of her breasts. Breasts that seemed to swell beneath the bodice of her gown. To ache. Filling Amelia with an unaccountable restlessness.

Gray caught himself up short as he realised exactly what he was doing. As he sternly reminded himself that Amelia was his ward and, as such, must be completely beyond his sexual interest.

He scowled darkly. 'I shall be going out shortly, and I do not expect to be back until later this afternoon.'

'I— But— I thought we were going to talk this morning, My Lord?'

Gray still had every intention of talking to Amelia—on several subjects, but not until he had all the appropriate answers to give in response to the questions she would no doubt ask him! 'We will talk when I come back, Amelia,' he assured her sternly.

'Come back from where, My Lord?'

The problem of servants well in hand, as well as a locksmith to deal with the front door, it was Gray's intention to ride over to Wycliffe Hall this morning to offer his apologies to the Earl of Stanford for not having believed the sincerity of the concerns voiced in the other man's letter to him. It was the least Gray could do when he considered the terse reply he had sent two weeks ago!

It was also Gray's hope that by his visiting Wycliffe in person the Earl's bride of less than a year might be of some help in the problem of what Gray was to do with Amelia…

Something Gray did not feel the need to share with his overly curious ward! 'I am not in the habit of having my movements questioned in this way, Amelia.' He eyed her haughtily.

'I was merely curious, My Lord.'

'Then might I advise a little less curiosity and a little more discretion?' Gray eyed her coldly. 'It is time, Amelia—past time!—that you resumed your proper place in this household.'

'My proper place, My Lord…?'

Exactly what *was* Amelia's 'proper place' in his household? Gray considered. At nineteen, she perhaps believed herself too old to be referred to merely as his ward. But she certainly could not be referred to as the mistress of the house!

She raised curious blue eyes at Gray's frowning silence. 'My Lord?'

Gray's irritation with this conversation grew. Along with his inability to find a suitable answer to her previous question…

'Or perhaps I might call you Uncle now that we have finally met?'

'Certainly not!' Gray gave a shiver of revulsion at the mere idea of being addressed as 'Uncle' by this young lady. Damn it, it made him sound as old as Methuselah! 'If you feel you must call me something else, then my associates usually refer to me simply as Gray,' he invited stiffly.

'If you please, My Lord, I believe I would rather call you Gideon…'

Gray stiffened. 'No!'

Amelia eyes snapped mutinously at his obvious coldness. 'I do not understand why not, when you call me Amelia…?'

'I refer to you as Amelia because that is your name.'

'And is Gideon not your own name…?'

It may well be, but no one ever called him by it. Not any more. Not since his brother Perry had died…

Amelia eyed Lord Grayson from beneath lowered lashes, aware that she must have said or done something to bring about that grimly bleak expression upon his rakishly handsome face. Simply because she had asked if she might call him Gideon…?

It had seemed like such a small thing to ask—especially as he had already given her permission to address him as Gray. 'I had not meant to offend you, My Lord…'

He eyed her impatiently. 'I am not in the least offended, Amelia, merely impatient to be about my business without further hindrance from you or anyone else!'

'But should you not stay and have breakfast first—?'

'Mrs Burdock supplied me with an ample breakfast several hours ago,' he assured her quickly.

This did not fit in at all with Amelia's image of Gideon Grayson as an inveterate rake and a gambler, either. Was it not the habit of rakes to remain out at their clubs or with their mistresses all night, before spending the day in bed sleeping off their excesses?

Perhaps rakes behaved differently when in the country?

Or perhaps Lord Gideon Grayson was not the rake and gambler he was reputed to be, after all…? His earlier mockery on the subject certainly seemed to indicate he was not.

Then what *was* he? How had he spent these last years in London? And could those pursuits possibly have something to do with the scars Amelia had discovered the evening before…?

Chapter Five

Gray was not in the best of moods as he handed the reins of his grey to the groom who had thankfully appeared as soon as he rode into the snow-covered stableyard on his return to Steadley Manor. Evidence that Ned, and hopefully Mr Davies, too, had been successful in persuading some of the servants into returning to the estate. As Gray strode purposefully towards the house he could only wish his own day had been spent as fruitfully.

To give the Earl of Stanford his due, the man had been only too happy to accept Gray's apology—both for doubting the truth of his information and for Gray's terse letter of response. And Alice, Stanford's wife, had been warm in her sympathy. So warm and sympathetic, in fact, that after eating a delicious luncheon and imbibing far too much of a first-class wine Gray had felt comfortable enough in her company to broach the subject of Amelia. Most especially Gray's immediate problem as to what to do with her whilst he spent Christmas at Mulberry Hall with the St Claire family.

A subject which in retrospect, Gray now accepted grimly, would have been far better left unsaid.

'Will you join me for tea, Gideon…?'

Gray stiffened in the act of handing his hat and coat to the footman who had—again, thankfully—appeared as soon as Gray entered the house, slowly turning to face Amelia as she stood in the doorway of the Blue Salon. As usual she looked charmingly enticing, in a gown of cream silk, and the colour of her eyes was bright as she returned his gaze with innocent enquiry.

An innocence Gray would do well to remember in the future, he admonished himself firmly. 'Tea?' he repeated, with a delicate curl of his top lip.

'Tea.' Amelia gave a gracious inclination of her head. 'Now that you are returned, I thought we might talk together as you suggested earlier…?'

The ride home had helped to dull some of the effects of the wine Gray had imbibed over lunch, but certainly not all of it. Neither was he any further forward—having totally dismissed Alice Wycliffe's solution to the problem—in knowing what to do about Amelia whilst he travelled into Gloucestershire for Christmas.

'We will only discuss how you wish to decorate the house for Christmas, if you would prefer, My Lord…?' Amelia suggested tentatively as she obviously saw his frown of displeasure.

Gray's scowl deepened just at the mention of Christmas, and he felt the beginnings of a headache pounding at his temple. 'I have absolutely no interest in the subject of Christmas decorations!'

Amelia gave a lightly teasing laugh. 'But we must at least bring in some holly and mistletoe! It will smell so wonderful, and— You *had* realised that Christmas is only a week away, Gideon?'

Of course Gray had realised. In truth, it had been part of his reason for visiting the Wycliffes. In the hope that they might offer to have Amelia with them at Wycliffe Hall for the holiday…

A hope that had been completely dashed once Daniel Wycliffe, a close friend of Hawk St Claire, Duke of Stourbridge, had informed Gray that he and his wife had also received and accepted an invitation to spend Christmas at Mulberry Hall. In fact it was their plan, due to Alice Wycliffe's 'delicate condition', to begin a slow and leisurely four-day journey there on the morrow, in order that the Countess did not overtire herself.

'You *do* intend being here for Christmas, Gideon…?' Amelia looked uncertain at Gray's continued silence.

That was a question Gray no longer had a straightforward answer to. His initial decision to come to Steadley Manor, deal with whatever needed dealing with here, ensure that his ward was being cared for, and then depart to Mulberry Hall for the Christmas holiday was no longer as clear-cut and decisive as it had once been.

Obviously some of the servants had returned to Steadley Manor whilst Gray had been with the Wycliffes, which would ensure Amelia's comfort whilst he was away. But could Gray *really* just up and leave her here alone, apart from the servants, over Christmas? The warm and sympathetic Alice Wycliffe had not seemed to think it even a possibility.

The Countess's solution to the problem?

Why, that Gray take Amelia to Mulberry Hall with him, of course! Which was utterly unacceptable!

'Gideon…?' Amelia prompted at his continued silence.

He did look wickedly handsome today, she acknowledged as a delicious shiver ran the length of her spine. So tall and darkly rakish, his hair slightly windswept from his ride, and his elegantly tailored clothes emphasising the width of his shoulders, the narrowness of his waist, and the long length of his muscled legs.

Elegantly tailored clothes that ably concealed that scarred chest and back…

And, of course, the bandage upon his arm, where Amelia had shot him the previous evening!

He gave her an impatient glance as he strode purposefully across the entrance hall. 'I suggest we retire to the privacy of the Blue Salon for this discussion, Amelia.'

She did not much like the sound of that, Amelia acknowledged with a grimace as Gideon stood to one side to allow her to precede him into the blue and cream room. She had deliberately chosen this room in which to wait for his return, knowing that the blue drapes and chaise were a perfect match in colour for her eyes. An effect that, at the moment, seemed completely lost on the stiffly forbidding Lord Grayson.

'Perhaps you prefer not to celebrate Christmas, Gideon…?' Amelia sat down upon the blue chaise and leant forward to pour tea into the two cups she had requested in the hope that Gideon would return in time to join her.

Gray would prefer not to celebrate *this* particular Christmas! Would prefer to forget its very existence, in fact. 'I believe I told you to call me Gray…?'

She gave a ruefully dismissive shake of her head, blonde curls brushing against her cheeks and nape. 'I consider it too impersonal for our particular relationship—'

'We do not *have* a relationship!' Gray glared down at her fiercely as he stood with his hands clasped tightly together behind his back. And felt as if he had just kicked a defenceless kitten as he saw the sudden tears that welled in Amelia's deep blue eyes at the fierceness of his tone. Except this young woman was anything *but* defenceless; she had shot him in the arm the previous evening!

She blinked long-lashed lids in an obvious effort to prevent those tears from falling. 'It has become obvious to me that you resent having been burdened with my guardianship—'

'I did not say that, damn it!'

She bowed her head, revealing the vulnerable curve of her nape as she murmured quietly, 'You did not need to put it into words, My Lord.'

Gray did not need to do a lot of things. Mainly he did not need to take out his temper, his frustration with this situation, on someone who was completely innocent—at least in this particular matter. After all, Amelia had not *asked* to become his ward. Circumstances had placed her as much as he in their present position. Besides which, Gray could not stand to see those tears balanced so precariously upon the long sweep of her lashes…!

He crossed the room in long, impatient strides to sit down beside her on the chaise. 'I am a surly devil this afternoon, Amelia. Please do not cry—' He broke off abruptly as, with a choked sob, Amelia launched herself into his arms to bury her face against his chest, and her slender arms moved tightly about his waist as she clung to him.

Gray had managed, in his brief respite from Amelia's physically disturbing presence, to convince himself that he had made too much of his attraction to her the previous evening. He had only felt it because he had thought to punish his ward's companion for threatening to shoot him. The fact that he had enjoyed holding Amelia more than he ought was merely an indication, he had assured himself, of the fact that he had been too long without a woman.

Learning that the woman he had held in his arms and held so intimately was in fact his ward, should have completely nullified Gray's response to her.

But now, as Gray's arms moved slowly—against his every instinct for caution!—about the slenderness of Amelia's waist, drawing the softness of her curves against him, her gold curls were an enticement he could not resist. He rested his cheek against their softness and knew that he had only been deceiving himself. That it was the creamy perfection of Amelia's skin that tempted him, the touch of Amelia's silky hair that enticed him, the heat of Amelia's body through the soft material of her gown that aroused him and once again caused his thighs to harden and ache.

So much so that Gray wanted nothing more than to lay her down naked upon the chaise this very minute and make full and satisfying love to her!

Lord help him…!

Having spent several months revelling in not having to answer to anyone for anything she did or said, Amelia had surprisingly found herself missing Gideon Grayson's forceful presence today.

No doubt, considering what he had revealed to her of Sanders' behaviour, Gideon had been busy with further estate business. Indeed, the fact that so many of the servants had already returned to Steadley Manor, and that Mr Davies was once again about his business on the estate, including having arranged for a locksmith to come and repair the lock on the front door, showed Amelia just how busy Gideon had been in those hours before she had even come downstairs this morning.

There had been a welcoming rush and a bustle about the house all day and the maids had cleaned and polished all the main rooms downstairs, as well as lit all the fires. Mrs Burdock was preparing them a veritable feast for dinner this evening now that she had at least some of her kitchen maids to help her.

The fact that everyone about Amelia was so busy had only succeeded in her feeling her aloneness more keenly. To have had Gideon return so cold and so distant had only added to those feelings of alienation. A feeling that had disappeared the moment she'd pressed her cheek against the warmth of his chest and felt and heard the strong and steady beat of his heart.

She burrowed closer against that protective chest now. 'I really am sorry that you have been burdened with my guardianship, Gideon,' she told him emotionally, the tears still falling hotly down her cheeks, no doubt soaking his pristine white linen. 'I would offer to relieve you of that burden—except I have no one else and nowhere else to go—'

'Do not give it another thought, Amelia, please!' His arms tightened about her. 'I am the one who is at fault for having ignored my responsibility to you for so long.'

His responsibility...

Yes, Amelia accepted heavily, that was all she was to Gideon Grayson—a tiresome responsibility that had come about simply because his brother had been married to her mother for merely months before her sudden and unexpected death.

No wonder, then, that Gideon Grayson had chosen to ignore her very existence for all this time. No surprise, either, that he now found her presence here in his home irksome. He certainly could not be enjoying having her cry all over him and making such a mess of his elegant clothing!

Amelia raised her head slightly as she lifted a hand to wipe the tears from her cheeks before raising her lashes to look at him. Her breath caught in her throat and her lips parted in a silent *oh* as she instantly found herself mesmerised by the deep grey of

Gideon's eyes. Eyes that were fixed, intent upon her own slightly parted lips...

'My Lord...?' she breathed shallowly.

'Gideon,' he encouraged gruffly.

Amelia swallowed hard before obeying the invitation. 'Gideon.'

He really did have the most beautiful mouth, Amelia decided breathlessly. She found herself unable to look away. So firm, and yet at the same time sensuous, the top lip slightly fuller than the bottom, hinting at a passionate nature. The passionate nature also hinted at the previous evening.

A passion she found herself longing to experience. To explore. To know. As she longed to experience the feel of that hard and yet sensual mouth moving passionately against her own...

He had to stop this now, Gray recognised in some alarm. He knew himself on the point of giving in to the temptation to lower his head and claim the fullness of Amelia's parted and slightly raised lips with his own. He should distance himself now—before he stepped over a line he had no business stepping over.

Except...

There was always an *except* where this particular young woman was concerned, Gray realised self-disgustedly. A part of him that wanted to say to hell with it and kiss her anyway, before he explored and tasted the nakedness of her full and ripe body.

And once he had? What then? What would become of their tenuous connection then?

Amelia was his ward, a young and unmarried lady of quality—not an experienced or married woman of the ton whom Gray could dally and flirt with, possibly bed, before moving on to another conquest.

In a word, this attraction Gray felt towards Amelia Ashford was dangerous!

Holding her in his arms last night, when he'd had no idea who she was, had been a mistake. Kissing her now, knowing exactly who she was, would be nothing short of a catastrophe!

Damn it, if Gray had found any other man in this compromising position with his ward then he knew he would have had no choice but to either demand satisfaction or an offer of marriage from that man. He had no intention of offering either of those things!

Gray moved back abruptly, taking a grasp on the tops of Amelia's arms to hold her firmly away as she would have swayed towards him. He had to shift slightly in order to ease the uncomfortable bulge in his pantaloons as she looked up at him in pouting disappointment.

Perhaps Alice Wycliffe's suggestion was the right one after all…?

Obviously Gray could not remain here alone with Amelia any longer than he absolutely had to. Nor could he leave her to her own devices whilst he went on his way to Mulberry Hall. Perhaps the best thing *would* be to take Amelia with him.

No!

Every part of Gray flared up in protest at the idea of introducing Amelia to the St Claire family. Hawk St Claire, the aristocratic Duke of Stourbridge, was as austerely handsome as he was intimidating. Lucian St Claire was considered as broodingly attractive as he was taciturn, and had also been a hero at Waterloo. And Sebastian St Claire, a charming rake before his marriage, had been Gray's closest friend and companion during those nights in Town when he had reputedly gambled and womanised!

Nor did Gray consider the wives of the three St Claire brothers to be any more of an example for Amelia to emulate. Jane, Hawk's Duchess of just over a year, was a ravishingly beautiful redhead who cared little for the dictates and restraints of Society. Grace, Lucian's recent bride, was as wilfully determined as she was beautiful. Sebastian, the wildest of the three brothers, had surprised everyone two months ago, when he had married Juliet, an ethereally lovely young widow who already carried his child.

As for the youngest member of the St Claire family…

Arabella, the young sister of the three St Claire brothers, despite now being married to the devilishly handsome Duke of

Carlyne, was also a perfect hellion. And Gray knew firsthand exactly how managing and forthright the beautiful Arabella could be when she chose!

For Gray to take Amelia into the midst of *that* arrogant and aristocratic family would be complete madness on his part.

And he did not believe himself to have been driven completely mad as yet...

Chapter Six

Amelia knew just from looking at the hard implacability of Gideon's expression as he turned to face her that she was not going to like what he said next. Any more than she liked the fact that he had moved away from her so abruptly when it had looked as if he might have been going to kiss her…!

'You really have no one else to stay with?' he rasped. 'No other family? Grandparents? Uncles or aunts?'

Perhaps an old family friend, or even just an acquaintance, who might be persuaded into taking responsibility for her? Amelia inwardly finished with a proud straightening of her spine. 'There is not even an old family dog who might be brought here to keep me company!' Her eyes flashed.

Lord Grayson's mouth firmed. 'There is no need to take that tone, Amelia—'

'There is every need if I have correctly understood your reluctance for my company!' Amelia stood up abruptly. 'But do not be alarmed, sir. I have my own rooms, and if necessary can easily remain in them for the duration of your stay here!'

She looked beautiful as she stared him down so proudly, Gray acknowledged ruefully. Every inch the lady she undoubtedly was.

Every inch of her too beautiful and desirable for his own peace of mind.

'Do not be so melodramatic, Amelia.' Gray affected a bored tone. 'The fact that you no longer have a companion here with you is, I admit, a little…inconvenient—'

'It is not inconvenient to me, sir.' She gave a determined shake of her head. 'You can have no idea of the constraints that have been placed upon me since I first entered your brother's household.'

A reminder, Gray recognised, of his complete lack of thought or understanding for what Amelia's life might have been these past years. Or what her life had been before that time…

'Tell me,' he encouraged huskily. 'I know nothing of either your mother or your own life before she and Perry were married.' Gray's admission caused him some discomfort as he acknowledged that he should have made more of an effort to meet his brother's wife and stepdaughter. 'Where did you and your mother live before you came here?' He moved to sit in one of the pale blue chairs set beside the fire, crossing one leg over the other as he looked up at Amelia enquiringly.

Her shoulders lost some of their stiffness. 'We had a cottage beside the sea in a small village on the Devonshire coast. My father's family came from there originally. He was the son of a vicar, but always wanted to be a soldier.' She gave a rueful smile at that irony.

A cottage set beside the sea in a village on the Devonshire coast…

The complete opposite, Gray acknowledged, to a manor house set alone in the flat and often bleak Bedfordshire countryside.

Amelia gave a shake of her head. 'My mother was the daughter and only child of the local squire. He died before I was born, so I never knew him, but according to my mother he had high expectations of his only child making an advantageous marriage. He would not even entertain the idea of her marrying the soldier son of the local vicar! My mother and father ran away together, and were married when my mother was but seventeen. It was a happy marriage.' Her chin rose defensively, as if she expected Gray to challenge the statement.

Which he had no intention of doing. 'They returned to the village following their marriage…?'

'Not immediately, no.' Amelia gave a smile. 'My mother accompanied my father on his campaigns for a year or more, and I believe it was only decided my mother must return to England once they knew she was expecting a child. Her father— my grandfather—had been killed in a hunting accident several months earlier, unfortunately without there having been any rec-onciliation between the two of them, which resulted in his leaving all his wealth to a distant cousin or some such.' She shrugged delicate shoulders. 'But, having returned alone to England, it was my mother's wish to live in the village she knew, with people she was familiar with.'

'That sounds…sensible.' Gray nodded, having more of an understanding now of where Amelia had come by her indomitable spirit. With a soldier for a father, and a mother who had known and determined her own heart even in the face of parental disap-proval, Amelia had been sure to be of similar determination and courage. That same determination and courage that had enabled her to face down an intruder with a pistol the evening before!

Amelia nodded. 'I am sure that my mother must have missed my father deeply, but it was an idyllic childhood as far as I was concerned. Months when I had my mother completely to myself, followed by weeks of excitement and outings when my father, now a sergeant in his regiment, was able to join us.'

The wistfulness of her expression told Gray just how idyllic, how happy, that childhood had been.

Her chin rose proudly. 'My father was killed four years ago. At which time his commanding officer, Major Lord Peregrine Grayson—' she smiled affectionately '—wrote to my mother, expressing his deepest sympathy at the loss of such a gallant soldier as he considered my father to be, and promising that he would visit her in person as soon as he was able.'

That sounded like Perry, Gray acknowledged with sad affec-tion, knowing that his brother had been a man who'd felt the loss of each and every man in his own regiment and, once it had been believed the fighting was over, had tried to visit the close relatives of all who had died whilst fighting alongside him during those bloody years of war.

'Obviously it was a fortuitous visit…?'

Those blue eyes narrowed. 'I trust you are not implying—'

'I assure you I am not implying anything, Amelia.' Gray held up silencing hands. 'From Perry's account of things, he and your mother fell in love with each other on sight.'

'Yes.' Amelia sighed sadly at the memory of how her mother's second marriage to Lord Peregrine Grayson had lasted only for a few brief months before her mother was taken ill with influenza and as quickly died.

'Which brings us back to here and now, and what to do with you.'

Amelia eyed Gideon Grayson warily. 'What to do with me…?'

He gave an autocratic inclination of his head. 'It has been suggested to me, as you are nineteen years of age, that come the spring you might like to have a Season in London.'

'A Season? Really?' Amelia eyes lit up with excitement at the prospect of going to London. Until she realised exactly what Gideon had said. 'Been suggested by whom…?' she prompted suspiciously.

He glanced down to brush a speck of lint from his perfectly tailored pantaloons. 'An acquaintance.'

What acquaintance? Amelia wondered with a frown. And when and where had Gideon met this acquaintance? Had it been this morning? Or had this already been decided upon, discussed with a third party, before Gideon even came to Steadley Manor? Perhaps—Amelia felt a pained contraction of her chest—with the mistress in London who currently shared Gideon's bed…?

'That is the reason I asked a few minutes ago if you had any relatives—older female relatives, obviously—who might act as chaperone during that time,' Gideon continued coolly.

'I am sorry, no.' There was a complete lack of apology in Amelia's slightly defiant tone.

Gideon had discussed her—what to do with her!—with a third party. As if she were some unasked-for package that had been delivered to his door by mistake. An unasked-for and unwanted package that Gideon Grayson obviously now wished to rid himself of at the earliest opportunity!

Amelia looked at him coldly. 'And is it your intention that during this Season I attempt to find myself a husband…?'

He looked momentarily disconcerted, before nodding abruptly. 'If that is your wish, yes.'

Exactly as Amelia had suspected.

Gray could see by the rebellious glitter that suddenly entered Amelia's expressive blue eyes that he had somehow spoken out of turn. Again. Although what could be wrong about following through on Alice Wycliffe's suggestion that come the spring he take Amelia to London and rig her out with a complete new wardrobe before launching her into Society, Gray had absolutely no idea.

Although it had not occurred to him until Amelia questioned his motives that she might possibly procure herself a husband during that time…

Damn it, *he* should be the one who was put out by the very idea of having to introduce Amelia into Society, when doing so would mean having to put himself to the inconvenience of attending the numerous balls and parties given by the ton that he usually made such a point of avoiding. As a wealthy and titled bachelor, Gray knew that showing his face in Society meant that every marriage-minded mama in the country would trample over anyone who stood in her way in order that she might reach his side and extol the virtues of her daughter as his prospective future wife!

But, instead of appearing excited at the prospect, Amelia looked as if Gray were suggesting he accompany her to the gallows!

He stood up impatiently. 'I am sure this is what my brother Perry and your mother intended for you—'

'That is unfair!' Those incredible blue eyes were once again awash with tears.

Gray shook his head. 'I do not think so. My brother Perry left provision in his will for your marriage dowry—'

'My *marriage* dowry!' Amelia repeated incredulously.

'Of course.' Gray gave a haughty inclination of his head. 'When your mother married my brother you became the step-daughter of a lord, so—'

'Do not touch me!' She moved sharply away as Gray would have reached out and lightly grasped her arm, and raised her chin proudly as she looked down the length of her nose at him. 'You have made your feelings very clear on the subject, and, as you are my guardian, if it is your wish that I go to London in the spring so that I might search for a husband, then of course I must go.'

'You were the one who suggested that you might find yourself a husband!' Gray glared his frustration with this conversation.

'You were the one who mentioned a marriage dowry!'

'I was merely—'

'Putting forward a way in which you might be completely rid of all responsibility for me?' Amelia finished scathingly.

Gray gave an exasperated snort. 'I made no mention of being rid of you—'

'You have made it perfectly clear that is your intention.' She swept her gown to one side.

'Damn it, Amelia—'

'If you will excuse me, My Lord?' She eyed him coldly. 'I believe I would prefer to spend the time before dinner upstairs in my bedchamber.'

As far away from him as she could possibly be whilst still remaining in the same house, Gray acknowledged impatiently. 'I have not finished talking to you yet, Amelia—'

'But I have finished talking with *you*!' she assured him, giving him one last scathing glance before walking from the room with her head held disdainfully high.

Leaving Gray no choice but to stare after her in complete frustration. Alice Wycliffe had assured him earlier that any young lady of nineteen years would be thrilled at the prospect of going to London and being introduced into Society. That she would be ecstatic at the suggestion of a new wardrobe. Of attending balls and parties and meeting all the handsome rakes with whom she might dance and behave the flirt.

Obviously when Alice had made this observation she'd had no personal knowledge of the stubborn and self-willed Amelia Ashford!

Chapter Seven

'You look as if you wish that your aim had been truer than it was yesterday evening!'

Amelia looked down the length of the dining table at Gideon Grayson, very aware of Watkins, the butler, standing silently near the door. 'Nothing so violent, I assure you, My Lord.'

'No?' He quirked a dark and disbelieving brow, looking very handsome in his black evening clothes.

It was true that when Amelia had reached her bedchamber earlier she had been so angry she had not known whether to throw something or simply to sit down and cry. In the end she had done neither of those things, but had instead paced her bedchamber as she tried to understand why it was she was feeling those contradictory emotions.

A Season in London, being introduced into Society and attending balls and parties in beautiful new gowns was surely every young woman's dream? It had certainly been one of Amelia's fantasies when she was growing up in Devonshire and had heard of the balls and pleasures to be had in London. But it was something as the daughter of a mere soldier and the disinherited daughter of a squire Amelia had known would only ever be that to her. A fantasy.

Amelia knew she should have been thrilled at Lord Grayson's suggestion of taking her to London in the spring—aquiver with joy at the thought of buying new gowns in which to attend all those balls and parties, meeting and flirting with the ridiculously handsome men of the ton.

Instead Amelia felt angry. Disappointed. Hurt.

It was that latter emotion that troubled Amelia the most. And as to the reason *why* she felt so hurt at Gideon Grayson's obvious effort to do what he believed was best for her…?

One look at his arrogantly handsome face before dinner, at how elegant he looked in his dark evening clothes, and Amelia had realised exactly why it was she felt the way she did. A London Season held no interest for her because she was *already* more than halfway in love with a ridiculously handsome man of the ton—with Gideon Grayson himself!

'No,' she assured him huskily now. 'I may be a soldier's daughter, My Lord, but I do not believe I have any real tendency towards violence.'

Gray eyed her sceptically. 'Indeed? Then perhaps you made me the exception!'

A delicate blush heightened her cheeks, but her gaze remained very direct as she answered him. 'Undoubtedly.'

Gray could not help but chuckle at the complete lack of apology in her tone. In truth, he was relieved that Amelia was at least talking to him once again; the first two courses of their dinner had been eaten in complete and awkward silence. 'No matter what you may choose to believe, Amelia, you obviously have the makings of a bloodthirsty little baggage!' He raised his wine glass in a toast to her before taking an appreciative sip.

An excellent wine, served to him by an attentive butler. And Watkins and two footmen had also served the delicious meal prepared for them this evening by Mrs Burdock. In fact, Gray noted with satisfaction, the household had been returned to at least a manageable state in just one day.

Now if only he could persuade Amelia into being as amenable…!

She looked very beautiful, in a gown of cream silk that left her throat and the swell of her breasts bare above an overlay of cream lace, making her skin appear the colour of ivory, her eyes bluer, and her mouth a perfect red bow. Her hair was dressed more elaborately this evening, too. A cascade of blonde curls was swept back from her face to fall enticingly against her nape and about the delicate shells of her ears and her temples.

Indeed, looking at her now from between narrowed lids, Gray could not help but appreciate how utterly and deliciously desirable Amelia appeared as she faced him down the length of the dining table…

'I have not enquired concerning your—injury this evening, My Lord.' Amelia had noticed, however, that his left arm appeared to be a little stiffer than the right. 'It is healing well, I hope?'

His mouth firmed. 'No doubt it will.'

Her brows rose at what she was certain was an evasive reply. 'But you do not know…?'

He scowled darkly. 'I said it would, Amelia!'

'Has the dressing been changed since yesterday evening?' she persisted.

'I assure you that I am perfectly well, Amelia.' He gaze was a frosty warning against pursuing the subject.

A warning Amelia chose to ignore. 'You do not appear so to me, My Lord. You are pale, and your left arm seems to be a little…uncomfortable.'

He gave a dismissive shake of his head. 'If my arm aches a little this evening then it is probably because I overtaxed it by riding for so long today.'

'Perhaps I should see for myself—'

Those grey eyes glittered. 'Amelia—'

'Did you allow your valet to at least redress it today?'

'Damn it, Amelia—'

'Would you leave us, please, Watkins?' Amelia turned to smile graciously at the butler. Having only secured his return a few hours ago, she did not think Gideon would appreciate having the butler leave again because he had taken offence at her tone! Besides, it was Gideon she was cross with, not Watkins. 'I will ring when you are needed again,' she assured the older man warmly, waiting as he had vacated the room and closed the door softly behind him before she placed her napkin upon the table and stood up.

'Amelia—'

'My Lord?' She deliberately held Gideon Grayson's gaze with her own as she walked slowly down the length of the room.

A nerve pulsed in his tightly clenched jaw as he watched her approach through narrowed lids. 'I swear, Amelia, if you do not stop "My Lording" me in that superior tone—'

'Shall I return to calling you Gideon, then?' she murmured throatily as she halted beside him.

Gideon would not do, either!

Gray wished that Amelia were not standing quite so close beside his chair. So close, in fact, that he was once again assailed with that perfume that was uniquely Amelia: elusively floral and utterly feminine! So close that he could see the rapidly beating pulse at the base of her throat. So close that the ivory swell of her breasts was on a level only inches away from his narrowed gaze.

So close that just her proximity caused his body to stir!

'You will need to once again remove your jacket, waistcoat and shirt, Gideon,' she prompted.

Dear Lord…!

How much was a man expected to stand? Gray wondered achingly. To resist? And he must surely resist where Amelia of all women was concerned…!

'I have absolutely no intention— What do you think you are doing?' He turned to look at Amelia as she moved to the back of his chair and placed her hands upon the collar of his jacket.

She raised challenging brows. 'Helping you, of course.'

'Damn it, Amelia—'

'You should not swear so often, Gideon.' She tutted reprovingly.

'Your stubbornness is enough to make even a saint swear, Amelia,' he assured her through gritted teeth, and he resisted her efforts to tug the tightly tailored jacket back over his shoulders despite the added discomfort it gave to his aching arm.

She gave him an exasperated look. 'And those scars upon your chest and back attest to your never having been *that*!'

Gray stilled at this reminder that Amelia had seen his scars the evening before. Honourable scars, if she did but know it, from injuries he had received during his years of working secretly for the crown. Years when Gray had necessarily allowed all who knew him—including his brother Perry and his family—to believe he was something of a rake and a wastrel who preferred not to involve himself in the messy business of war. No wonder, then, that Amelia had twice now referred to those scars as having been gained dishonourably rather than honourably...

'Your waistcoat and shirt now, if you please,' Amelia murmured with satisfaction, having taken advantage of Gideon Grayson's brief distraction of thought to pull the jacket ably down his arms before removing it altogether.

'I have no intention of taking off any more of my clothing in your presence—Amelia, cease this instant!' He raised his voice as she moved to stand in front of him and deftly began to unfasten his waistcoat.

Amelia ceased. Not because Gideon had instructed her to, but because of a sudden awareness of the tension that emanated from him; his jaw was set grimly, eyes blazing darkly, and his hands were clenched into fists until the knuckles showed white as they rested on his muscled thighs.

She moistened her lips with the tip of her tongue. 'I am only trying to help, Gideon...'

He breathed deeply as he continued to glare at her, that nerve pulsing rapidly now in his tightly clenched jaw. 'What you are doing, Amelia, is playing with fire,' he warned her harshly.

Amelia could barely breathe as she looked searchingly into that arrogantly handsome face. At the way the unhealthy pallor of Gideon's skin gave his eyes a dark and dangerous appeal as they blazed up at her. At the grim set of his jaw and those sculptured and sensuous lips.

She began to tremble, to shake at how desperately she wanted to feel those lips against—devouring!—her own...

'Do *not*, Amelia!' Gray groaned as she stepped between his

parted thighs and even the light brush of her gown became an unbearable torment against his ultra-sensitive erection.

'Do not what, Gideon…?' She placed her gloved hands on his shoulders beneath the silk of his waistcoat.

A touch that instantly burned, seared through the thin material of Gray's shirt. Making him long for there to be no barrier at all between Amelia's hands and the bareness of his chest.

She easily held his gaze with hers as she stepped closer still, the warmth of her legs a delicious torment now as they pressed softly against the inside of Gray's thighs, causing him to become harder still.

Gray had been in one state of arousal or another since first setting eyes on this beautiful and desirable woman. Physical. Emotional. Temporal. Amelia—with her courage, her honesty, her undeniable beauty—challenged him on each and every one of those levels.

He closed his eyes briefly before looking up again. 'If you do not step away now, Amelia, I cannot be responsible for what happens next!'

Instead of doing as he asked, Amelia smiled. Slowly. Invitingly. The softness of her lips parting slightly as she moved so that the fullness of her lips were now mere inches away from Gray's own.

'Do not say I did not warn you…!' Gray gave a brief, self-disgusted shake of his head even as his hands moved to fasten tightly about the slenderness of Amelia's waist to pull her in tightly against him, so making her completely aware of the fullness of his erection.

Her eyes widened slightly as that arousal pressed revealingly against her, before her tongue once again moved moistly across those red and parted lips. 'I promise to say nothing at all, Gideon, if you will only kiss me…!' she invited breathlessly.

It was too much—Amelia herself was too much!—and with a low groan Gray moved the short distance that separated them and claimed her mouth with his own.

Amelia gave a deep and satisfied sigh in her throat, and her fingers clasped tightly onto Gray's shoulders even as her lips parted beneath his. It was an invitation Gray readily accepted as he deepened the kiss.

She tasted of warmth and honey. Unlike anything Gray had ever tasted before. A taste as unique as Amelia was herself, and just as addictive…!

Gray drank of her hungrily, deeply, as he crushed her breasts against him, running his tongue lightly across her lips in warning before venturing inside the heat of her mouth. Her tongue met his shyly, gently duelling, before ceding to his dominance. Gray's tongue surged inside, taking, claiming, in deep and rhythmic thrusts that matched the deep and aching throb of his thighs pressed so intimately against her.

As Gray had known would happen, he wanted more. Wanted to feel the silkiness of Amelia's skin beneath his hands, to see and touch the ivory softness of her breasts.

Even as he continued to kiss her his hands were busy with the tiny buttons at the back of her gown. One. Two. Three. Until her gown was unbuttoned halfway down her back. A shift in position, an easing away, and Amelia's gown fell gently down to her waist.

Gray dragged his mouth from hers, placing kisses upon her neck, her throat, before raising his head to look at the fullness of Amelia's breasts revealed beneath the thin material of her chemise. His hands moved up instinctively to cup beneath those orbs. Her breasts seemed fuller tonight, heavier, and the nipples were already hard beneath her chemise.

A light tug of that material revealed those breasts in their full glory, allowing Gray to gaze upon her nipples, his breathing becoming ragged as he looked on their fullness and likened them to the colour and ripeness of raspberries.

And Gray was fond—very fond—of raspberries…

Amelia knew she should be shocked, possibly outraged, at the things Gideon was doing to her. But instead she had been thrilled to her core when he had kissed her. Had trembled with anticipation when her dress fell down about her waist. And now she could only gasp in pleasure as his lips closed about the bareness of her breast as he drew the aching tip deep inside the heat of his mouth.

Her hands moved instinctively to cup the back of his head, to hold him to her. She entangled her fingers in the darkness of his hair as he feasted upon her, first suckling, then gently biting, before rasping his tongue across her sensitive flesh and suckled her again, whilst all the time his hand caressed the rosy tip of her other breast.

Pleasure such as Amelia had never known, never guessed at, coursed through her body. Her arms tensed, her back arched, and a fire seemed to burn in the pit of her belly. An aching heat, a need she did not completely understand but knew well enough that only Gideon could assuage.

'Gideon—I need…!' she groaned.

Gray was reluctant to relinquish the honey taste of her breast, lingering to bite gently before slowly raising his head to look at her. 'What do you need?' he encouraged hoarsely.

Amelia's cheeks were flushed, her eyes a wild, deep blue. 'I do not know!' She shook her head. 'I ache, Gideon. *Here.*' She took one of his hands in hers and moved it lower, cupping the heat between her legs.

Her gown was so thin and silky that Gray could feel her curls as he cupped her there, pressing his palm gently against her in a slow, rhythmic caress.

'Gideon…?'

'Feel, Amelia,' he encouraged throatily, and his hand left her briefly to move beneath the hem of her gown and travel the silky length of her legs, seeking and finding her most sensitive spot before caressing it rhythmically.

Gray drew her nipple back into the heat of his mouth as he heard her gasps of pleasure, the rhythm of his hand matching the movement of his mouth on her breast.

'Open your legs for me!' Gray encouraged hungrily, groaning low in his throat as she did so, opening herself to him as he continued to caress her.

Amelia cried out as pleasure such as she had never imagined ripped through her body in wave after surging wave. She felt the long slow thrust of Gideon's finger inside her. Clinging weakly to his shoulders, she moved instinctively with him until she was so sensitised to the pleasure she could no longer bear it.

Amelia allowed her damp forehead to drop down weakly onto one of Gideon's muscled shoulders as he moved his hand away from her. Only the sound of their erratic breathing now filled the otherwise silence. Low, throaty gasps on Amelia's part, as tiny ripples of pleasure continued to consume her. Loud and hoarse on Gideon's as he—

As he what? Amelia wondered sinkingly. She had allowed Gideon to touch her with an intimacy that made her blush to think about it. And what had Amelia given him in return?

She could feel the hard warmth of his thighs still pressed against her, knew that Gideon had not reached that same earth-shattering release as she. Her inexperience in such matters, her lack of knowledge, gave Amelia no indication as to how she might achieve that. What did a woman do? How did she progress in pleasuring a man? Perhaps if she were to touch him as he had touched her—

'No, Amelia!' Gideon's voice rasped harshly in the tense silence as she reached down between his thighs, his fingers biting painfully into the flesh of her upper arms as he put her firmly away from him.

Amelia was trembling, shaking as she looked down at the blaze of fury in that hard and arrogantly handsome face. Gideon's eyes were a glittering black, his cheekbones standing out in the raw savagery of his face, his mouth a thin and angry line above a tense and clenched jaw. 'Gideon—'

'Not a word, Amelia!' He turned her firmly, to readjust and refasten her gown. 'There is nothing you can say—no justification for what just happened,' he bit out in disgust as he stood up abruptly.

'But—'

'I should never have come here.' Gideon looked down at her coldly. 'Never have—' He gave a tense shake of his head. 'It was my original intention to spend only two days at Steadley Manor before travelling into Gloucestershire to spend Christmas with friends. I had thought, after I arrived here, to change those plans. But I think it better, in light of what has just happened, if I proceed with my original plan.'

Amelia's heart sank. 'You are leaving…?'

His eyes narrowed. 'First thing in the morning.'

She swallowed hard as she blinked back the tears that were threatening to fall. Knowing that there was nothing she could say, nothing she could do, when Gideon was so disgusted, so shocked by her behaviour, that he could barely stand to look at her, let alone spend any more time in her company.

Chapter Eight

⧼⧼⧼⧽⧽⧽

In the event, it was much later than first thing before Gray was able to take his leave of Steadley Manor the following day.

Aware of the need to stay completely away from the vicinity of Amelia's bedchamber, Gray had instead waited downstairs for her to appear in the breakfast parlour. When eight o'clock and then nine o'clock passed, without any sign of her, Gray was forced into sending one of the maids upstairs with a request for Amelia to join him immediately.

Her reluctance to be anywhere near him was made more than obvious when she appeared a few minutes later, pale and beautiful where she lingered in the doorway, as if half prepared for flight.

Gray tightened his mouth at the reason for her reluctance, knowing he should not have kissed Amelia the previous evening, let alone touched her as intimately as he had. No doubt he had frightened her out of her wits with the intensity of his passion, he acknowledged.

He thrust his hands behind his back. 'I have been waiting to leave these past two hours, Amelia.'

The same two hours, probably, Amelia realised, during which she had been crying as if her heart would break. As she had cried long and hard the previous night. Hot, shameful tears that had left their mark this morning in the dark and bruised look to her eyes and the deathly pallor of her face.

She had not wanted to see Gideon again before he left. Had not wanted to see the coldness in his eyes when he looked at her. To know, to feel the disgust he must now feel towards her. It was too cruel of him to demand that she be present now, when he departed for Gloucestershire.

Her chin rose proudly. 'I am sure that you and I have nothing left to say to each other, Gideon.' She met that narrowed and cold gaze unflinchingly as she defiantly continued to call him by the name she always had.

'If that is your wish,' he finally allowed remotely. 'Right now my only concern is how soon I can expect you to be ready to leave.'

Amelia gaped at him. 'Leave for where…?'

Gray eyed her impatiently. The situation between the two of them was difficult enough, his temper already frayed from waiting overlong for Amelia to come downstairs, without his having to repeat himself. 'I am sure that I told you I intended to start our journey to Gloucestershire first thing this morning?'

She shook her head, her golden curls tightly confined this morning, held in place by a ribbon the same golden-brown as her long-sleeved gown. 'You made no mention of my accompanying you.'

'Well, of *course* you will accompany me!' He snapped his impatience. 'What sort of monster do you think I am, Amelia, that you imagine I would leave you alone here over Christmas?'

Unfortunately Gray already knew the answer to that question. As he knew the reason why Amelia was so reluctant to be anywhere in his vicinity this morning. It was a reluctance that was perfectly justified when Gray knew he only had to look upon Amelia's loveliness to want to make love to her all over again.

Damn it to hell!

'Well?' he demanded.

Amelia looked across at him, a puzzled frown between the deep blue of her eyes. 'I do not understand. You said you were going to stay with friends. Surely those friends will not want an unknown woman foisted upon them? Especially at this time of year…?'

He gave a hard and humourless smile. 'I have no doubt the St Claire family will welcome you with open arms! Besides, you are my ward,' he added bitterly.

Amelia shook her head. 'But—I do not know the St Claire family. I have no gifts for any of them.'

'I have gifts for them,' he drawled. 'You are my ward, Amelia, and as such the gifts will come from both of us,' he added impatiently as she still frowned.

Much as Gray might not have liked Alice Wycliffe's suggestion that he take Amelia with him to Mulberry Hall for Christmas, as reluctant as Gray still felt to introduce her to the St Claire family, with their arrogant disregard for the unwritten rules of Society, he knew that he no longer had a choice. He could not stay alone here with Amelia any longer—just as he could not just depart for Gloucestershire in the knowledge that he was abandoning Amelia to spending Christmas alone at Steadley Manor.

As much as Gray knew he should keep his distance from her, he simply could no longer even bear the thought of leaving Amelia alone here…

If Amelia had thought, hoped, that three days of travelling across the country into Gloucestershire would allow herself and Gideon to reach at least the same amount of understanding as had existed between them before those intimacies had taken place between them, then she was to be disappointed.

Two coaches travelled into Gloucestershire: one bearing Amelia and the maid who had been chosen to accompany her, and the second carrying Gideon and his valet. The trunks containing the clothing they would need for an extended stay were divided between the two carriages.

Their two overnight stays at coaching inns were equally as lacking in private conversation between them, as on both evenings Gideon ate his meal in silence before leaving Amelia to the attentions of her maid by retiring early to his bedchamber.

So it was that by the time the two coaches turned into the gates of Mulberry Hall, late on the third afternoon, relations between Amelia and Gideon were still tense and unresolved. Unless, that was, one accepted that this coldness, the remoteness that now existed between them, was how their relationship was to be in the future…

The driveway to the house itself seemed never-ending, and Amelia's eyes widened once the coach had come to a stop and she stepped out to look up at Mulberry Hall itself. It was a veritable mansion, huge and at least four floors high, with extra wings having been built onto the east and west walls.

'How beautiful!' she gasped breathlessly. 'You did not tell me we were coming somewhere so—so magnificent, Gideon.' She turned to him reprovingly as he alighted from his own carriage.

Gray gave a derisive smile as he moved to Amelia's side and took a firm hold of her arm. 'No doubt you will find the St Claire family equally as magnificent. The Duke of Stourbridge can be especially—imposing,' he acknowledged with a grimace. And he intended having a conversation with Hawk St Claire at that gentleman's earliest convenience. A conversation during which Gray would no doubt learn—and deserve—exactly how imposing the Duke of Stourbridge could be…

Amelia's response was to clasp her cloak more tightly about her. 'A duke?' She shook her head, her eyes wide. 'You did not say— You should not have brought me here, Gideon—'

'What else was I to do with you?' Gray eyed her exasperatedly.

Amelia's chin rose defiantly. 'I have lived at Steadley Manor without the company of family or friends for some two and a half years; I have no doubts I could have continued to do so for another Christmas!'

Gray gave an impatient nod. 'No doubt you could. I, on the other hand, decided otherwise.'

Her cheeks flushed. 'You—'

'Could you save any more arguments for later, Amelia?' Gray rasped grimly as the front doors of Mulberry Hall were thrown open and the St Claire family began to emerge—the three St Claire brothers and their wives, their sister Arabella and her husband Darius Wynter, and aunts, uncles and cousins too numerous to mention. 'Or, alternatively, forget them completely!' he added with hard dismissal as he turned to greet their hosts.

The cutting reply Amelia had been about to make remained unspoken on her lips as she stared up at the imposing body of people coming down the steps to greet them. Well…to greet Gideon; the St Claire family had not even known of her presence until now.

Amelia was sure she had never seen such handsome men as the three St Claire brothers and the blond-haired Adonis who accompanied them down the steps. The haughty and aristocratic Hawk nevertheless gave her a charming smile when they were introduced, and the darkly brooding Lucian gallantly kissed her hand. The rakishly handsome Sebastian St Claire stood on no such ceremony, but pulled her into a friendly hug, and the man who had the appearance of a Greek god—Darius Wynter, the Duke of Carlyne and husband to Arabella—kissed her warmly on both cheeks.

The wives of these overwhelming handsome men were, as might be expected, all as beautiful as their husbands were handsome, from the tall and stately redhaired Duchess and the mischievous dark-haired beauty who was married to the brooding Lucian, to the serenely lovely Juliet, wife of the rakish Sebastian. But Arabella, Duchess of Carlyne, a young woman who appeared to be of a similar age to Amelia herself, was without doubt the loveliest of them all, with her gold and molasses curls and impish dark eyes.

Within minutes Amelia felt totally overwhelmed at being surrounded by so many handsome men and such beautiful women.

'No doubt you will wish to freshen up before joining us for tea,' Jane, Duchess of Stourbridge, remarked kindly once they had all finally entered the magnificent marble entrance hall.

'May I be allowed to escort Amelia to her bedchamber, Jane?'

Arabella proposed warmly as she appeared at Amelia's other side. 'The Blue Suite, do you think…?'

'Of course.' The Duchess affectionately gave her permission.

'I am not sure…' Amelia turned in search of Gideon, and saw him standing a short distance away, talking softly—and obviously privately—in conversation with Hawk St Claire.

Gray sensed rather than saw Amelia's slightly bewildered gaze upon him. As he had been aware of everything about her these past three days as they had travelled through the snow covered countryside to Mulberry Hall. Most especially the pallor that remained in Amelia's cheeks. The guarded expression in her eyes now whenever she looked at him beneath those silky long lashes. Her complete silence unless he deliberately engaged her in conversation.

All of them, Gray knew, were caused by his unbridled—frightening?—show of passion three evenings ago.

Dear Lord, Amelia was aged but nineteen years—a protected and innocent nineteen years—whereas Gray was eight and twenty, with a wealth of experience behind him both in and out of the bedchamber. His actions three evenings ago, the intimacies he had subjected Amelia to, must have scared her witless!

He excused himself to Hawk St Claire before striding over to Amelia's side. 'Is something wrong, Amelia?' he asked softly.

'No. I—'

'I believe Amelia only wished to make you aware that I am taking her upstairs to her bedchamber,' the feisty and beautiful Arabella teased.

Gray was not sure that allowing Amelia to become too well acquainted with the self-willed and forthright Arabella Wynter was in his best interests, but in the circumstances he had little choice in the matter. Especially as Amelia herself appeared to have nothing to say on the subject. 'Yes, by all means go upstairs with Her Grace, Amelia.' He scowled his impatience with her inability to even look him in the eye. 'The Duke and I have some business that we need to discuss,' he muttered distractedly, before striding off to talk to Hawk St Claire in his study.

Just as if she were his dog or his horse, to be dismissed and then forgotten, Amelia inwardly fumed as she glared after Gideon's retreating back. Or perhaps not… If Amelia had learnt anything this past three days then it was that Gideon took a far greater interest in the comfort of his horses than he did her own!

'Men can be so impossibly boorish when in the company of other men, can they not…?'

Amelia turned her attention back to the patiently waiting Arabella Wynter, Duchess of Carlyne. 'I am sorry, Your Grace. I have no idea—'

'You shall call me Arabella, as I intend to call *you* Amelia,' the other woman announced imperiously. 'And you know very well what I meant,' she continued, her arm still tucked warmly into Amelia's as the two of them began to ascend the wide staircase. 'My darling Darius is perfectly manageable when the two of us are alone together, but once he is in the company of any or all of my brothers he seems to feel that he has to demonstrate how capably he manages me. When, in reality, it is the other way around!' Arabella gave an unladylike snort.

Amelia had trouble envisaging the golden godlike creature who was Arabella's husband as ever being in the least manageable!

'I insist you tell me everything, Amelia!' Arabella's eyes lit up conspiratorially. 'Gray has made absolutely no mention of a ward until today…'

Amelia's explanation as to how she had come to be Gideon's ward was made in as few words as possible, by which time the two women had arrived at and entered a beautiful bedchamber decorated predominantly in blue with touches of gold—exactly Amelia's own colouring.

'How beautiful.' She looked about her raptly. 'I—'

'Do not change the subject, Amelia!' Arabella laughed reprovingly. 'I absolutely refuse to allow you to leave me with so little information to relate to my sisters-in-law when I return downstairs. You know, of course, that Gray is our guest of honour?'

Amelia's eyes widened. 'He did not say…'

Arabella gave another of those inelegant snorts as she dropped down upon the bed. 'He is a man—his sense of pride would not allow him to do so!' She patted the bed beside her invitingly. 'Gray is my hero. He is the whole family's hero! And we shall be forever in his debt,' she added softly.

Amelia sat down abruptly, more bewildered than ever. 'That does not seem to fit with the stories I have heard of his behaviour in Town...'

'A word of advice, dear Amelia.' The other woman patted her lightly on the hand. 'Ignore whatever gossip you may have heard about him. Especially gossip that has been deliberately nurtured by the man himself,' she added enigmatically. 'I am not allowed to relate all the details, because I do not wish to hurt the feelings of innocents, but several weeks ago a madman attempted to take my life—and would have done so, I am sure, if Gray had not shot him dead first.' Those beautiful brown eyes glowed with satisfaction.

'Gideon shot a man dead...?' she repeated faintly.

Arabella's smile widened. 'It is all perfectly true, I do assure you, Amelia.'

She shook her head. 'I did not doubt your word—it is only... As I have already told you, Lord Grayson and I have not been acquainted for very long—only a matter of days.' Though it seemed so much longer to Amelia. It seemed, in fact, as if she had known Gideon all her life. 'But on the night we met I am afraid that it was I who shot *him*!'

Arabella Wynter sat back in surprise. 'Truly?'

'Truly.' Amelia nodded miserably.

Arabella's attempts to hold back a smile totally failed her as first she smiled, and then chuckled, before bursting into joyful unrestrained laughter. 'How wonderful! How truly wonderful!' She continued to chuckle, her brown eyes aglow with merriment. 'I believe, Amelia, that you and I are going to be the best of friends!'

Amelia saw absolutely nothing to laugh about. In fact she was totally bewildered.

Arabella Wynter's advice to her was to dismiss any gossip she might have heard of Gideon. The other woman had described him as a hero. As the man who had saved her life.

Amelia felt as if she understood Gideon even less than she had previously...

'You and I need to have a private talk as soon as dinner is over, Amelia!' Gray took a firm hold of his ward's arm in order to escort her into the dining room as she reached the bottom of the staircase, wearing a silk and lace gown the same blue as her eyes, and a single strand of pearls about her throat.

She looked up at him from beneath lowered lashes. 'A private talk concerning what, Gideon?'

Gray had joined the other gentlemen in the library several minutes ago, with the intention of enjoying a relaxing drink before joining the ladies for dinner. After the awkwardness of his earlier conversation with Hawk St Claire he had felt as if he could drink a whole decanter of spirits and not even notice!

It had not taken Gray long, however, to realise that his friend Sebastian, his two brothers, and the dashing Darius Wynter all seemed to be sharing a joke at his expense.

He had wondered at first if perhaps Stourbridge had revealed the details of their earlier conversation, but one look at that austerely handsome face had reassured him that Hawk was not a man who broke his word. And the Duke had given Gray his assurances earlier that their conversation would remain private between the two of them.

Which only left the impishly troublesome Arabella Wynter as the possible source of the joke...

'It is enough, Amelia, to say that I wish a few minutes of your time as soon as is convenient after dinner.' Gray glowered down at her impatiently.

She gave a gracious inclination of her head. 'How fortuitous, when I wish for a few minutes of your *own* time "as soon as is convenient after dinner"!'

Amelia had spent several hours alone in her bedchamber before it had been time to change for dinner. Time in which to go over that earlier conversation with Arabella Wynter.

To question as to why Gideon had allowed her to continue believing the gossip she had heard about him.

To wonder once again, in light of what Arabella had told her of Gideon's having shot another man in defence of her life, exactly how he had come by those scars upon his chest and back...

Chapter Nine

Gray's mood had not improved in the slightest by the time he and Amelia were at last able to slip away to the warmth of the heated conservatory, whilst the men enjoyed their brandy and cigars in the library and the ladies retired to the drawing room.

How could it, when Gray had spent the past three hours watching as Amelia had been flattered and flirted with by several other men invited to the St Claire Christmas festivities? Jeremy Croft, son and heir of a neighbouring estate, for one. And several of the male St Claire cousins. Even the Earl of Whitney, Jane St Claire's charming widowed father, had shown Amelia some marked attention.

Gray, seated as far down the long dining table from Amelia as possible for him to be, had been forced to watch in brooding displeasure as she had obviously enjoyed those attentions. And why should she not? Was it not for this very reason that Gray had suggested giving Amelia a London Season? So that she might meet other men and enjoy their attentions?

Perhaps it was—Gray had just not realised at the time how much he was going to detest having to sit back and watch!

Several candles had been lit in the conservatory for those guests who wished to escape there for either peace or privacy from the festivities, and Gray now found himself glowering down at Amelia as she perched primly on the edge of one of several cushioned wicker garden chairs. 'You appear to be enjoying yourself…?'

She gave a slight inclination of her head. 'Everyone has been very kind.'

Gray's eyes narrowed. 'Implying I have not?'

'Implying whatever you wish it to imply,' Amelia came back tartly.

It did not take too much intelligence on Amelia's part to know that Gideon was spoiling for a fight. He had been glaring at her for most of the evening, and he had made their excuses to the Duchess as soon as it had been polite to do so before dragging Amelia off to the quiet solitude of this conservatory. A place, presumably, where he might talk to her in private.

His eyes glittered silver between those narrowed lids. 'You have only been here a matter of hours, Amelia—it usually takes much longer for the St Claires to incite the same outspokenness in their guests as they themselves possess!'

Amelia laughed softly. 'They are truly wonderful, are they not?'

'Wonderful is not a word I have ever before heard associated with the St Claire family!' Gideon grimaced.

'Well, you have heard it now,' Amelia assured him primly. 'I like them all very much. Arabella is especially engaging,' she added softly as she watched him from beneath lowered lids. Gideon appeared as arrogant and imposing as the St Claire brothers, in his dark evening clothes and snowy white linen.

'Yes…Arabella…' He paused, his jaw tight. 'Did you happen to mention, during your earlier conversation with her, the way in which the two of us met?'

Ah. Amelia had only realised after Arabella Wynter had left her rooms earlier this afternoon that she had not extracted the other woman's promise not to mention the shooting incident to anyone else. An oversight on her part, it would appear, that Gideon was now also aware of…

Her chin rose challengingly. 'I do not understand your—displeasure, considering I am the one who was at fault for shooting you.'

No, Gray did not suppose that she did. Amelia could have absolutely no idea of the teasing that he, an agent of the crown who had in the past survived several attempts upon his life, was going to suffer at the sarcastic tongues of Darius Wynter and Sebastian especially for allowing a woman to pink him.

'It did not occur to you that perhaps the incident might have been better kept to ourselves?'

'Not in the circumstances the conversation came about, no.' She continued to face him challengingly. 'Arabella had just finished telling me how you had saved her life several weeks ago. How you have become a hero in her own and her family's eyes.'

Gray's mouth tightened at the young Duchess's indiscretion in having revealed even that much. 'And reciprocating by confiding how you had shot me seemed like a natural response to that disclosure?'

'No, of course it did not!' Amelia stood up impatiently, those beautiful blue eyes snapping with anger. 'You have deceived me and lied to me, Gideon. As I believe you deceived and lied to your own brother before he died. In other words, sir, you are not at all what you seem!'

Gray's breath caught in his throat at Amelia's astuteness. At her ability, armed with so little information, to see through the charade his life had necessarily been these past seven or eight years. 'You are talking nonsense, Amelia—'

'No, Gideon, you are once again attempting to deceive. And I will no longer be deceived.' She gathered up her gown before turning. 'I have been pleased these last few days to see that your arm has obviously improved, but I have no wish to talk with you again—on any subject—until you are willing to tell me the truth!'

With a swish of her skirts she turned on her heel and marched proudly from the room.

Leaving Gideon to stand alone and frustrated in the conservatory…

* * *

'You seem somewhat sad this evening, Amelia.'

Amelia looked up to smile at Lady Grace, the self-confident and dark-haired wife of Lucian St Claire, as she paused to speak with her once the ladies had retired to the drawing room the following evening after another sumptuous dinner. 'I am probably tired,' she excused. 'It has been a busy day.'

'But an enjoyable one, I hope?' the other woman prompted softly as she sat down beside Amelia on the chaise.

'Oh, yes.' It was the eve before Christmas, and first thing this morning Jane, Duchess of Stourbridge, had gathered all the ladies in the house to help her in delivering baskets of food and presents for all those on the estate. Something she had apparently begun upon her marriage to the Duke almost two years ago, claiming that the tenants and their children would appreciate the food and gifts more before Christmas rather than after it.

Seeing the adults' pleasure, and the excitement on the faces of the children as they received this largesse, Amelia could not help but agree with the Duchess.

She had also spent an enjoyable hour before dinner in the nursery, not only with Jane St Claire, but the recently arrived Alice Wycliffe, Countess of Stanford, and Arabella's sister-in-law, Margaret, Dowager Duchess of Carlyne. The older woman had no living children of her own to provide her with grandchildren, but she obviously doted on Alexander, the six-month-old Marquess of Mulberry. And, being pregnant herself, Alice Wycliffe had obviously enjoyed being around such a beautiful baby as Alexander.

Amelia had also learnt, as she drank tea with Alice Wycliffe, that it was she and her husband whom Gideon had visited the day after his arrival at Steadley Manor. And that it was Alice Wycliffe who had suggested to Gideon, during that visit, that Amelia might enjoy a Season in London.

It had altogether been an enlightening as well as a busy day for Amelia.

But a day when she had seen nothing of Gideon...

He and the other gentlemen had been busy cutting down and

bringing in holly, mistletoe and boughs covered with berries, so that the house was now filled with their beauty and festive perfume. A bittersweet reminder to Amelia that tomorrow was Christmas Day.

'You know, Amelia—you do not mind if I continue to call you Amelia…?'

'Not at all,' she assured her warmly; indeed she had become on first-name terms with all the female guests as they had rushed and bustled together throughout the day.

'I do not profess to be knowledgeable when it comes to men—'

'Oh, please—'

'To be fair, Lucian is the only man I have ever desired to know really well,' Grace continued, with obvious affection for her broodingly remote husband. 'But I am sure that Lord Grayson has his dark side, too.'

'I— Yes. Perhaps…' Amelia was deeply uncomfortable with this conversation.

'On the outside arrogant, and at times remote.' Grace nodded. 'But underneath a man of deep honour and loyalty.'

Amelia grimaced. 'I do not believe that Gideon would appreciate our discussing him in this way.' She was all too aware of his displeasure concerning what he had obviously considered her indiscretion in speaking of her own rash behaviour five days ago, and Arabella's in discussing the events of a few weeks ago.

Grace tilted her head quizzically. 'You call him Gideon?'

She could feel the colour warming her cheeks. 'He would prefer that I did not.'

The other woman nodded. 'But he has not forbidden you to do so?'

'Not forbidden, no.' Amelia gave a rueful shake of her head.

Grace smiled briefly. 'My husband tells me that Lord Grayson has allowed no one to call him by his given name since his older brother Perry—your stepfather—was killed at Waterloo.'

'I did not know that.' Amelia swallowed hard. 'I have made so many mistakes, it would seem.' She sighed, disheartened.

'I believe I might go to bed now—if you think no one will mind?'

'I am sure they will not. But you yourself might have cause to regret it…'

She frowned. 'Why so?'

Grace rested her hand gently upon Amelia's. 'I noticed that Lord Grayson did not seem inclined for company this evening, either. He left the house as soon as we had finished eating,' she explained, at Amelia's questioning look. 'I believe he walked in the direction of the boathouse. Without his hat or a coat.' She glanced out of the huge picture window. 'It has started to snow again, so perhaps you should take them to him?'

Amelia gave the other woman a puzzled frown. 'Why are you telling me these things…?'

Grace laughed softly. 'Because tomorrow is Christmas, my dear Amelia, and no one should look as unhappy at Christmastime as you and Lord Grayson have looked this evening!'

Amelia grimaced. 'I know Gideon is unhappy with me—'

'It is himself he is unhappy with, not you,' Grace assured her softly. 'Several weeks ago Lord Grayson did this family a great service, for which we are all very grateful. Knowing the St Claire men as I do, I am sure that Gray has not confided those events to you?'

Amelia frowned. 'Gideon is not a St Claire…'

'He is now,' the other woman said with certainty. 'As much a brother to Hawk, Lucian, Sebastian and Darius as any of them are to each other.' She stood up, a slight and regally graceful figure. 'Lord Grayson believes himself committed to silence on a certain subject. I am sure that I speak for all the St Claire family when I urge you to tell him we release him from any such commitment.'

Amelia shook her head. 'I really do not think—'

'I have found that sometimes it is better to act than to think, Amelia,' Grace urged firmly. 'Pride is all very well, my dear, but it will not keep you warm on a snowy winter's night.' She gave a husky laugh. 'And there is a warm and comfortable loft above the boathouse…' she added softly, before turning to walk gracefully across the room to help Jane serve cups of tea to the other ladies.

Leaving Amelia with many more questions in need of an answer...

Gray stood in the shelter of the boathouse, looking out across the lake. The edges of that lake were frozen, and already covered in the snow that was once again gently falling. Not that Gray saw any of the beauty of that bright moonlit scene before him. His thoughts were all inward. Troubled and contradictory thoughts that only served to make him feel even more out of sorts than he was already.

He had been unhappy for days with the way he and Amelia had parted the other evening. He liked even less the strained silence that now existed between them. Not that he had seen very much of Amelia throughout his day; she had been as busy as he with other things. But he had heard her husky laughter several times, and known that she was at least enjoying herself. Perhaps Gray should be satisfied with that. After all—

'Gideon...?'

He turned sharply to see Amelia standing in the shadowed doorway of the boathouse, a cloak pulled up over her golden curls and about the slenderness of her body. 'What the devil are you doing here?' He frowned as he stepped forward into the boathouse. 'Come inside at once, out of the cold! Do you not know better than to walk outside in the snow wearing only that thin gown and cloak and those dainty slippers?'

She laughed ruefully. 'Which question would you like me to answer first? But before I do—I have brought you a coat and hat.' She held the two garments out to him almost shyly.

'Never mind those now.' Gray took the hat and coat and tossed them down onto an old rowboat that had been pulled out of the water and stored for the winter. 'Why are you not back at the house with the other ladies, enjoying the warmth of the fire and drinking tea?'

She looked up at him reprovingly. 'That is three questions

you have asked now, without letting me answer a single one of them!'

Gray could see her quite clearly in the moonlight, her skin appearing more ivory than ever, her eyes clear and sparkling. He reached out to clasp both her hands in his as he saw her give an involuntary shiver. 'There—I told you it was cold!' He frowned down at her. 'You must go back to the house immediately—'

'Will you return with me?'

To the confines of his bedchamber? Knowing that Amelia was somewhere in the house, as out of reach to him as that moon shining so brightly above them? 'No, I am not ready to return just yet,' Gray answered hardly.

'Then I will not go back, either.'

'Do not be so stubborn, Amelia—'

'*I* am stubborn?' She gazed up at him incredulously, her eyes blazing with temper now. 'I have been assured by not one but two of the St Claire ladies that you are far from the rakish gambler you allow Society to believe. Have been told that the St Claire family all consider you to be a member of their family—an honour I do not believe they would have bestowed lightly. I am also told that you are a man of great honour and loyalty. That, furthermore, you are a hero. And you—you do not even *attempt* to tell me any of these things yourself, but prefer that I continue to believe every bad thing I have ever heard about you! You—'

Her tirade was cut short by Gideon pulling her into his arms and bringing his mouth down firmly upon hers.

Amelia gave a choked cry as she returned the fierceness of his kiss, her arms up about Gideon's shoulders as she clung to him.

By the time they broke apart, long minutes later, Amelia was crying and laughing at the same time, as the emotions she had held in check all day threatened to overwhelm her. 'You— You— You *man*, you!' She frowned up at him exasperatedly.

Gray chuckled softly, his arms about her waist still as he refused to release her. 'Is that the worst insult you can level at me?'

'Probably not,' Amelia allowed with an attempt at sternness.

'But for the moment no doubt it will suffice. I insist that you tell me the truth, Gideon. *Now.*'

'You insist?' he repeated softly.

She nodded firmly. 'I do.'

Gray gave a rueful shake of his head. 'I knew that the St Claire women would be a bad influence on you!'

Amelia eyed him challengingly. 'I do not believe that any of them can claim to have shot the man they love on their very first meeting.'

'No, I— What did you say, Amelia?' Gray stared down at her incredulously.

Amelia gave a pained groan. 'I spoke out of turn.' She pulled out of his arms to turn away from him. 'Please forget that I—'

'Amelia, I have no inclination to forget, when I have loved you from the very moment you shot me!'

'Do not tease me—please, Gideon!' She huddled down in her cloak as she moved sharply away from him. 'I believe I will go back to the house after all…'

'Amelia, I assure you I am completely in earnest!' Gray crossed the distance that separated them in two long strides and reached out to clasp the tops of her arms. 'You have no idea how much I have regretted—how deeply sorry I am—that I frightened you the other evening with the depth of my…my passion.' He gave a self-disgusted shake of his head.

Her eyes widened. 'Is that the reason you were so cold towards me afterwards? Because you believed me to have been *frightened* by what we had shared?'

He nodded grimly. 'I should not have touched you in the way that I did. You are a young and innocent young lady, completely unaware of—of such intimacies. A young and beautiful woman who deserves to be spoilt and petted by any number of men, your beauty appreciated and admired, before you make any choice concerning where you do or do not love.'

Amelia looked up at Gideon searchingly, knowing by the fierceness of his expression that he believed the things he was saying. 'You will *dare* to stand there and admit to deciding what

I do or do not need without so much as consulting me on the subject?' she demanded incredulously.

'I am only thinking of you—'

Her disgusted snort interrupted him. 'For your information, Gideon, I received my first offer of marriage on my seventeenth birthday. From the eldest son of Lord Rotherford—perhaps you know of him?' She could see by Gideon's stunned expression that he had indeed heard of the wealthy Lord Rotherford and his estate in Norfolk. 'I received my second offer a month later, from the Earl of Radcliffe. Perhaps you have heard of him, too?' She gave him a scathing glance. 'Shortly before my mother was taken ill and died I received a third offer, from Sir Charles Montague. I see by your expression that you have heard of him, too,' she noted with satisfaction. 'In the space of four months I received, and refused, three offers of marriage. You had not realised, had you, that although we lived so far from London, we were not lacking in social invitations?' She gave an impatient shake of her head.

Gray was astounded. Speechless. Every single one of the men Amelia had mentioned was as young and wealthy, if not more so, than he was himself. And all had offered for Amelia before he had even *met* her?

He found himself filled with a black rage at the mere thought of those other men paying her such attentions.

Amelia gave an exasperated sigh. 'I only tell you these things, Gideon, to show you that I am not a young and impressionable girl, to imagine herself in love with the first handsome gentleman that she meets. Indeed, I knew—have always known—as my mother did before me, first with my father and then years later with Lord Peregrine—that when I met the man I was destined to love then I would know him instantly.'

Gray could barely breathe. 'And did you...?'

Her expression softened. 'Oh, yes, Gideon. I knew you.' Her gaze remained steadily fixed upon his. 'And nothing—absolutely *nothing*,' she repeated with emphasis, 'that has occurred between us since has shaken or diminished that love in the slightest.'

His darling, wonderful Amelia—

'I am instructed by Lady Grace,' she continued softly, 'to inform you that she and the rest of the St Claire family free you of any obligation of silence you might feel on their behalf. Now, will you tell me what is so secret that you would lie to all who care for you rather than reveal the truth? Do you still doubt me, Gideon?' she prompted as he hesitated.

'Of course I do not doubt you! Damn it, Amelia, I—' He broke off, shaking his head in frustration. 'I *will* tell you the truth—all of it—but first let me tell you that I do love you. I love you deeply and truly. It was because I love you that I spoke to Hawk St Claire when we arrived, to ask him if he would act in my stead as your guardian. To give his permission for me to woo you. To allow me to make you an offer of marriage when you have come to know me better. I have been trying to do the right thing, Amelia!' he insisted as she stared up at him incredulously.

'And how long is this wooing to take?'

'I had thought perhaps six months would be a respectable period of time—'

'Six months! Oh, no, Gideon. If you wish me to even consider such an offer then I insist you make it now and not in six months' time.'

He frowned darkly. 'But you have not heard the truth about me yet…'

Amelia looked up at him steadily. 'I believe in you, Gideon.'

'You…?' Gray swallowed hard. 'And it is seriously your wish for me to go down upon one knee and propose to you in this wet and draughty boathouse…?'

'The idea does have some appeal…' She eyed him with relish. 'But, no, Gideon, I am assured by Grace that there is a warm and comfortable loft above us.' She looked up pointedly.

Gray drew in a sharp breath. 'Lady Grace appears to have been very free with her information…'

'I prefer to think of it as helpful.' Amelia turned in the direction of the wooden staircase leading up to the 'warm and comfortable loft'. 'Coming, Gideon?'

'You are sure you do not wish to wait six months…?'

'I am very sure, Gideon!' she said exasperatedly.

'In that case…' Gray moved forward and swept her up in his arms. 'I love you very much, Amelia,' he murmured throatily as he carried her up the wooden stairs.

Her arms curved up about his neck as she smiled up at him in delicious anticipation. 'Show me!' she encouraged.

Once upstairs, Gray laid Amelia down upon the old sofa that he presumed was being stored there—although perhaps not, bearing in mind Lady Grace's fondness for the place—before moving down on one knee beside her. 'Will you marry me, Amelia Jane Ashford?'

'Oh, I most certainly will, Gideon James Grayson,' she assured him fervently, and she gently pulled him down beside her on the sofa.

Gray's mouth captured hers as he became lost in the wonder of kissing and caressing the woman he loved.

'I am so very proud of you, Gideon,' Amelia told him softly a long—very long!—time later, as she lay warm and replete in his arms.

Gideon had found a blanket and Amelia's cloak to place over their nakedness as he'd talked to her of his years of working secretly for the crown, and the shocking events that had led to his saving Arabella Wynter's life some weeks ago.

'I know that your brother would have been, too,' she added gently as her arms tightened about him.

'I hope so,' Gray murmured huskily.

'I *know* so,' Amelia repeated firmly. 'Do you believe now that I love you?' she added teasingly.

'I believe it, my darling!' It would be difficult for Gray not to believe in their love for each other after the beauty and wonder of their lovemaking, Amelia had given all of herself to him, as he had given all of himself to her.

'And you really are not going to insist on this silly idea that Stourbridge must act as my guardian for six months?'

'No.' Gideon groaned at the very thought of being apart

from Amelia for even a quarter of that time. 'When shall we be married, do you think?'

'Well, there is a church here at Mulberry Hall, is there not...?'

Gray smiled in the darkness. 'There is.'

'Then perhaps at the start of the New Year?'

'I will speak to Stourbridge immediately we return to the house.'

Amelia laughed huskily. 'It is the middle of the night, Gideon!'

His arms tightened about her possessively. 'Then I will speak with him when we return in the morning.'

She snuggled down comfortably in his arms. 'A happy Christmas to you, Gideon.'

'And a happy Christmas to you, too, my love.' Gray smiled. 'And many more happy Christmases to come, I hope!'

A lifetime of them, Amelia vowed silently.

Together...

See below for a sneak peek from our classic Harlequin® Romance® line.

Introducing DADDY BY CHRISTMAS by Patricia Thayer.

MIA caught sight of Jarrett when he walked into the open lobby. It was hard not to notice the man. In a charcoal business suit with a crisp white shirt and striped tie covered by a dark trench coat, he looked more Wall Street than small-town Colorado.

Mia couldn't blame him for keeping his distance. He was probably tired of taking care of her.

Besides, why would a man like Jarrett McKane be interested in her? Why would he want to take on a woman expecting a baby? Yet he'd done so many things for her. He'd been there when she'd needed him most. How could she not care about a man like that?

Heart pounding in her ears, she walked up behind him. Jarrett turned to face her. "Did you get enough sleep last night?"

"Yes, thanks to you," she said, wondering if he'd thought about their kiss. Her gaze went to his mouth, then she quickly glanced away. "And thank you for not bringing up my meltdown."

Jarrett couldn't stop looking at Mia. Blue was definitely her color, bringing out the richness of her eyes.

"What meltdown?" he said, trying hard to focus on what she was saying. "You were just exhausted from lack of sleep and worried about your baby."

He couldn't help remembering how, during the night, he'd kept going in to watch her sleep. How strange was that? "I hope you got enough rest."

She nodded. "Plenty. And you're a good neighbor for

coming to my rescue."

He tensed. Neighbor? *What neighbor kisses you like I did?* "That's me, just the full-service landlord," he said, trying to keep the sarcasm out of his voice. He started to leave, but she put her hand on his arm.

"Jarrett, what I meant was you went beyond helping me." Her eyes searched his face. "I've asked far too much of you."

"Did you hear me complain?"

She shook her head. "You should. I feel like I've taken advantage."

"Like I said, I haven't minded."

"And I'm grateful for everything…"

Grasping her hand on his arm, Jarrett leaned forward. The memory of last night's kiss had him aching for another. "I didn't do it for your gratitude, Mia."

Gorgeous tycoon Jarrett McKane has never believed in Christmas—but he can't help being drawn to soon-to-be-mom Mia Saunders! Christmases past were spent alone…and now Jarrett may just have a fairy-tale ending for all his Christmases future!

Available December 2010, only from Harlequin® Romance®.

HARLEQUIN®

A *Romance*

FOR EVERY MOOD™

Spotlight on

Classic

Quintessential, modern love stories
that are romance at its finest.

See the next page
to enjoy a sneak peek from
the Harlequin® Romance series.

REQUEST YOUR FREE BOOKS!

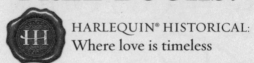

HARLEQUIN® HISTORICAL:
Where love is timeless

2 FREE NOVELS PLUS 2 FREE GIFTS!

YES! Please send me 2 FREE Harlequin® Historical novels and my 2 FREE gifts (gifts are worth about $10). After receiving them, if I don't wish to receive any more books, I can return the shipping statement marked "cancel." If I don't cancel, I will receive 6 brand-new novels every month and be billed just $4.94 per book in the U.S. or $5.49 per book in Canada. That's a saving of 20% off the cover price! It's quite a bargain! Shipping and handling is just 50¢ per book.* I understand that accepting the 2 free books and gifts places me under no obligation to buy anything. I can always return a shipment and cancel at any time. Even if I never buy another book from Harlequin, the two free books and gifts are mine to keep forever.

246/349 HDN E5L4

Name _____ (PLEASE PRINT)

Address _____ Apt. #

City _____ State/Prov. _____ Zip/Postal Code

Signature (if under 18, a parent or guardian must sign)

Mail to the **Harlequin Reader Service:**
IN U.S.A.: P.O. Box 1867, Buffalo, NY 14240-1867
IN CANADA: P.O. Box 609, Fort Erie, Ontario L2A 5X3

Not valid for current subscribers to Harlequin Historical books.

Want to try two free books from another line?
Call 1-800-873-8635 or visit www.morefreebooks.com.

* Terms and prices subject to change without notice. Prices do not include applicable taxes. N.Y. residents add applicable sales tax. Canadian residents will be charged applicable provincial taxes and GST. Offer not valid in Quebec. This offer is limited to one order per household. All orders subject to approval. Credit or debit balances in a customer's account(s) may be offset by any other outstanding balance owed by or to the customer. Please allow 4 to 6 weeks for delivery. Offer available while quantities last.

Your Privacy: Harlequin Books is committed to protecting your privacy. Our Privacy Policy is available online at www.eHarlequin.com or upon request from the Reader Service. From time to time we make our lists of customers available to reputable third parties who may have a product or service of interest to you. ☐ If you would prefer we not share your name and address, please check here.

Help us get it right—We strive for accurate, respectful and relevant communications. To clarify or modify your communication preferences, visit us at www.ReaderService.com/consumerschoice.

HH10R